About the Author

Henry Chikwuji Edebeatu is a Management Consultant. He holds a Postgraduate Diploma in Public Relations and second degree in Industrial Relations with a number of certificates in Conflict Management and related areas. He is an accredited Mediator of the International Institute of Mediation and has written numerous articles on various social issues. He is the author of 'Ogbuefi - Endless Chase'.

Henry Chikwuji Edebeatu passed away 4th February 2020.

A Giant Cross

Henry Chikwuji Edebeatu

A Giant Cross

Olympia Publishers
London

www.olympiapublishers.com
OLYMPIA PAPERBACK EDITION

A CIP catalogue record for this title is
available from the British Library.

ISBN: 978-1-78830-486-3

This is a work of fiction based on a true-life experience but all
characters are fictitious and any resemblance to real persons, living
or dead is purely coincidental.

First Published in 2023

Olympia Publishers
Tallis House
2 Tallis Street
London
EC4Y 0AB
Printed in Great Britain

Dedication

To my daughter, Hannah, for making me proud despite all that she suffered in a foster home. And my mother, Theresa, who passed away on the 11th of July 2019.

Acknowledgements

I am tremendously grateful to God for giving me the grace to write this novel. I know that without Him it would never have been possible.

My appreciation also goes to my daughter, Hannah, for going through some parts of the initial drafts and coming back to me with what I initially felt were unpleasant and harsh comments of hers. Her constant request for updates on my progress was a great motivation to me.

I appreciate my son's criticism of the initial title and his interest in wanting to see the novel published as quickly as possible.

I do not want to forget my wife, Bridget, for her continuing support.

Last but by no means the least, my sincere thanks to my editors, publishers and all others who assisted or inspired me but are not mentioned.

Note from Author

The author has written this novel in the hope that it will touch the hearts of the heartless and abusive spouses and make them realise that their actions and habits bring both mental and physical pains to sufferers.

It is hoped that such people, after reading this novel, will at least acknowledge that they are cruel and recognise that no wrong doer would ever go free.

On the other hand, this novel will strengthen men, women and children who suddenly find themselves in hostile homes.

"Marriage is a warfare."
– My late father

Prologue

It was a Saturday morning in the middle of harmattan. The sun rose early, with signals that it was going to be one of those blistering days. The whistling of the breeze woke me up with a throbbing headache that weighed me down until later that morning.

Nkem, my adorable wife, sat on the double sofa in the living room attending to nothing but her fragile fingernails. 'Nkem!' I called very graciously. 'What are we having for breakfast?' I asked.

She lifted her head nauseatingly and sent out a long hiss without any words.

'Nkem, was my question out of context. Why the fizzle?'

'Has leprosy ruined your fingers so much that you can't prepare breakfast yourself or do I look your housemaid?' she fumed.

'What has overtaken you this morning? Aren't you my wife? Besides, you know quite well that I'm not feeling too well.'

'That's your cup of tea.'

Meanwhile, dust moles danced in the air and had penetrated even the tiniest holes, covering the furniture and photographs that hung on the walls. Would Nkem ever have the time to dust them and tidy up the house with her present unwarranted rage? I doubted it very much.

With an empty stomach, I decided to stroll across the road, to where my best friend, Matthias, lived, to momentarily escape the looming screeching of Nkem, the horrendous woman I brought into my home as my better half.

Matthias lived in a three-bedroom cottage on a large piece of land fenced with barbwire lying around the outside walls. Inside were massive decorations covered with different species of green, red and pink flowers, including red roses. The family kept the living room nicely, with baskets of wine floras and wind chimes, together with the national flag in front of the balconies sitting opposite the dining window. Trailing plants enveloped their facades and shrubs grew through them. It was a classic dwelling place meant to be lying on a strictly preserved zone for the elites.

Matthias, a middle-aged man, devout Christian, and a famous esteemed senior worker of our denomination treasured the companies of others because of his peculiar circumstances. There he was, stooped with perforated singlet slung over his shoulders, and baggy knickers covering his waist down to his knees, whistling and grinding some fresh pepper with the handmade grinding stone. Nearby was his partly amiable wife beside the motorcycle garage, her face looking plump and expressionless. She dressed like an adolescent lady waiting to become a bride-to-be, positioned on a collapsible armless chair, switching her eyes aimlessly all over the premises. Right beside her was her guest whom she was entertaining with some fresh orange juice and biscuits.

The woman with her cheeks heavily decked with brunette

powder, lips coloured with light black cosmetic, appeared in immodest attire. Her hair looked as if she was carrying dreadlocks. She was dark of face, with restless eyes glittering and staring at every moving object, a thin nose and a neck that protruded above her collarless top. Indeed, every part of her was defined. Her face was flat with what appeared like an oblong head standing on her lanky neck. I froze from the chest up. Was I seeing the world from the depth of the valley? How could such a married woman in her mid-forties bear such worldly looks? To start with, why should Matthias' wife keep such a swanky, rough-looking woman as a friend, knowing that Matthias, her husband, was a senior worker in the church? I asked silently but at once remembered that was not my mission at that very moment.

'Ah! Matthias,' I squeaked nervously as soon as I sighted him.

He looked up, temporarily adjourning his task. 'Yes, Chidi,' he responded.

'Why are you doing a woman's job instead of going through the Sunday school book against tomorrow's church service? What about your wife?'

'Please, Chidi, don't trouble yourself,' he said with a forced grin. 'It's my cross and no one else would bear it but me. Every man has his to bear and this is mine. I'm focusing on heaven,' he spoke like a man already inured to ridicule.

'Hmm!' My mouth stayed shut for a while as I stood ruminating over my home. I knew it was not different. I nodded my head countless times, so intensely like the male Jamaican anoles, with a threatening extension of a colourful flap of skin on its neck. 'So, the story is the same everywhere?' I mumbled.

'I judge my case to be mild,' Matthias claimed. 'Not like Martin's situation, his wife can lock him out at will and abuse him, releasing curses upon him, at the top of her voice, not caring about the peace and rights of their neighbours. The irony is Martin's unwillingness to utter a word so that he disappoint those who see him as a committed Christian and senior worker in the church.'

From my earliest remembrance, my upbringing was Christian oriented, but I had never before seen men so tenacious in their faith like Matthias and Martin, even on the face of clear dereliction of responsibilities by their women and abuses like the one I witnessed on that day. As I pondered over that incident, I concluded that no home is immune, where such fire does not burn, even in the household of heads of big congregations. Any man who pretends that his relationship with his better half is impeccable simply wants to get a deceptive public admiration. For the respectable men kept picking the unruly women and the virtuous women pick the domineering men.

'My brother, Chidi,' Matthias continued. 'The truth is that on the face of a severe test, compassion and compromise would be endangered, yet the paradigm for peace in homes remains forbearance. So, go in, take your seat and wait for me until I'm done.'

I was dumbstruck.

Chapter One

One of the earliest crises caused by the northern herdsmen in my country caught my parents by surprise while they were still living in the hinterland of the cattle merchants. I kept wondering what took them to that region so early in their lives. For life was not, at that time, as taxing in the south where we belonged, as it later turned out to be. It would be a big task for me to make any effort now to recollect how old I was at that time. The only thing I remembered was my mother not being comfortable enough letting me walk alone down the lonely and rocky path that led to my school.

So, every morning, on each school day, she would wake me up very early, when I would have loved to sleep more, and lead me to the bathing room, even as I staggered, with my eyes half closed and starving for the deferment of that routine. She would then brush my teeth, bathe me, clean my body, rub me with the popular petroleum gummy jelly called Vaseline before dressing me up in my white and navy-blue cotton uniform.

One morning, it was very foggy and drizzling. Every child, I presumed, would have loved to be at home on that particular day. Especially me. Instead, my mother had woken up to get me ready for school. She got to where I was still lying in bed and pulled me up gently without procrastination. As I dilly-dallied, stretching my body, especially my neck, and striving to be firm on my feet, there came an unexpected darkness everywhere. The National Power Company had turned off the light, and soon there followed a loud rocket of thunder and flashes of lightning. It was threatening to rain again and that must be the reason for the lights-out this time around.

The rain was becoming too frequent and people were getting a bit agitated. It was heavy the previous week, with strong winds lashing the town, and trees crashing down at different locations. Again, within a few hours, the previous night, a significant amount of precipitation occurred, leading to severe flooding risk with numerous hazards, which included loss of crops and livestock.

I thought with all of that, going to school on that day would be put off but instead, my mother made for a candlestick and as she picked up a match to ignite it, the men restored the power again. So, I had no choice but to follow and as soon as I got under the shower, the light went off within a few seconds, for the second time. The National Power Company was famous for erratic power supply. So, my mother left me standing on the bathroom floor that was slick with all kinds of slime substance and went for the candlestick she had left behind. When I had showered, she got me dressed and took me to school.

Not long after she had dropped me off, one could see many other parents trooping down the major road leading to the various schools and nanny centres. Though the sludge still covered the ground, everyone strove to move as quickly as possible, evading every small pool of water that punctuated the whole arena.

Suddenly, there was confusion everywhere, which awoke some deep fearful responses from parents. We could see many, all fidgeting, puffing and panting like an old steam engine, without any hope, triggered by the uneasy stifling atmosphere. No one knew what was happening and how best to respond to the threat.

My mother, who never crossed the school's gate whenever she brought me to school or collected me, joined the others, got to my school's gate and walked straight to the corridor in front of the class where I was. She pushed, and without any decorum, burst into the class where I sat hitting one of my teeth with the unsharpened pencil in my hand, staring at the broad blackboard, wondering how to get over our usual first mental exercise of the day. As she stood by the door of the classroom, the tiny silver necklaces round her neck, which dropped on her chest, pushed up and down, revealing clearly the tempo of her heart rate and making it so easy to count. Her heart was pounding. It was pounding swiftly. It was obvious. She clearly had abandoned all the pending tasks she need to accomplish that day.

The ugly news spreading, as wild fire, did not seem to have reached anywhere near the school's environment. Therefore, everyone was taken by surprise as she stood akimbo, facing the teacher who was briefly dumfounded but very quickly switched to a countenance full of smiles which anyone could erroneously take for being friendly but to us, who knew him very well, it was the opposite. Initially, my mother was silent but her silence was roaring with the way she stood. Soon, we watched as she began to demonstrate her impatience when she broke her peace, exhuming not only command but also logic.

'Mr Teacher, would you please discharge every child here and let them be on their way to their different homes, unless you want the looming crisis to consume them,' she burst out and we were all flabbergasted.

'Calm down, madam,' our class teacher, Mr Clifford, persuaded. He was a man who ordinarily earned the respect of anyone who came across him, even for the first time. He was tall, gaunt but full of strength with a straight stare and loping strides. My mother did not pay any attention to those features. By then, the school's bell had sounded and everyone knew that all the pupils were quickly to be on the assembly ground. The way the bell went, almost every one of us knew, without any doubt, it was an emergency gathering.

'Chidi!' my mother called with a loud and thundering voice. 'Gather all your belongings and let's be on our way.'

This time her eyelids blinked unnaturally, and she was beginning to bounce like a table tennis ball with her hands clipped to her chest as if she was protecting her two breasts. I realised immediately she had lost her composure. She was tying a single wrapper instead of two as most African women usually do. She must have left the house in a great rush. Also, she must not only have walked very fast on her way but would have ran to beat the time for her face down to her neck was still coated with perspiration.

I was already on my feet as soon as I heard her raucous voice calling my name. It was no longer time to hearken to the school bell or my class teacher. I quickly moved towards her and half way she met me, grabbed my hand and dragged me with a genuine intention and passionate feelings of care. But her grip felt like iron pincers. That time, others were moving fast to the assembly ground. As I walked away with my mother and my heavily-loaded school bag, some of my mates were waving at me and I could not help but look back to catch all their hands.

By the time we got to the school gate, so many outsiders had begun to troop into the school premises. That was when the school headmaster realised that some serious crisis had broken out, especially when one of the parents came, exhibiting a quiver of fear that was running through her as she kept shouting, 'The herdsmen are at it again!'

That would not be the first time they would be fermenting trouble for very feeble excuses. They hated to see anyone in their town who was not yet a member of their sect or faith. Besides, they were frowning at parents who dared put their daughters in public schools because to them, schooling was an importation of western culture. To crown it all, the news that got to them that hazy morning, that in some parts of the country many villagers were disallowing their friends and family members from grazing their cattle on other landowners' field aggravated their fury.

Those herdsmen usually moved in procession through every bush path with their large number of livestock without caring whether they step on crops or not. In many cases, they allowed their cows and sheep to feed on other people's farm harvest. So, no doubt, the grazing had damaged a lot of plantation in many parts of the country and in order to resist those farmers, fighting had broken out resulting in some countless number of killings. Such killings had occurred several times in the long past with properties worth thousands of hard currency, destroyed. Majority of the victims were

Christians who would never fight back because of their faith but believed that vengeance is God's. The worst was that law enforcement agents never brought to book any of them who perpetrated that evil, simply because those monsters were from the same tribe with those who had the power to make them pay for their crimes. That must be why they were at it again.

The last time a similar incident happened was three years before when some of the herdsmen deliberately butchered farmers, who were mainly Christians, and burnt their houses. The worst being that they waited for the people to conduct the burial of those they killed in order to launch another attack, which increased the casualty.

The claim of the herdsmen was that farmers often kill their cows. At one time, they asserted that the farmers killed one hundred of their cows when it was actually two. The government compensated them with huge sums of money for each cow, for the one hundred cows they claimed were lost, without any recompense to the farmers who lost about one hundred and seventy farms.

Someone opined then that ours was a country where human beings were sacrificed for the loss of a cow and the value of a cow was far more sacred than that of the people.

Later, the rumour spread that those killers were not from communities within the country but from the neighbouring country. Some people claimed that the herdsmen recruited them as mercenaries and they already knew how to handle sophisticated weapons.

Soon, parents were all scrambling to locate their children and hardly allowed the school headmaster to address the pupils. The pupils, nearly all, had instantly spread out; anticipating the appearance of someone coming for them.

Then we pushed out of the gate.

I was now beginning to feel the firmness of my mother's fingers over my wrist; yet, I dared not object as I realised she meant well. Although, I perceived she was not going to accept any resistance at that time.

As we stepped further and continued to hurry down the road, we noticed a stretch of human traffic moving towards the direction we had left. On the other hand, there were still a good number of people, including fruit hawkers peddling their wares, looking unruffled despite the height of the confusion on the ground. Thoughts started gnawing into my head. 'Why are these people hiding their worries behind an air of insouciance while others are rattled?' I asked my mother very calmly, like a toddler.

'Most of them are the indigenes,' my mother responded virtually with muzzle velocity, as if she was in a boundless haste, and then slowing down for breath, leaving no doubt that she was already getting fatigued by the protracted rolling gait. 'They are the Fulanis', the owners of the land. Their brothers are the ones fermenting the trouble and they have the assurance they won't be hurt. Those who appear to be in great haste are the non-indigenes, like us,' she said.

'Aren't they bothered about the crisis?'

'They can't be and even if they are, they have no place to run to because this is their land,' my mother replied.

By this time, it was apparent all the schools in the town had closed. In some places, nobody seemed to have ordered the closure. The atmospheric hullabaloo necessitated it. Some shop owners secured themselves by locking the iron bars which barricaded their stores from the outsiders and were then peeping from inside their stores. But was it safe for them?

Nobody was asking that. People had already deserted the major market centres.

When we got to the house, it was as quiet as a graveyard. None of the tenants were in the house. We did not know their whereabouts. My mother had expected my father to be home by then seeing the huge number of residents pacing up and down the streets of the city. Meanwhile, she made for a short bench. She had been overcome more than I had by both physical and mental exhaustion, so intense that she started to feel pangs of a headache throbbing. 'My limbs are beginning to ache,' she confessed. 'Chidi, remain here while I go and look for your father,' she persuaded me. 'Make sure you don't step outside until I return.'

'Okay, Mama.'

As she crossed the narrow sewage channel in front of the house, she could see my father walking lackadaisically towards her as if nothing was at stake. 'Thank God you are here. I was coming to look for you,' she uttered as soon as my father got closer to her.

'There is no single soul in Jones Street,' he exclaimed.

'So, you know that and yet you remained at the shop without being bothered,' my mother replied, discourteously.

My father went for the small table radio and tuned to his regular station, FM 93.7. Just then, the voice of a radio announcer came, 'Some herdsmen were seen by some of our reporters this morning burning houses and killing people who either failed to get converted into their sect or disallowed them from grazing their cattle on private farmlands. The crisis has escalated to more villages and many are envisaging that unless the government take drastic action, the situation could get worse. A representative of the herdsmen told our reporter that the destruction would continue unless the government considers creating cattle colonies in all parts of the country.'

More and more people were beginning to flee the small city of Jos, especially those living at the outskirts, in order to escape the massacre. 'Start putting together important stuffs for you and Chidi and by tomorrow morning, I will take you to the train station where you will board the train straight to Enugu and from there you will head to our village, Mbauku,' my father stated.

'What! Aren't you coming with us? What would you be doing behind?' my mother tabled her concern. 'I'm sure by this time tomorrow, there won't be any more strangers left in Jos,' she asserted.

'Don't worry. I shall have all my machetes well sharpened and I shall be indoors henceforth. No man born of a woman would ever escape the glittering edges of my cutlasses if they dare step into this apartment,' my father boasted.

Ours was a self-suited apartment in a stand-alone building, housing five other tenants in a very remote area of the city. Apart from the turntable and the cushion, which my father just purchased on a hire purchase basis, it will be correct to say that the apartment was unfurnished.

'Please, my dear, we must all leave this city tomorrow,' my mother pleaded.

'If you are not ready to leave with Chidi by tomorrow, then you have the freedom to remain here with me but find a way of conveying him across to my uncle in the village, for he is all I have got for now,' my father declared.

'I beg of you, my love, I'm on my knees,' my mother implored in her frantic desire. My father smiled at her sheepishly as if he loved those caring words but not the idea.

My mother sat in silence on a stool near the living room window. She could still hear the footsteps of some passers-by clattering like the sound of water into a bucket. She could hear loud and clear yet from the distance, the distressed voices of others like the sound of monkeys faced with the hunter's gun in the thick forest whose slippers were clicking noisily on the paths littered with leaves. She quickly went into the room and started to gather whatever belonged to her and me. She knew that once my father said something twice, he meant it, and no one could change his mind.

Like a theatre that could only exist in a nightmare, my father went to where he housed his cutlasses and brought them out. He began to look for his files with which to sharpen them. He could not remember where he had kept them. 'Could it be I didn't bring them back?' he sighed.

He then realised that truly, he did not bring them back from his store in the market after Musa, his friend, had borrowed and returned them. Would my father ever have the opportunity of going to the store again? Could he ever regain those files? The chances were slim. His store contained two of his grinding machines. He used the big one for grinding pepper and the medium sized one for corn grinding. According to him, people with that kind of grinders were very few and because of that, he was never able to meet the demands of his customers. Any wonder that he stayed back at the store grinding for customers while others were running away from public vicinity for their own safety. From the grinding alone, he made a sustainable living. He left our village, Mbauku, soon after getting married to my mother and went to Aba, in the south-eastern part, to settle. He was an apprentice under one of the famous spare parts dealers before one of the market women's riot brought large-scale destruction to lives and properties. The devastation greatly affected the dealer's stores. So, a friend of the dealer encouraged him to go with him to Jos, which used to be a quiet and peaceful small city in the central north of the country. Now, after only six years of being in Jos, this crisis erupted.

***

The next morning, all was set for my mother and me to say goodbye to the lovely outskirts of Jos. My mother ensured that she safeguarded her loved sewing machine. That was the only possession that was of value to her at that time. With the machine, she hoped to sustain herself and her only son back in the village. The machine had a suitable light metal container that could shield it from any abrasion, worthless wreckage, should the acceleration of the train, or vehicle become overly swift. The other things we went with were just some of my mother's dresses and shoes as well as mine apart from a few kitchen utensils, which my mother said she loved so much. I did not forget my school bag, which was heavily loaded with books, most of which were so old they had their covers ripped off.

Travelling with excessive luggage from the outskirts to the train station was not going to be an easy task, particularly for people living in the eastern part of the city where we were because commercial vehicles were not very frequent in those areas. We were, however, hopeful that through my father's influence, we would be able to get a free ride.

My father was famous among the Hausa and Fulani communities. In less than a year of arriving at Jos, he could speak Hausa fluently and it was not difficult for him to make a great number of friends, one of whom was Musa. My father was already nursing the feelings that at least one out of his many friends would be willing to give him the maximum protection and support he needed should the crisis become uncontainable. As predicted, Musa was the one who came and drove us from the house to the train station on the day my mother and I were to depart from Jos.

Musa was a man with a very small stature and a round face, half of which the moustache and whiskers veiled, though he claimed he was a Christian but not many could believe him because of his slovenly appearance, especially his repulsive shaggy face. He breathed very hard and incessantly pants each time he took a short walk. But he was cheerful all the time and surprisingly combative with excellent heavily accented English. It was not common then to see people from his tribe who were very good in spoken English. He must be one out of a million of them. He appeared like a man who was more interested in his thoughts than in things outside himself. Yet, he was a person apparently with a finger in every pie and with contacts to match even the most popular monarch.

There were trunks of human beings at the station, racketing like the bleating of the flocks among the sheepfolds. The queue for the train ticket was unimaginable. Every passenger appeared to be a non-indigene. Just then, a train officer picked up the microphone and announced with a voice many at the station abhorred. He sounded more or less like one speaking in his native dialect. 'Only ten *fickets* more, the *quoaches* would be filled to *quapacity* and the rest of the *fassengers* would have to wait for the next train to *Enuku* which is due to arrive by six a.m. *chumorrow*. However, it is *imfortant* to let you know that the train is *quarrently* being delayed due to *chechnical itches* which are being *avressed.*'

Despite the tense situation, many people burst into laughter, not because of what he said but the manner he uttered it; like someone who had never seen the four walls of a school.

People now began to panic as chances were shrinking rapidly. No single non-indigene wanted to remain at that station any day longer and some were beginning to shunt. The initially organised queue was now in great disarray. Musa, the man who drove us to the station alighted after parking the van in a secured spot. He reassured us that we would secure two of the ten tickets left. We were not quite sure what magic he was going to perform. He walked into the station's office and after a couple of minutes came out. The look on his face could not give us any measure of hope. As he drew closer to the van, he nodded his head. My father could not instantly interpret his gestures until he got to us and said, 'I told you, two of the remaining tickets would be allocated to you.'

Musa now leaned on the van and turned his back on us. My mother looked at my father with a defined expression, which my father easily understood. 'Didn't he come with any ticket?' my mother asked slowly.

'Young woman, can you be patient for once.'

Meanwhile, the crowd appeared to be growing every second and there was no sign that people were going to stop trooping in. In my sight, it was like gangs of extras in a Nollywood presentation. The stage confused me more when I could not easily understand the nature of the crisis that was making so many people run for their dear lives. In my child's mind, it was difficult for me to picture correctly. All I could see in every matching face at the station were anxiety and desperation to distance themselves, as fast and far as possible, from the impending chaos and doom, which they were all anticipating.

Then Musa walked into the station main hall again and minutes after we could see him coming out of the station's main entrance, making his way towards us, with his face brightened up and full of smiles. This time, it was so easy to ascertain what the result was. As soon as he got to us, he handed over the tickets to my father who in turn, tendered them to my mother who very quickly picked her favourable purple handbag and slotted the tickets in it. Instantly, she held my left hand and we began to move towards the departure lounge. I would be lying if I claimed that I was used to the firmness with which she constantly gripped my wrist.

Musa and my father began to haul our luggage one after the other to where they would be loaded on the train. After many minutes of being at the train station, the heavy sound of the horn of the train was heard. The horn was to remind all the passengers to get on the train and any pedestrian who may be crossing the rail line to be mindful, that in a matter of minutes, it would be on its way to Enugu.

My father came close to me, held me tight to his body, sweeping me off my feet in a huge hug. Seconds after, he let go but held my two hands, swung them several times and lifted me up, holding me in the air for minutes. He dropped me and stooped to give me a peck on my forehead. It was hard not to smirk.

I got a glimpse of my mother from the corner of my eyes and her eyes were glistening with water, rolling down her cheeks unrestrained. Could that be tears? I was baffled for a while as intermittently, she was coming up with smiles that were lasting only a few seconds. Gradually, her grins entirely disappeared and that was soon after one of the train officers blew the final whistle, indicating that it was time for the train to be on the move and all doors were to close.

My mother and I quickly jumped on the train. As soon as the automatic doors closed, she brought out her head from the narrow window, after parting the plastic tinted curtains, to say her final words to my father. 'God be with you and keep you until we see you again.'

Some tears dropped off again. It was then it dawned on me why she was very emotional about the parting. Would my father return to us again or was it going to be the last they would see each other? Yet, she had been unable to overpower his strong desire to remain in Jos even in the face of obvious insecurity. I could not fathom why he was so hard and would not even consider my mother's soft emotions. None of those thoughts bothered him anyway, he, in a jiffy, walked close to the window, gave my mother a kiss and bade us goodbye.

My father and Musa walked back to the car. My mother and I gazed as Musa drove him off, stretching away into the distance until we could see them no more.

The coach where my mother and I sat had a sickening smell mingled with fumes of smoke coming from the outmoded locomotive, for we were near the head of it. However, the fumes never lasted for too long as it disappeared as soon as the train increased its speed, but the nauseating smell remained, or do I say that we rather quickly got accustomed to it. Later, I found out that the smell was emanating from the bodies of some of the passengers. Many of them had neither brushed their teeth, nor taken a bath for the past twenty-four hours or even more, owing to the crisis.

For that reason, I became so anxious that we reach the end of our journey in good time.

We passed many other towns and the first one we passed showed that all the rumours we had heard were true. It was Fada, a town barely one quarter the size of Jos. One should thank God that the train track did not pass through Fada's main town centre. The station was crowded with people when we got there and I felt it was only the non-indigenes, mixed with some mobile police officers, who were there to safeguard travellers. If not for that, it would have been difficult for any train to pass without the arrows of those protesting herdsmen hitting their targets.

As we passed, we could see some buildings still in fresh flames, and many billboards pulled down with others swaying in the wind. It was so easy to discover that a good number of the residents must have suffered some big losses.

Some of the towns were quite big with others not more than a hamlet. I could also see towns and villages in various stages of dilapidation and I began to wonder if we were still in the same country. In some places, I could see some tall and beautiful buildings far better than the ones I had ever seen before in my life. I could see gardens with flourishing flowers, crops and other plants.

A few moments later, I stared off into the distance beyond a small canal and could see a large group of cattle, some severely dehydrated with their heads bent towards the withering grass. Soon, we came around a very narrow, fragile looking bridge across a deep and stretched stinking ditch as the train passed by and it felt as if it was not going to pull through.

As the train continued accelerating, in a great discharge of smoke and blaze, flashes were spraying upwards from its funnels. It was splendid to watch, and I incessantly fixed my eyes on it with astonishment and the doubt of a little boy. We passed towns upon towns, villages upon villages, spending very long hours on the road, until we got to Enugu train station where we had to alight to take a bus going straight to Mbauku, which was about one hundred and seventeen kilometres away.

My mother, who had barely said a word throughout the twelve-hour journey, once again retreated to herself as soon as we boarded the bus to Mbauku. This time, she hung her jaw on two of her palms. Her eyes glittered as she stared steadily at me. For some reason, I did not give her the occasion to realise I was identifying with her worries. For her, life was holding some measure of uncertainty and without much hope. She was so bottled-up in the sudden family division that she had wished it were all a dream.

Now as the bus zoomed, we soon began to perceive the distant smell of the mucky Asaba beach market. It wasn't long before the appetising natural bouquet of the famous River Niger took over and seemed to be welcoming us. I began to feel some kind of strange excitement as we prepared to step down on to the land of our fathers. In my heart was an ardent desire to witness and discover my new home, the dwelling of my fathers and all our ancestors.

As the bus eventually pulled over at the town's small garage, we stepped out, the eyes of a young woman walking towards the mini-market caught that of my mother. The woman, whom I later found to be my father's niece, shouted and without hesitation or modesty ran to the family compound to inform my uncle of our arrival. Before one could mention Casablanca, a number of young boys reached at us to transport our luggage to where would now be our permanent home. It was to the great delight of everyone in the village that two of their own had arrived home safely.

'Where is Diji, your husband?' was the first question my uncle asked my mother.

'He's staying behind but he's fine and likely to join us in a couple of weeks,' my mother replied in a great exhibition of faith. That response saved her from numerous other questions that would have followed.

My mother was not sure where to move. My uncle lived in a small mud house that was still attractive, cemented and painted but it was not difficult to reveal that the building had gone through a series of renovation. Despite all that, it was the best for a moderate, cosy village dwelling place.

The house was a bungalow with two rooms and a living room which had housed my uncle with his wife and five children who were all still in their teens. The wife was fat, huge and red-eyed, whom I later had to see frequently acting like a bulldog. She was also frumpy and didn't care less. Everyone in the village had the highest fear of her, including her husband, who could match her in everything, height, size and strength except for bullying, but he was always refraining from challenging her about the way she acted for fear she would blow up. She was constantly sulky even when she was talking about her husband. But then, it was she who offered that we temporarily move in to one of their two rooms, sounding almost kindly. What surprised me most was the great hospitality she showed us despite the widespread opinion of her unsteady character.

Although, hospitality appeared to be king amongst our people, no one could have given her the benefit of the doubt that she would have proved to be so nice. Otherwise, how else would one explain the facts that began from the day that followed. We received donations of different kinds from her and other villagers, yam, cocoa yam, yam flour, rice, beans, even dried fish, and numerous soup ingredients were in abundance for us. Days later, my uncle, an acclaimed local farmer showed my mother a large part of his barn from where she could take as many yam tubers as she required. He cultivated large acres of land. Land was not a problem for anyone willing to cultivate it.

My uncle planted different species of food crops, including assorted kinds of vegetables and fruits. He seemed to be producing the meals of hundreds of non-farmers. Therefore, according us the opportunity of eating out of his surplus farm yields was not a problem for him in any way.

Chapter Two

I woke up the following morning to discover that every person appeared in layers of the red sand common in that area. It was particularly on the children and worse during the dry season. One of the symbols with which to identify strangers was dress colour and appearance. Anyone spotted in bright, pleasant coloured dress was definitely unaware of the dusty vicinity of Mbauku, therefore, a stranger.

My mother spent the initial days teaching me some of the culture of our people. She had a lot of time to spend with me. She would often say to me, 'Chidi, don't put your hands in your pocket while greeting an elder.' Often displaying how I should bend or stand. Any time I forgot to do it in the way she had taught me, she would raise her voice, not wanting anyone to blame her for not raising an only child according to the expectations of the people. Nevertheless, she was such fun to be with.

Days later, she approached my uncle to get his concurrence on her plans to start her dressmaking business.

'I have a sewing machine, and I am wondering if I could keep it under the cashew tree in front of the house to get my business going,' she told him.

'Look, Chioma, you don't need to ask for my endorsement. The whole of this place belongs to your husband and me,' he told her. 'As you know, your husband and I are the ones left of our parents, so we own things together. When he was to leave for the north, after the Aba women riot, I told him to remain here with me and till the land, but he dumped the idea. He wanted the white-collar job. Look at it now. I pray God brings him back safely.'

Days rolled by and even weeks, and there was no word from my father. By then, a good number of people known to be residing within the neighbourhood of the crisis area had returned to the village while others had fled to safer hamlets in the outer north. In fact a swarm of refugees were pouring into my small community of Mbauku. Nobody could tell how safe my father was.

My mother's worries grew day after day and her anticipation reduced her appetite. Every morning, she woke up with trembling lips, feeling a certain heat in the pit of her stomach and her heart beating like a retired sportswoman who had been compelled to do a one hundred yards race. Her brain seemed to be constantly cracking and every state of her nervous dread was visible. Life had become uninteresting to her without the lover of her heart.

My mother's frightening moments slowly began to decline, as she seemed to resign to fate. As soon as it became noticeable that she was no longer lamenting much over my father's absence, came a huge surprise though, the news of more genocide in the north had spread. Many doubted the possibility of anyone who had not made contact at that time being in a safe condition.

One night, after many months, some of the people had

ruled out the possibility of my father still being alive. Someone came thundering at the door, beating at it. At that time, it was traditional for everybody to be indoors with entrances and windows well secured as pockets of vigilante groups in the village kept parading the entire vicinity to ward-off those who might intend to inflict troubles and burgle homes or stores.

Everybody had gathered around the lantern kept on the quadrilateral stool in the centre of the large living room, listening to the folktale my uncle was telling us. He then paused as the knock came repeatedly. 'Who is that?'

A voice responded in a very quiet tone, 'Please, open the door.'

'That sounds like Diji, my husband,' screamed my mother who without hesitation or any reservation jumped up and headed to open the door.

'Stay back, Chioma, and let me open it myself for security reasons,' my uncle commanded without waffling or any procrastination.

My mother who had already reached the door pulled the handle towards herself despite my uncle cautioning her. Amazingly, there stood my father in the popular Fulani regalia, with a hat, black hood round his neck and brown rubber footwear. He looked ruffled, worn out and dejected. He had so suddenly grown lean with an uneven and hoary-looking moustache nearly halfway down his neck like someone who had mourned for months. He hugged my mother in a manner that left no one in doubt he had the greatest appetite for her more than anyone else did. Minutes after, he beckoned to me. As I got to him, he lifted me and threw me upwards, lifting me in the air, and as I was going to land, I was in his two hands again. He then released me for a few seconds and again cuddled me to himself.

'Thank God your indecision has not caused you any trouble', my uncle said to him. 'You had the opportunity to come back peacefully with your wife and son but you chose not to do so. We are all so grateful to God that you finally made it back safely. Chioma, please don't disturb him with any further questions until he has put something in his stomach. So, organise some water for him to have his bath and then prepare some food,' my uncle suggested.

My mother got up to go to the kitchen, but she could not hold her peace. 'Where are your sharpened cutlasses?' she asked as she stared at him with distinct curiosity, but not with bitter spirit. She then left and stood near the kitchen's door, waiting for the water she filled the black kettle to get hot on the fire. 'Where is the sack containing the heads of those you captured and slaughtered?' she further enquired.

My father who was once known for being resilient at all cost now plunged his head downwards, deeply haunted by remorse. With a gentle and perhaps forced smile of penitence, he stood up and walked to my mother with his broad chest directly facing her as he spread out his arms to embrace her, reminding her that all of that show of brag was gone.

He then started to relate how his Hausa friends helped him. He told us how he disguised himself in the popular Fulani attire to escape shortly before the herdsmen started moving from house to house in search of the non-indigenes.

'Thank God you can speak Hausa very fluently,' my mother pointed out.

Not only could he speak the language very well, he was very popular amongst the large community. He narrated how he saw dozens of corpses flung on the roads as he tried to flee.

He was naturally strong and brave but his present experience appeared to have diffused his courage and made him lose confidence in himself. As I watched him, I could see that his encounter had tamed the combatant in him and it was going to take days before he could empty his memories of all that he went through.

A short while after, the water in the kettle which was on the fire was boiling and my mother went and emptied it into a waiting bucket, half full with cold water. After my father had taken his bath, he ate his food like a hungry lion that had not eaten for days, and when he had sat for a moment, he asked for a mat to stretch himself on the floor. He did not converse again until the next morning.

The next day, nobody reminded him that he was back to where he ran from years back, where both the weak and strong men spend their days on the farm, under the scorching sun, the vicinity of the no-nonsense thunder, the whirlwind and the showering of the rain. Vast measure of farmland awaited anyone who chose to return home and follow the path of bucolic existence.

So, it soon became apparent to my father that he was starting life afresh in the land of his fathers. It would have been different if he had returned with his cassava-grinding machine. Maybe, the story would have changed a little. Nevertheless, he was game for what would befall him.

'Don't get disturbed so much, Diji,' my uncle comforted him. 'I have excess yam seedlings and cassava stems to pass over to you,' he said. 'I shall organise some men who will assist you clear any dimension of land you may want to till,' he reassured him.

I had never before seen a man who had so much

unpretentious affection for his brother, like my uncle who did not even bear any physical resemblance to my father. He was short and fair in complexion with a pointed nose like that of an Italian figurine and he spoke extremely fast, as if through his nose.

With those words, my father spent the weeks that followed without the anxiety and nightmare which he had returned from Jos. So, he resolved to make life better from the uncompromising difficult struggle of that time. So did my mother, I could imagine.

***

Very quickly, my family became accustomed to the routine of village life. Though life was rugged and severe for us. My mother would constantly sit under the cashew tree with her sewing machine displayed very conspicuously. Yet for hours, no one would come to patch any torn clothes, not to speak of sewing new dresses. At times, she would sit all day without one customer. She would catch sight of a number of other village women who would have woken up at the third cock-crow returning from the farm in the evening, some with bunches of palm fruits and others with basins and sacks of cassava tubas, all of which they would process and take to the central market. Some would later trek with the processed items, carrying them on their heads to some other nearby villages that were some kilometres away.

Occasionally, some of the women would wave at my mother, as they passed, where she usually sat behind the sewing machine as she greeted them one after the other. The looks in their eyes would often confirm to her that they were all thinking she would not be able to make ends meet, unless she made up her mind to join them in making the early morning trips to the long distant cassava plantation.

As for my father, he would have to wait until the next farming period before he could begin to cultivate because it was already the middle of the ploughing season. Meanwhile, he became his brother's errand boy, though gleefully, in order to obtain the required yam seedlings and seedlings of other crops. Somehow, he moved on but it was not an easy experience.

As I grew up, I longed for the surplus cornflour food I used to enjoy in the north, the fine smelling onions, the delicious fresh milk usually obtained directly from the cows, called *fura* by the natives, the pure and organic honey extracted directly from very active and dexterous looking bees and the local rice pudding. I also longed for my friends, Audu, Kabiru, Sikiru and Yakubu. I missed them all and I had lost everything.

It was not so easy growing up in the village. Soon, I found that my parents were almost as if they were hustling on the streets to provide everything that I needed as a child to bring me up in a proper way. I knew that they loved me and wanted me to become an eminent person in the society. I wondered if they ever fathomed how obliged I was in my heart with the little they were already doing for me. Sometimes, my father would sit by my side in the evening when he returned from his activity and would tell me stories about my grandfather and great grandfather. It was my greatest joy to be with such a warm and comic father.

After staying in the village for a while, I found that most parents often sit with their children at nightfall to tell them interesting stories. Some would stay out under the moonshine or as soon as the stars were out and the owl hooting as if it was midnight.

Many times, my father would shrug his shoulders and appear very worried for a moment. I never understood why until months later when I realised that it was an expression of intense emotions for me as his only son and the stretched physical efforts with which he was battling with at the time. Often, he would end such mutual closeness with the warning, 'Chidi, my son, you must try to be a good boy and make me proud in the future.'

After my parents were stabilised, they fixed me back in the local school called The Baptist Primary School and wearing a brand-new blue and white tartan patterned top and khaki shorts on my first day was my greatest delight. From the outset, I was top of the class in every subject; doing very well in Mathematics, English Language, and most especially Religious Education. My biggest obstacle was the newly introduced vernacular, which I had to study with total neglect of other subjects.

I was very good in sports and months after I'd started the school, the games master chose me to be part of the school's football and volleyball teams, even though I was still very small. I loved those games with all my heart and against my parents' desire and pleasure, who felt they only sent me to school to face my studies. If they were proactive, they would have acknowledged the recognition and value placed on sports men and women.

Later, I joined the choir at the Baptist church located inside the school's premises and many people found that I was greatly talented in music. They believed that I had one of the strongest voices in the whole school. The choirmaster who tested my voice said he was including me in the choir because of my tuneful baritone. Initially, I felt flattered and shy too. I was constantly touched when I watched the lives of our choirmaster and others who truly lived very decent lives. Seeing their kind, calm and easy-going lifestyle reinforced my desire to become a Christian. I was highly impressed when the choirmaster approached me one day and told me that I would make a very good Christian if I continued with the same zeal for singing in the church. He encouraged me to face my studies and obtain the best educational qualifications so that I would be able to contribute more to the development of whatever church I would find myself part of in the future.

I understood exactly what hopes my parents had for me and I went about doing what was required of me, both at home and in school. I ate whatever was put in front of me no matter how poor it tasted.

On my part, I swept the house, dusted the tables and chairs, washed my school clothes, completed my school assignments on time and answered the teacher's questions correctly. Above all, I kept to myself at school more than ever before, standing alone in the corner of the field every breaktime, reserved, knowing the son of whom I was—poor parents.

However, as time went by, I began to come out of my shell and started making a few friends. In particular, I met Chike who was slightly older than I was and already in year six; ready to pass out from the primary school at the end of the session, while I was still in year five.

It was not easy growing up in the village as I discovered life was not just tough for us but almost impossible to scale with the constant struggle of getting enough to eat. It was also harsh for a number of other families like the one Chike came from. As young as some of us were, nobody advised us to look for ways of supporting ourselves. We did realise it ourselves and that was to be of great relief to our parents.

Each time we got back from school, and would have completed all our homework, I would accompany Chike to the bush to hunt for animals like rabbit or cockerel. Sometimes we also went to the nearby small river to fish. Chike was a nice fellow who also was serious with his studies, hardworking and always wanting to relinquish his parent's responsibilities over him. He had three siblings that I had not yet been acquainted with. I discovered that his parents and mine had almost the same zeal for fighting to survive life. It therefore seemed fitting for both of us to be friends. We dominated the surrounding bushes in search of rodents, in our efforts to make a sustainable living in accomplishment of our parents' wishes. We set traps here, there and, indeed, everywhere. Any day we failed to visit our traps; we would definitely bury at least a rodent in the bush before returning home because the traps we set never missed their targets. Besides the financial relief it afforded us, it provided pleasant delicacies in our homes.

One Saturday morning, Chike suggested that instead of going hunting or fishing, we should go in search of menial jobs at building construction sites, as we got the news that young teenagers who could give support to professional masons were usually welcomed. Anything Chike said was always good for me, so we went.

As soon as we got there, we found that the site supervisor would critically observe each person who came and make a declaration of 'yes' or 'no' as the person passed his front when he instructed the person to do so. Those who heard the 'yes' went to the right and those with the 'no' to the left. At the end, those with the 'yes' for which Chike belonged got the job and were asked to come every weekend as their slots would always be kept for them.

Though Chike was only slightly taller than I was, he was stout and it was often easy to see the lines of his muscles stretching on both arms. He had fat legs and a strong physique and as he walked, it appeared he was rocking backwards and forward like a chimpanzee. If anyone had asked both of us to run, I would undeniably be faster than he would, most likely because of his bowlegs.

The site supervisor asked the rest of us who could not meet the standard requirement to go home, as we did not qualify for the job by his evaluation. Truly, those of us the site supervisor discharged were evidently tender and possessed all the traits of adolescence.

The site supervisor required no oracle to know that we were too young and unfit for the nature of work required on that site. While others left, I remained there, pleading frantically with him. As I begged and wept, he saw my desperation and then said, 'Okay, I'll give you a chance to work on this site if you pass our normal stage two test for all applicants. That is the test we usually give to intending casual workers whenever we have a large number of them clamouring to be taken.'

'I'm ready sir,' I said to him without any hesitation. 'Sir, I'll give you a surprise today,' I said, unflinchingly.

'Okay, go over there,' he pointed. 'And remove the tarpaulin covering those bags of cement, and lift one, carry it to where they would be used over there,' he stated.

With every enthusiasm and hope, I hurried away to where the bags of cement were. I had the greatest assurance in myself that I would undoubtedly lift one as directed and most probably surprise the site supervisor. 'If not two bags, at least one, just one would get to where it was required and that would do,' I soliloquized.

Meanwhile, Chike who had started work was already perspiring. I could see that he kept his ears to the discussion that went between the supervisor and me. When I looked at him, his countenance showed that he was entreating for me. At another time, I looked at him and he was focusing on his work but I caught him making a sign of the cross. He was very curious of me getting the job or perhaps it could be he was anxious that we should continue to keep each other company as much as was possible.

I now bent forward to lift the bag containing the cement with all the energy in me, though mindful of my spinal cord. For me, it was a *do or die* affair. Quickly, I counted, 'One, two, three, go!' as though my strength depended on the tot up.

The hefty bag remained where it was, and if it were a living object, I was sure it would have let me know that my efforts were not having any impact. My palms were still very soft just like any other boy in his teens. I tried again and again and soon realised there was no way I could lift any of those massive bags of cement, even if I was allowed the opportunity to attempt as many times as possible.

In anguish, I went back to the supervisor to release the bad news. My thoughts that he would empathise with me sunk. He simply said, 'No sentiment, my boy, go home and come some other time.'

The rest of my day was ruined. My primary goal was to work and get some money, but that prospect had suddenly eluded me.

The good news was that Chike later came to our house that day to give me some money from his day's earning. After a couple of days, I still went to the construction site to try my luck. There was no success despite several attempts and I continued to try until one blessed day, the whole misery came to a halt, as I was able to cross the hurdle the supervisor placed on the path of every job seeker who went to that site for the first time.

Chapter Three

After the second farm harvest, my father could irrefutably say that he had overcome his earlier consternation as he looked back. That harvest was bountiful and everybody in the village acclaimed his accomplishment. That year alone, he was able to make a sale that helped him raise his own small brick apartment within a few months in which we later moved in. From then on, he kept showing my uncle that he owed him something more than gratitude.

We were not better than an average small family toiling on a daily basis to have the important aspect of our needs met. Nevertheless, food was never lacking on our table. It was always there.

My mother was a model of the olden day's woman, cut out to be a homemaker who honoured and loved her husband and a mother who cared so much for her only son. She was the third of her parents' daughters and, judging from some of her long-standing collections in her old-looking smeared plastic albums, she appeared to be much prettier compared to her other sisters. She was of average height and a good body size, with natural long hair, which she constantly flicked back, and she had inviting pouting lips. She was what one saw, very calm and humble. Her walk was gentle and admirable, striding often like one in a fashion parade. She was always all smiles, and nothing ever annoyed her.

From the way I saw my father look at her at times, it was obvious that he acknowledged her beauty. She had a perfect figure, I must confess, and she would not have encountered any problem attracting any man no matter how handsome or highly placed that man might be. Sometimes, when I looked at her and glanced at my father, I would feel that my father was not good enough for her, because of her splendour and character. My father must have counted himself lucky to marry such a woman whose beauty was admired by all and envied by many.

In contrast, my father was tall and stout; about five feet and seven inches with conspicuous muscles and fat legs that made him look masculine like his grandfather, according to him. He had very long and wide feet, so much so that no one's feet could ever fit in his shoes. He looked unbearably older than his age, perhaps because of the stress life brought to him so early, still, no one dared challenge him to a brawl. Merely the hairy looks of his chest would chase challengers away. His cheeks were flabby, his neck thick like that of a pig, his hair was already turning white, which caused confusion as many mistakenly referred to him as an old man. In any way, that did not remove the fact that, though not so conventionally handsome, he had a moderately attractive face.

I remembered stumbling upon some old pictures that my parents took together, showing them posing in different styles that seemed to symbolise enjoyment of the fruits of their marriage. In one of the pictures, they were both dressed in a crisp, purple, typical Nigerian hand-woven white top with sharply tailored gown and trousers. They looked like everyone's wish—contented and full of affection for each other. Truly, they were pictures of contentment. From that time and until the period I found myself staying with them, I never witnessed them explode at each other in a hot argument. I never saw either of them expressing primitive anger or using vulgar words.

I could still recall what happened between them one day, the day I thought that our home would be on fire. The time was about a few minutes passed seven p.m. in the evening. The whole of the outside was to some extent visible as the dusk fell but the inside had become dark, though not completely. My father had just finished taking his dinner and was relaxing in his usual sitting position in the living room, on a multi-coloured bamboo deck chair which my mother and I dared not sit on, not because he forbade us but as a mark of respect.

My mother had already placed the kerosene lamp on top of the centre table, slowly burning to give light to the entire area. As I passed, my unbuttoned shirt hooked the handle of the lamp and pulled it down, quenching the light and leaving the globe shattered on the floor. My mother who was at that time coming out from the kitchen with an empty glass in her hand, quickly placed it on the floor beside the chair where my father was sitting, in order to return to the kitchen for a broom and parker to clear the pieces of the globe.

At the same time, my father remembered that he had a torch light and stood up to go for it only to kick the empty glass dropped by my mother. The glass cracked and pieced into my father's right foot. He shouted and was calling for light as he realised the damage to his foot was severe. When my mother and I rushed to the scene, we could see blood gushing out like water from a tap.

'I'm so sorry, my dear,' my mother continued to say, repeatedly. One could catch her conspicuously showing signs of remorse. 'It's my entire fault as I should have told you to be careful when I dropped that empty tumbler,' she blamed herself.

'Don't worry, my dear; it's not your fault. I should have been more careful. Next time it won't happen like that,' my father stressed.

As I kept saying, 'Sorry, Father, sorry, Mother, for not being very watchful when I passed by the lantern.'

They both echoed at the same time saying it was not my fault either. I became even more astounded. The home was constantly quiet and when we were in, people who passed by would hardly hear any voice from the house.

As I grew up, I prayed and wished that when I became old enough to marry, I would be able to find a woman like my mother who would not pretend to be what she was not at first sight. Yes, I would want to marry a woman, whether gifted with splendour or inappropriate looks, who shall be virtuous enough to maintain peace and tranquillity in my home. But I prayed that God would give me the grace to emulate my father's forbearance.

The understanding between my father and mother helped us to live happily and manage our affairs without outside intervention. It made it simpler to wade through all the difficult challenges which confronted us as I went through my secondary school.

Hardship could sometimes transform into good tidings. Though my parents were good moralists, the difficulties and challenges that confronted us further made them to turn to

God. Indeed, their steadfast faith developed through hard circumstances. They started going to the old time Baptist church in my village, which had existed even before they were born. As they went, I went with them. There, the men of God taught people to have faith in a God who is able to make the impossible things possible.

I will never forget all they taught us in that church. They taught us as children that God is able to make someone live a life without evil thoughts or acts. Those young Sunday school teachers taught us that God could make someone love others sincerely without feelings of revenge. They also taught us that the Divine Trinity consists of three persons, God the Father, God the Son and God the Holy Ghost, and the three are as one. They taught us that there must be godly sorrow for sin and a renouncing of it. That justification is the act of God's grace through which we receive forgiveness for sins and stand before God as though we had never sinned. That we can be made holy; that divine healing of sickness is provided through the atonement; that Water Baptism is by immersion and that Jesus is coming again to take all the good people to heaven.

We were told that we would eternally be lost if we did not experience the new birth. For me as a teenager, I felt that fear and conviction in my heart. One day I yielded, I promised God as I knelt in one corner of our home that if He would save me, I would serve Him for the rest of my life. The glory of the Lord came down. It seemed like a beam of light pierced through the old enduring roof of that house and went down into the depths of my soul. The condemnation, worry and care were gone and the joy of another world filled my heart. That choice my parents made established a spiritual heritage for me.

However, when I was through with my secondary school

education, it was evident I had temporarily reached the end of my education because of lack of financial support. Therefore, I decided to look for a job with my secondary school certificate. I wrote applications and sent to all the private firms and government offices that I knew at that time. Over three-quarters of them did not consider my application. The remaining gave me the opportunity to attend their interviews, but they all later came back with almost the same acknowledgement of:

'Dear Chidi,

Thank you very much for attending an interview at our organisation. However, we regret to inform you that on this occasion, we will not be progressing with your application because there were other candidates who matched more closely the skills and experience required for this role.

We wish you the best of luck in your job search.

Best regards.'

I began to wonder how a deprived secondary school certificate holder, like me, would have obtained the relevant experience they were looking for. The work experience I acquired at the construction site, membership of the football team in my school and the choir group were to me, sufficient to bridge any skills gap. By any standard, I knew that I had gained employability skills like effective communication, team spirit, interpersonal relationship, among others.

One day, luck opened its door for me at a time when I was getting frustrated. I received a letter from the State House of

Parliament that I was successful in my interview. They offered me the position of Clerical Support Officer on a level that was three steps away from the minimum. My parents were very elated. It was in the state capital at Enugu. I had not travelled to Enugu before where the State House of Parliament was located at the government-reserved vicinity except on the day when my mother and I were returning from Jos, some years back.

My uncle connected me to the son of one of the village chiefs so that I could stay with him until I found my feet. A day before the day I left, my uncle and my father sat me down to educate me. It was very important to them and I enjoyed the special attention they were both paying to me. The children of my uncle were still very small, and I was like the hope of the entire family.

'Be careful not to mix with bad people,' both of them had told me. 'Don't allow wayward girls to distract your attention,' they both emphasised.

'When it's time for you to get married, you must pray until God convinces you of the right woman,' my father stressed. 'It's not going to be by outward appearance but by God Himself pointing the woman to you. When you get to Enugu, face your work and always remember whose son you are. Don't neglect God. Keep your salvation and do not give the devil the chance to ruin your blessings. Find a Baptist church and make sure you always go to church,' he highlighted.

'I promise, Papa, I will be fine. I know that your hearts will go with me. I thank you so much, Papa, and thank you, Uncle.'

The next morning, it was a Saturday and the weather started with being bright but that fine climate suddenly changed. The sky became thick and wrapped with light floating smoke. I quickly prepared and went into the room to bid my father goodbye. 'Chidi, God will go with you,' he said.

I also went to say the same thing to my uncle and his wife. They were all very happy that I had something to do. They saw it as a big opportunity for me to earn something that would enable me to assist my parents and them too.

I hurried to the motor park with no minutes to spare. My mother raced after me shouting, 'Chidi! Chidi! Wait! I must see you off to the motor park.'

I looked back and saw her running after me and at the same time attempting to adjust her wrapper. I felt for her. I began to measure the level of her affection for me. It was immense. At that point, I could not hold my sob, yet I hid my face away from her eyes. Then I stood and uttered, 'Mama, hurry up. I don't want to miss the first bus and I don't want the rain to catch up with me too.'

'It won't, my son,' she said. As she reached me, she grasped my small handbag quite unexpectedly. She then held my hand as was traditional of her.

'Mama, leave my hand, let me walk by myself. I am no longer a child,' I insisted.

'You will be my baby forever, Chidi,' she said.

As we drew closer to the motor park, we could hear the motor boy shouting, 'Enugu! Enugu! Enugu! One more seat left to go.'

Both of us hurried at the same pace. The motor boy met us midway and took over my moderate leather bag containing a few of my belongings. I walked to the bus and jumped in. Where I sat was close to the door as I was the last person to board, and the motor boy shut the entry. My mother stood, gazing at me. Her eyes became very red and they stared awfully as though she was seeing not just me but something beyond.

'Mama, go and take care of my papa,' I told her.

As the bus driver sounded the horn to alert passengers that he was about to take off, my mother spun round and started to go back home. I sat yawning, and as I turned and gaped back towards that road, I could see her striding gently. I felt utterly dejected at that moment. I could imagine how bleak spirited and lonely she must have started feeling. But I was more concerned with one task which I set for myself, my future.

***

It was around four p.m. in the evening when we got to the ancient city of Enugu, which was to be about three hour's journey from my village but because of the bumpy roads, we spent nearly the whole of that day on the road. There were plenty of ditches everywhere and in some cases, the road had been cut in two by gully erosion, compelling every motorist to stop and ponder how best to evade the trenches. Besides, most parts of the road were muddy and slippery, constraining every driver to decelerate. Along the journey were many areas where the bushes from both sides of the road had nearly come together to cover the path. Though it was a lonely road, the only joyful thing was that it was quite safe to wade through.

At Enugu, the air was dry and already blistering as the sun had suddenly emerged soon after the early morning drizzling. As I passed, there was a weird smell oozing out from overflowing bins. Part of the city appeared to be filthily rich and the entire atmosphere enveloped with the horrid odour.

Everywhere I went, I stumbled on loathsome sights and the despicable stench. Some of the wastes contained solid and gaseous gases, which were toxic and radioactive. I was convinced that the negative attitude of the government towards the efforts to maintain a hygienic environment had continued to inspire citizens of that age-old city to advance in dirty culture and become nonchalant towards good sanitation.

At another place, I saw a middle-aged woman emerge from a narrow path and go to the side of the major road then she dropped off her sack of refuse without weighing up the aftermath of her action. Indeed, the city was quite unlike Mbauku where there was a continuous sweet-smelling breeze saluting everyone who resided there or came to visit.

I walked through the narrow streets trying to locate my destination until finally the sun set. The evening light illuminated every nook and cranny so I could dodge some of the spilled over litter bins.

I followed the description handed over to me and moved as smartly as I could as if I had lived my life in that strange city, until I got to the door of my host. On knocking, Amaka was readily present to welcome me. I found myself at once in a most pleasant and convenient apartment. The light was on, the hoary standing fan blew freely from the corner and assorted DVDs were neatly stacked on a medium height rack near the television, with a charming piece of classical music coming from two speakers placed adjacent to the television. There was a sofa, centre glass table, oblong in form with flagrance artificial flowers in its centre. There was a desk and another reading table made of mahogany wood, a soft armchair, and numerous books in the shelf that was standing on a nice Taiwan rug upon the under-layer foam. Everything was completely different from what I had already been used to. I was still scrutinizing intently the whole lounge when Amaka interjected my thoughts. 'Take your bag into the room,' he suggested.

'Let me rest a bit,' I responded. I then sat on the armless chair near the reading table. As I watched, my two hands were tucked in-between my legs, and Amaka could notice how I was admiring his tasteful minimal studio-like apartment.

Amaka was exactly the same age as Chike's elder brother, whom I left in the village. He had quite a cheerful and pleasant personality. He grew up in Enugu where he was born and stayed with his parents until he finished his education, started work and moved out into his one-bedroom flat. There was little account of his parents' background and lives other than that they were well to do and had stayed away from Mbauku all the days of their lives.

My luggage was still by my side, and for a moment all my anxieties and weariness were briefly gone. I could then hear the bell of the wall clock ringing and reminding us it was already seven p.m. It was a lovely melodious tone, like a soothing pill capable of luring one to go to bed without dilly-dallying. I continued to explore the rest of the apartment, and anyone could easily have described it as adequately appealing.

'Please go inside and drop your bag and come with me so that I can show you round my apartment,' Amaka said. 'Make yourself very comfortable. Keep your bag here,' he pointed. 'I have left some spaces in my wardrobe for you to hang some of your clothes. Over there is the bathroom. Go in and refresh. There is cooked rice already in the microwave, when you are done, I'll serve you...' Amaka went on and on.

It was too much hospitality for me to comprehend and

rather than being elated, I was nervous. Would the reception continue the same way? Was I going to part with Amaka in peace in the end? Or shall we go our different ways when the time comes for me to leave his place? I prayed for the good. Inside me, I was very eager for the night to roll fast so that I could rise and go to my first job, save some money and get my own apartment.

I finished in the bathroom, had my dinner and the bed was wide enough to contain two young relatives and friends. However, sleep would not easily come, as I was so anxious to experience first day at work. I remained calm and never wanted Amaka to know that I was struggling with sleep, though I securely closed my two eyes.

As I lay, I remembered my parents, especially my mother whom I could bet with anything that she would not have found her sleep too because she must have been worried about me. She would obviously be concerned with my general welfare. I quickly mumbled a few words of prayer that God should grant me favour on time so that I would prove to her how much I love her. As I focused on those thoughts, I fell into deep sleep.

Amaka was still in bed, stretching from one end to the other, when I sneaked out at exactly five a.m., to have my shower in readiness for work. I got prepared, putting on what I felt was my best outfit and left. It was a day I would never forget.

The office was a large government department but as soon as I arrived, an officer I met in one of the offices directed me straight to the unit where I was to work. As a junior clerical support officer, I was to be registering all the incoming and outgoing mails, tracking their movement and doing the filing for the entire members of staff of that department. For me, it was quite an enjoyable exercise.

When I got home that day, enough issues kept Amaka and me conversing until midnight.

After the first month, I shared my first salary into five— among my father, mother, uncle, and the church where I belonged. I then retained the fifth part. It was quite delightful to all of them because I had done that which was conventional.

But the things I witnessed while working as parliamentary junior staff gingered me to consider furthering my education in order to do something for my dear country. I discovered that those elected to serve my beloved country were not right-thinking persons. They were all the wrong people, without conscience, without vision, carting away the goods that belonged to all and sundry, and turned back to be selling the same goods to the people who owned them, like in the days of Jeremiah in the Bible. While they relish in wealth and affluence, there were thousands of marching faces of economically deprived citizens.

Our politicians were shady and consistently displayed deceit and lies like the infamous mafias. Rather than legislate for the good of the people, they slept in their statutory chambers, only to awake when it was time to loot the national treasury. It was quite awful. Those were the same stooges, who, from the outset, were swift to pledge heaven and earth for the costly votes of our people but were scarcely able to deliver the earth. They had made our once great country poorer. My country that was like the prince of the continent became then like a widow.

Those plunderers were making the precious sons and daughters of our fatherland weep and beg for bread on the streets. Their tears were very visible on their cheeks as their fine hopes dimmed. Those promising young men and women who previously were comparable to fine gold, suddenly turned out to be as esteemed as earthen pitchers.

Our leaders had greatly committed iniquities and all who used to honour us then despised us because we were no longer worthy of anything in their eyes. They saw our nakedness.

The wickedness of those men and women who called themselves politicians showed even on their attire.

My eyes ached with tears because our God given treasure had become like dung and the bowel of our citizens were being troubled.

Those who had the power to speak and confront the perpetrators of evil kept silent.

A number of children, and even the suckling, swoon in the streets and appeared to be asking, 'Mother, Mother, where is our bread and butter?'

My country's breach was as deep as the sea and there was none to heal her. All who heard of our woes clapped their hands, hissed, and wagged their tongues with questions like, 'Is this the nation that men called the giant of Africa, the former joy of the whole continent? Is this the centre of the black populace?'

Our leaders were cruel like the ostriches in the forest as they cared less for our young ones who fainted with hunger in every lineage and the tongues of the suckling children bit the tips of their mouth for thirst.

The people exterminated by the sword were fewer than the ones taken away because of hunger, stricken through for want of the fruits of the field.

The kings of the earth and the inhabitants of the world would never have believed that the adversary and the enemy were able to penetrate the land of an oil rich country, all because of their leaders.

And the hopes of many as yet failed for vain help. In waiting, they waited for a country that could not deliver them because the perpetrators were swifter than the eagles of the earth.

They drove away the innocent who would have redeemed our country and safeguard the crown. Rulers became servants and servants became the rulers. Yet, none could lift up their eyes towards the heaven and cry for mercy.

Those things pained me so much. So, I got inspired to pursue journalism part-time at the University of Enugu. It was going to afford me the chance to join the fearless who dared challenge those rogues called the politicians.

In due course, I gathered some money and moved out of Amaka's flat. But I must state that from the first day and until the last I stayed with him were treasured. He had made every sacrifice to make my stay pleasurable.

Working and schooling at the same time was not something palatable in those days. Most of the time, lectures for some courses that I enrolled in would have ended before I got to the classroom. My workplace and the university location were kilometres apart. Often, the traffic would stretch over a long distance, constantly halting for hours before any vehicle could move and within a few minutes of easing off, it would come to a halt again. Hawkers seen at both sides of the road would occasionally block the views of many drivers. Sometimes, by the time I reached the university main gate, I would see some of my university colleagues already making efforts to board any available bus to get to their different homes, leaving me with no option than to find my way back too. For that reason, spending four years in the university was like a nightmare.

I was sure it was my parents' prayers which probably kept my zeal and energy going. They could not offer anything but their regular petition to God.

At that time, my father had become the assisting pastor of the Baptist church in my village while my mother was a senior minister. They never missed attending the church for one day. It was a constant reminder from my mother in all of her mails to me that I should never forget to attend church on Sundays. 'It will do you good,' she would always admonish, and all the time ending with a scripture quotation like, 'God is our refuge and strength, a very present help in trouble' or, 'Love not the world, neither the things that are in the world. If any man loves the world, the love of the Father is not in him. For all that is in the world, the lust of the flesh, and the lust of the eyes, and the pride of life is not of the Father, but is of the world.' Those words and their truth kept me going until I completed my studies.

After my graduation ceremony, I tendered my new degree certificate for an upgrade to a new position. Later, I was elevated to a senior position and posted to the liaison office at the country's capital city, Abuja. It meant I had to leave the naturally beautiful houses at Enugu and the hospitality and love that I had become accustomed. As I gathered my essential belongings, I was ruminating over the nervousness my mother would go through on receiving the news of my movement. Somehow, I suddenly became comforted on recollecting that their lives had become devoted to God.

The sun rose early, and the weather was very bright on the day I was going to travel. It meant that the roads would be dry and every driver's vision would be better because of the warmth of the day. After the journey had started, we had not gone half way when one of the tyres of the vehicle carrying us exploded. I was glad the vehicle was not at top speed and so no damage was done save for my palpitating heart. Everyone in that vehicle soon found themselves compressed like sardines in the back of a towing van pulling the vehicle to the next town where the tyre would be patched. Unknown to us, and as was common among the drivers in that part of the country, the driver had no spare tyre. When we got to the next town, none of us was prepared to wait for the roadside repairer to finish with the fixing of the tyre, so we all left to look for an alternative vehicle.

We stood for hours along that road under the gradually warming sun, waving down every passing vehicle. The other option would have been to go into the motor park, but we would not for fear of the high cost of the fare. After many hours, a black Peugeot 404 Station Wagon pulled up before us. It was not a commercial vehicle but a privately-owned car and the owner was ready to take as many passengers as were there and anxious to leave just for a token. We were ten passengers cramped together. Ten passengers were overload for a vehicle that would have only accommodated a maximum of six passengers, excluding the driver.

Soon after we all sat in that vehicle, I started reading a story in a magazine lent to me by one of the passengers. It was an interesting love story of a Nigerian top military leader and legendary hero, triumphant in coup plotting. He only came to the limelight after he showed himself as the spokesperson for the last coup plotters. His name was Lieutenant Colonel Haruna. He and his co-plotters succeeded because they used young military boys who were mostly commanders of various units. Most of those commanders asked their boys to come for a party and when they all arrived, they conscripted them into the group. Subsequently, they went to the armoury in Lagoon cantonment, close to the defence headquarters, got the people around that place, took all the guns and ammunition and every other thing they needed for the coup. So, the trusted military boys of the then President were the people that pulled his government down.

The high point of that coup was to curb corruption and many other anomalies in the society. For instance, some of the military officers who attended the choicest military training colleges in the world were not included in the government affairs because they were not from the privileged part of the country while the mediocre among them were greatly favoured. When those in authority celebrated mediocrities and pushed excellence to the background, it would be painful; and those were the things those young soldiers wanted to correct. When the politicians dethroned the sovereignty of the people for the sovereignty of the crooks, the so-called, *godfathers*, then they were, at the same time, creating lawlessness as well as perversion and injustice.

I had almost lost every remembrance that I was in a vehicle because of the captivating narrative when, without prior sign, there was a sudden explosion and that sound was the last thing I could still recount until I saw a good part of me roasted by flames, now looking like a leftover grilled chicken.

The two front tyres of the vehicle had burst and, together with the wheel, rolled off on their own, unstopped. Before one could realise it, the vehicle had started to somersault. One eyewitness testified that it did a cartwheel a number of times and when it stopped, the roof of the vehicle was on the ground with the four tyres facing the sky. As if that was not bad enough, it subsequently caught fire in a matter of seconds.

I was unconscious for a moment but was woken up by the harsh shouting coming from one of the passengers sitting by the side of the fuel tank. 'Fire! Fire! Fire!' he continued to beckon. It was coming from one of the passengers who was where the fire had probably started. Later, I discovered that nearly half of the passengers were asleep when the incident happened.

Soon the smoke covered the entire space, but luck showed me an opening for an escape. As I struggled to come out of the vehicle, I could feel the unbearable heat of the fire travelling from my two legs to my head. I screamed as I battled for my life. My face, my back, my left hand and part of my legs were all skinned and instantly became a nasty sight. I smelt like a male goat thrown into the fire to rip it of its hair.

As I lay by the roadside, I could still hear some voices in pain coming from the vehicle, shouting persistently, 'Help! Help! Help!' Some people were in great danger even as the flame had completely taken possession of the vehicle that all who stopped to render whatever help they could, stood helpless. Yet more and more echoes of 'Help! Help!' kept coming, again and again from the flame but they quietened as they lost energy to cry out.

Minutes after, some good Samaritans came who helped me, together with a number of others, to a local hospital where I spent a few days before the doctor transferred me to the Abuja General Hospital. Before that time, the news had reached my office and every one of them began praying for my quick recovery.

While at the Abuja General Hospital, I met someone who asked if I was interested in gaining employment in a sector most viable and enviable by many young people, the upstream sector. I quickly jumped at it and he requested that I complete an application. I asked for a clean sheet of plain paper. I scribbled some lines as much as my state of mind could carry me at that time and handed it over to that man. I was still at that hospital when I received a phone call that I should attend an interview. I had felt well enough to a point when the doctor could have discharged me but I was not, for some reasons which the doctor refused to disclose to me. When I explained to the head of the ward what my wishes were, he arranged with the matron to delegate one of the nurses to accompany me to the interview venue. A nurse I had not seen since I had been at the hospital. I later learnt that her name was Nkem.

Nkem had looks that any man would fall for at first sight. She was fair of complexion, with dimples on her cheeks each time she smiled. Each time she smiled, anyone close to her would be compelled to show their admiration. Her smile made it very appealing to look at her endlessly. Her eyeballs were dim, and her pupils glittered in such a manner that would make one think she was a half-caste. When she glanced at people, she did so as if she was sending out a free invitation to the young men among them who cared. She also bore some traditional tiny marks on both sides of her cheeks, which made it so easy for me, like anyone else, to guess her correct ethnicity.

She was tall and chubby. Her hair was dark and long, extremely suitable for any style of natural weaving. It appeared to be a special gift from God because it left her with no other choice than a continuously natural weaving shape and trying out any other style, which could require some woollen attachment, would be a waste of effort. Indeed, she had a perfect structure from her head to her toes. She certainly would qualify for a regional beauty contest.

From the way she was dressed in her immaculate white gown, I doubted if any other profession would have been more befitting to her than the one she had found herself. She was very nice to look at especially with a hat like that of an air hostess. Nkem was quite a pleasant and charming young lady, with a noble personality.

As we crossed the pavement in front of the hospital Nkem held me. 'Don't worry,' I said to her. 'I believe I can walk on my own,' I pointed out.

'No, Chidi, you are my patient and under my care and I must ensure you are all right,' she responded.

'Hope you have got enough money for the taxi fare,' she asked.

'Yes, of course,' I replied.

'Well, in case you are short of money, I can always augment for you,' she added.

'That won't be necessary. Thank you very much.'

Soon, we waved down a taxi and it pulled by. 'Where?' The taxi driver asked.

'Natural Gas Company.'

'The company's headquarters or its annexe adjacent to the stadium?'

'The headquarters.'

'Seven hundred,' he said.

'No, five,' Nkem responded.

'Make it six, and let's go,' he made the last offer.

'Please, five,' Nkem insisted.

'Two of you?'

'Yes, but we don't have any luggage, you know.'

'Okay, get in,' he said. We jumped in.

The taxi driver moved as carefully as he could but when we had gone just a little beyond halfway, we heard a loud sound at the rear of the vehicle. The driver pulled by the side to check where the sound came from and behold a cyclist had crashed his bicycle on the car, damaging the rear light as well as the bicycle's front light. To our surprise, before we could get out, more than ten other cyclists had surrounded the car and were demanding that the taxi man should pay for the bicycle's front light.

'How dare you make such a silly statement when it was your man, who ran into my car?' the taxi man blew up. Before we knew it, one of them opened the boot of the car and removed the jack. 'What do think you are doing?' The taxi man fumed. As he moved towards the man holding the jack, he sighted a traffic officer coming, and then he went to complain.

'You are both causing an obstruction,' the officer said. 'Move your car to the service lane and then we can settle the matter.' As the taxi man went into his car to move it out of the way, all the bicycle riders disappeared, leaving the young naughty rider who defaulted.

'I'm sorry,' he said to the taxi driver.

Nkem came out of the car, enraged. 'Why didn't you apologise earlier, but waited until you have wasted our time?'

The taxi man glared at him, exceedingly angry but went and picked his jack where a colleague of the defaulter dropped it. He then entered his car. As Nkem came in, we set off again. We had only fifteen minutes left to be on time.

Surprisingly, we were on time and Nkem would have to

wait for me until I finished the interview. As we stepped into the small reception office, we could hear the silent humming of two standing giant air-conditioners blowing out some chilly air that was not quite appealing to all visitors, particularly for people like me who had just entered the city. We both wondered how the workers could stay in that chilly condition without coming down with a cold, though they all appeared in well conventional tailored suits. There were eight altogether who came for the interview and I was the third to go in. After about half an hour of rigorous verbal drilling and tests, I came out only to meet Nkem nodding her head backwards. I tapped her on the shoulder and she quickly adjusted her head up, feeling a bit embarrassed.

'How was the interview? she asked.

'Oh! Good. Very good. I'm quite hopeful,' I told her.

'I pray God favours you today and always,' she whispered.

I became elated and full of strength and as we boarded another taxi back to the hospital, I was so pleased with the manner Nkem spoke to me.

'Where are you from?' I asked.

'Why do you ask?' she responded.

'Having spent almost all day with me, I deserve to know,' I said.

'You already know my name, don't you?'

'Yes, I know, but from which part of the country are you?'

'Does my name not say it all?' she asked. 'Look at my tribal marks.'

'Are you from Enugu?'

'No. I'm from the core Niger Delta area.'

'Cross River?'

'No. Rivers,' she stated.

'Okay, I see. That must be the Ibo speaking part.'

'Yes, you are correct.'

As soon as we got to the main gate of the hospital, we cut our conversation short. When we alighted, and as we walked into the hospital premises after I had paid the taxi driver, some of the staff were wearing welcome looks, interested in knowing the outcome of my interview as if I had become a member of the hospital family.

The entire staff at the hospital were all glad and treated me as one of their own until I left the hospital three days later. Even as I left, I was still carrying scars around my forehead and arms that would take a few more weeks to heal completely.

I was still recuperating in the State House of Assembly guesthouse, when again I received a letter from the Natural Gas Company that I should come for a second interview. When I got there, only three interviewers were at the table, one of them a woman. Only three of us who must have performed well came this time around. I had hardly taken my seat when the woman started throwing a catalogue of questions at me.

'Tell us why you think you are the right person to be hired for this job,' she asked. 'What is the greatest challenge you have ever encountered in your life?' she asked again, barely allowing me to complete the submission of my response to her first question before unleashing more questions. As I later learnt, her mission was to make me fumble as she favoured the candidate from the same tribe as hers. As luck would have it, the head of public relations, the man who later became my boss, preferred me. That was how I got that lucrative job.

I had not resumed at my new posting when I tendered my resignation at the State House of Parliament, and a few days after, I commenced work at the Natural Gas firm.

There, at the Natural Gas Company, the entire office setting was different. The people were unique and more business-like. Everybody appeared very serious at work, from resumption to closure. It was a company for anybody with aspiration to build a career. Not like the State House of Parliament where people exhibited indiscipline in no small measure. There, workers were known to be irregular at, and generally habitually late, to work with many of the junior ones covering their bosses' lapses. Despite their lateness, many would spend hours saying hello to friends and chatting away. Some who got to work hours late closed earlier to take care of their private business, most times using state owned cars. Some female workers would leave their desks to be hawking wares from one office to the other. Yet, no one did anything to correct the anomaly.

Chapter Four

After working close to two years at the Natural Gas Company, my parents began to put pressure on me to find a woman who would spend the rest of her life with me. That happened to be every parent's worry and dream in those days. It would fulfil the good old Biblical command of, "Be fruitful and multiply…" I succumbed to their insistence and I was then counselled by them to pray very earnestly for God's guidance and also cautioned not to look outside the Christian folks for the bone of my bone.

'You are our only child and so you must quickly marry to keep the lineage of your father alive,' my mother continuously sang this into my ears at every opportunity. Always adding: 'But you must pray until God shows you your wife'

I became very steady with attendance at the Baptist church, which was far-flung from the vicinity where I lived. I took part in virtually all activities. I could say that I was even lucky that there was a branch of the church in the city although I was ready to make all the sacrifices to attend it, wherever it might be located, since I knew my parents would be more than elated.

I remember my first day at that church. It was my greatest

pleasure. The branch was a revamped version of the one located at Mbauku, my village, but anywhere the Baptist church was, its viewpoints and tradition were the same. Generally, the members of the Baptist churches were not flamboyant. They were strictly conservative in outlook with the women not carrying jerry-curled hair, earrings or bangles. People knew them for their full-length, well-rounded blouses that rode up the neckline, which made it so difficult to reveal anything that was not to be.

It was always easy to identify any Baptist Church from a distance by the heterogeneous flowers and beautifications that often surround their vicinity, starting from the frontage. Everything about the church was unique and there were always people to welcome you as you step in, right from the gate to the main entrance leading to the auditorium where the great men of God ditched out the sermons on a weekly basis. Even some of the aged men and women were not discouraged because of distance, neither were they encumbered for their years, in trekking the long distances to get to those churches. They still preferred the many kilometres hike through the dusty roads, rather than worship in any other nearby churches.

The distance was usually a lengthy span for me to and from the church but it was something I craved to do. On one of those Sundays, I was going home after the service, I felt as if my two legs were heavy and unable to carry me, so I decided to use public transport. That day I stood for a very long time without catching a bus, as was usual due to the remoteness of the area.

After I waited for nearly half an hour, a bus came which was almost full to capacity and I sat at a spot next to the door, stretching my hand to give the fare to the bus conductor when someone tapped me from behind. It was Nkem, the nurse whom I had not seen since I left the Abuja General Hospital.

'Where are you going?' I asked.

'I'm on an afternoon shift today,' she answered.

'Do you work on Sundays? Don't you go to church?'

'Yes, I do work on Sundays, occasionally.'

'Okay, don't worry about your fare. The bus conductor will take it from the money I have handed in,' I told her.

'I can see that you are doing very well,' she stated.

'Well, I thank the Almighty God,' I responded. I felt some guilt in my heart that ever since I left the hospital, I did not make any attempt to check on her, at least to prove how grateful I was to her for all that she did for me. When I realised it was well over a year since I saw her last, I felt even worse. I quickly apologised. 'Nkem, I'm so sorry that I did not bother to check on you at the hospital knowing that if not for your kind help, I would not have got the job I'm doing today.'

'Never mind, it means nothing to me. I know you have been very busy with the work; though it would have been my joy to find out how you are doing, especially with the job.'

'I promise to check on you at the hospital one of these days,' I assured her.

'I'm getting off at the next stop,' I told her.

'Okay, take very good care of yourself,' she said.

'Goodbye,' I finally uttered as I got off the bus.

From that moment, my heart centred on Nkem as a woman who I felt could keep a home. Her beauty, her soft-spoken words and patience were all that set flame on my superficial mind to consider her as a possible life partner. I completely forgot my parents' constant advice that prayer was paramount before embarking on that journey.

The next weekend, I took a gamble and decided to pay Nkem a visit at the hospital. As I got there, the woman I met at the front office quickly recognised me. 'Please remind me your name,' I said.

'Esther,' she told me. 'But I still remember yours very well, or are you not Chidi Diji Dike?'

'Oh, yes, you are very correct. Ah! Esther Saraki,' I screamed. 'Please forgive me, your hair style has completely changed your look,' I appealed.

'How is life with you?' she asked.

'Well, God has been faithful to me,' I stated.

'Are you here to see the doctor?' she enquired.

'No. I'm now one hundred per cent healthy. I'm here to see Nkem,' I said. 'Is she at work?'

'Hope there is nothing wrong?'

'Nothing, just nothing,' I emphasised.

'The doctor is conducting a ward check and Nkem is going around with him.'

'I will wait then,' I stated.

'Fine,' now lowering her voice. 'I hope there is nothing serious between two of you?' she asked with all manners and the body language of an office gossip. I stared away, feigning a bit of indifference. She went further, this time increasing the tempo and level of her voice, 'Be very careful, Chidi, I must warn you about that lady. She has funny and strange behaviour. She doesn't get on well with anyone in this hospital. Everybody has something against her, or she has something against everybody.'

Esther spoke as if she knew Nkem from childhood; with such conviction that perhaps showed she was acquainted with some measure of her hidden identity, more than anyone else was. There was nothing, which Esther disclosed that resembled my perception of Nkem. The past images of her soft-spoken words on the first time we met and the day she went with me to where I was currently working as Public Relations Officer, flickered on my mind. I recalled her care and sympathy. A straight talker, very calm but engaging and very collected except that she was in some way tight-lipped. *Could all of that be deception?* I asked myself. *Could Esther be lying against her or exaggerating the facts to send me off?* One instant conclusion in my heart was that Esther must have told many tales about Nkem simply to thwart my intentions for reasons I could not yet spot. After not too long, Nkem passed by and waved at me, signalling that she would attend to me in a matter of minutes. I hung patiently until she came to meet me. 'So, you kept to your words,' she asked as soon as we embraced each other. She looked occupied with her work routine.

'It's very unfortunate you came at such a time I have so much to do,' she said. 'I won't be able to stay here in the waiting room with you for too long.'

'It's all right, just to fulfil my promise,' I told her. Then I got up and she followed me to the door.

'Would you allow me to pay you a visit in your home?' she asked.

'Why not?' I replied. 'Only make sure you keep me informed so that I would shelve all other commitments I might be having,' I said. We then parted.

In my next communication with my parents, I told them of my feelings for Nkem and requested that they join me in prayers. My mother again took me through the marriage process in the Baptist Church, warning me not to have anyone in mind while praying but to ask that God Himself should direct me and choose a wife for me. She encouraged me to seek the counsel of the elders in my church branch.

Sadly, whether I sought the counsel of the elders of the church or not, it seemed that my mind was already unwavering, my heart ruling my head. I had fallen head over heels in love with someone I had hardly been acquainted with. Nothing my mother said to me had sunk in yet.

A few months after visiting Nkem at the hospital, Nkem gave me a telephone call to inform me that she was going to return my visit by that weekend.

I had a one-bedroom flat near the city centre. I furnished the apartment very scantly because I had paid a very high rent to get it, which so many people had wanted. Besides, my primary objective was to save some money in good time.

The entire vicinity was decent; the surrounding roads tarred with concrete sewage channels at both sides. The apartment itself was in a well-fenced compound decorated with flowers. It was a one-storey building containing about five apartments. My apartment was on the top rear. The walls inside my flat had fresh fine light-green and white colour combination that stood out, coated with wallpaper in some places. The floors that were covered with fashionable tile designs kept sparkling, whether I mobbed them or not. I had very fine-looking curtains hanging at each door and window of the entire apartment.

The apartment appeared ill-furnished and there was nothing in it that would have made me encourage any stranger to visit me, save for very close people. But I did not mind Nkem visiting because my heart was already centred on her.

Predictably, when Nkem came knocking at my door, I

could see from her eyes that she had far more expectations than she met. She had already imagined that I had become well off owing to where I was working.

Her stay was long. I entertained her with a bottle of apple drink and some chocolate biscuits. Though she drank and ate the biscuits there was something on her face that told me she was longing for a bit more than those. 'Can I get you some more apple drink?' I asked.

'No. No. Not the apple drink again,' she responded. 'Don't you have something with just a little alcohol in it, like an original blended malt whisky or red wine?' she asked.

'Oh no,' I said. 'I thought you are a Christian?' I asked.

'Yes, of course. Does that mean you should not take just a little alcohol? Was Timothy in the Bible not admonished to take just a little wine for his stomach trouble?' she responded.

'That is a big misconception of the Bible. Anyway, I don't have any at home at the moment.' We then talked about the social life of the city, ranging from the constant road congestion to the growing insecurity caused by some hoodlums. We never stopped talking until she was about to leave. As she got up, I went closer to her and cuddled her without any hidden intention, thanking her for coming. She then held my two cheeks and drew my face close to hers until I could feel my chest against her breast. Suddenly, her rich dark hair and luring shining eyes carried me away. We glanced at each other for seconds and in the end, she clasped both hands round my neck and seized my tongue with her lips, kissing and holding me tight to her body. It was a quick clumsy and rough kiss of tongue-to-tongue. I quickly released myself, as I could no longer resist her.

'Start going!' I shouted, moving towards the door. She

pulled my hands and pushed towards me. I flung my hands away.

'Are you sending me away?' she asked.

'No. But you have to start going right now.'

'Okay, okay,' she consented. She took gentle short strides towards the door and as I followed, she turned all of a sudden, cuddled me, and began to caress me once again.

It was sad for me that before Nkem left my house, what usually happen between a young man and a woman of his choice took place, to my greatest fury. It broke down my spirit that day and I went about the whole of the weekend, sober and full of guilt, praying that God should forgive me and spare me from facing any public degradation.

As time went by, Nkem called me to let me know that I had put her in a family way. I screamed as I was staggered by that piece of information. Subsequently, I invited her to my house again.

I shook my head and pitied myself as I became very obsessed with what I was soon to confirm. My parents would feel betrayed and the church disappointed. *How would I even let the cat out of the bag?*

When Nkem came calling at my doorstep the second time, I prayed that it should be all a joke, but that prayer was not answered. As she stepped in, I could read her body language and it did not take long to realise that Nkem was very serious with what she had revealed to me. She was sure herself. There seemed to be no way out. Apart from having the intuition, she could feel her breast as tender as an overripe watermelon and heavier too, with occasional abdominal cramping. Her rejection of smell had increased especially with fried food causing her wave of nausea for her stage.

Sweat suddenly began to drip down my sleeve, and my heartbeat echoed fast as I made those discoveries myself. Anyone very close to me would hear the reverberation.

Nkem sat very quietly, with her stylish dress, on the easy-cushion chair near the entrance. She was very calm and was looking indifferent. There was a sudden moment of quietness by both of us as we starred away with faces of hate. Suddenly, our eyes locked in mutual animosity.

'Aren't you a man?' she uttered. 'Look at the way you are glaring morosely, panicking and shaking like a leaf. You better rise up, be a man and let's decide immediately on what next to do.' I remained speechless as I buried my head in my palms. 'Anyway, let's go and see a doctor for advice,' she chirped in.

'What advice?' I asked.

'For some pills, may be.'

'Pills for what?'

'Pills to get rid of the thing or are you ready to be a father?'

'Never!' I shouted without thinking over the idea twice. 'I am a Christian or, was, if you like,' I averred. 'My membership of the Baptist Church and earlier contact with God had enlightened me enough as to know what was morally right. I won't do a thing like that and fall into the mighty hands of God. That would be committing double iniquities.'

What I was more afraid of facing was the let down and reproach which I would soon be bringing to my parents and the church that had come to know me as one of its own. My eyes were dry and red and I started feeling as if something was knocking my chest against a rock and broken into pieces.

Nkem turned her face away from me, feeling very relaxed as it were. Perhaps, she had little or no idea what was going on inside of me. She had not known much of my background neither did I know hers. For me, it was an intense mental pain combined with feelings of severe dread as I contemplated how to manage the indignity.

How best to take the news back to my parents became a second major obstacle and next was the question of how Nkem's parents whom I had never met before would take the matter. They may feel that I had trapped their daughter with a man's wiles and wrecked her career prospects. They would hardly believe it was the other way around.

Nkem had dozed off by this time. I moved closer to her and tapped her on the shoulder. I detested her that very moment. 'You have to start going!' I yelled.

'Okay, but what's the conclusion of the matter?'

'Give me some days to think about the whole nonsense.'

'You called it nonsense? Something you knowingly did?'

'You enticed me into it.'

'See what you are saying. Better be a man and accept your fault.'

'Please go, I say go.'

'All right but I beg of you not to delay for too long, so that the public, especially my co-workers would not notice anything,' she said. She got up and held me, drawing her lips to give me a kiss. I pushed her away in fierce anger and saw her to the main door of my small apartment. She departed.

At work, in subsequent days, people began to spot out my low-spirited countenance and started talking about it behind me. I was therefore not surprised when my boss called me in to his office one day to talk about what was filtering into his ears.

'Sit down, Chidi,' he said. 'I have noticed that you are no

longer looking as cheerful as you used to be in the past. Is there anything going on in your life that you may wish to confide in me?'

'There's nothing, sir,' I quickly responded.

'I want you to be rest assured that it's going to be between only the two of us,' he pointed out.

'There's nothing, sir,' I insisted.

'Why I'm so concerned is because very lately I have noticed unusual errors in the reports and correspondences you prepared. It's unlike you, Chidi,' he noted.

'I'm very sorry about that, sir. I shall be more careful henceforth,' I promised.

'Okay, take this document. That's the last report you passed to me yesterday. I have made some corrections and comments. Please do the necessary adjustment and let me have it back as soon as you are done. Nonetheless, if there is anything you want me to explain further, do let me know.'

'Thank you very much, sir,' I said and left. I could tell he did not believe me and saw from his facial expression that he knew I was hiding something. As I got back to my desk, I stood backing it and was unable to take my seat immediately as cold gripped me over the sticky situation.

Just at the very point of sitting down, I heard footsteps inching towards me and I turned. It was Stella Isa, one of the senior officers in our Human Resources unit.

'I've been here before to see you but I saw you entered your boss' office so I decided to hang around and wait for you,' she hinted. 'I actually came to see you on a very personal matter, and I hope you have got a moment,' she enquired.

I quickly took my seat and adjusted myself, focusing raptly at her. She pulled the chair in front of me and sat down.

My face looked very strong but she smiled at me as if to cheer me up but hesitated, a bit like someone who did not know how to put the matter.

'I'm all ears, my sister,' I said to her.

'Well, Chidi, it is not anything serious, just that I noticed recently that you have been unusually quiet. Is there anything wrong?' I chuckled and managed to put up a nervous smile, pretending that all was well.

'How do you mean?' I queried.

'You are not as lively as you used to be and people in this office are talking about it. Did you receive a warning or reprimand from your boss?'

'Well, Stella, there is nothing like that,' I reiterated.

'Okay, I am happy to hear there is nothing. I just wanted to make sure, because you are one of the few in this office who have been placed on the fast track, and the company is always obliged to assist staff in this category achieve their goals. Anyway, let me go back to my office because I have got lots of tasks on my desk.'

'Thank you very much,' I said. *Holy Mary! So that which took place in the secret place is now in the public domain. I must do something about this matter before it becomes a nightmare*, I thought within me. I now realised I was a gibbering wreck as the bleakness of my depression was lifting.

Chapter Five

Three days later. I went to my boss as soon as I arrived at the office. 'Good morning sir.'

'Good morning, Chidi. I hope all is well?'

'Yes sir, just that I have an urgent need to travel to the village to see my parents.'

'That's no problem, Chidi. Complete the necessary absence form and I will sign it.'

'Thanks very much, sir.'

'That's all right.'

I walked out satisfied that he did not bother to ask for my reason for travelling to the village. I could now embark on the journey to break the unpleasant news. That was going to be the first time I would be going to see them since leaving my small hamlet of Mbauku after my secondary education. But look at what I would be taking home to them? I knew it would not make them happy.

The road to my village from Enugu had become worse. To get there on time, I had to wake up very early as if I was traveling to a neighbouring country. Not just that, it was no longer safe to ply anytime from five p.m. in the evening, through the night. Most motorists were arming themselves to the teeth, with machetes and locally made guns to confront any possible emerging hoodlums. Luck must be on anyone's side not to come across fake checkpoints manned by those hooligans.

Before I took off from the motor park, I made sure I got some assorted biscuits and chocolate sweets. I would find them very handy for the numerous children who were likely to come around to greet me when I got to the village.

After about eight hours on that road, I arrived safely. The driver drove straight to our family compound. My mother ran out from under the cashew tree where she was sitting behind her ancient sewing machine. Over a dozen children ran after her and now were surrounding me. They were all struggling to get hold of my small, travelling black leather bag as soon as my feet touched the ground from the vehicle. 'Don't destroy the handle of the bag,' my mother shouted at them. 'Let two persons carry it,' she told them. I left the bag for them and went into the medium size bungalow my father put up before moving out of my uncle's apartment. The smell of the house was a mixture of ancient wood and red dust common in that region, yet without an air conditioner, it was chilled and homely.

Everyone was happy to see me, especially my mother who kept on greeting me repeatedly, 'Welcome, my son, welcome, my son.' She was overjoyed.

'I hope you are in good health,' she asked.

'I am, Mama.'

'But you look so worried and not very happy as I used to know you,' she pointed out.

'I am happy, Mama, but...'

'But what? Speak to me, Chidi,' she begged.

'Where is Papa?' I asked. I tried to digress in order to have more time to gather myself and choose my words in a way that would catch the fancy of her sympathy rather than wrath.

'Your father has gone to see one of his friends. He would soon be back. You can go to say hello to your uncle whom I guess is indoors as he has not been feeling well lately.'

'I will do that later.'

I made for my bag and unzipped it, brought out some biscuits. I took a pack and handed it to my mother to distribute to the children who assisted in carrying my bag and were still hovering around. Already, the children playing within close proximity were sure they would get something for the helping hands they lent. My mother called the one who was the oldest among them and gave him the biscuit. 'It's for all of you,' she emphasised loud and clearly.

The children could notice my father coming from afar. One of them ran to meet him. 'Papa, Uncle Chidi just arrived,' the little boy revealed to him. My father, who was now very anxious, then looked up and saw a number of other children. He increased his steps and as he approached, still from a reasonable distance away, he asked in a voice shaking with joy, 'Where is Chidi, my boy?'

I got up to meet him when he was about to enter the house. We almost burst at each other by the door. He hugged me in a stiff kind of manner and as he held on to me tighter and tighter, I could see some blurry spots that drifted in front of his eyes. 'Hey! Papa, do you have eye problem?' I asked.

'Forget about that, Chidi, I'm glad you are here,' he uttered. 'It's now about seven years since you left us,' he opined.

'No, Papa, it's only six years now,' I asserted.

'What's the difference?' he asked. 'How time flies.' He now freed me and sat beside my mother. 'You're much welcomed,' he said. His hair, which was dark and coiled the last time I saw him was now mixed with white and looking very soft. It was as if some were falling off and later, when he attempted to comb it, some particles of dandruff were flying out.

'Papa, I will get you some cream for your hair,' I told him.

'Thank you, my son.'

'Chidi, let me get some water ready so that you can have your bath,' my mother offered. Immediately, it occurred to me that I had better table my mission.

'Before you go, please let me tell you one of the things that made me come home,' I said timidly.

'Hah!' my mother sighed. 'I said it… I was so sure as soon as I saw you that there is something special about your coming, more so when you did not inform us prior to this time,' my mother averred.

'Papa, Mama… a young lady is carrying my baby and that is why I've come,' I finally burst.

'What?' my mother snapped and scowled at me, unbelievably, clipping her two breasts with her palms and swiftly threw her legs apart, which were initially crossed. My father was silent for a while but his silence meant something I could not easily understand. Suddenly, he started pulling his hair with vigour as if he was determined to uproot them from their very base. Both of them were staring resentfully at the floor as if that was what they both planned to do at that material time. They must have both felt deeply disappointed, as that was the last thing they expected from me at that very moment.

'Why have you allowed the devil to have his way in your life?' my father asked with a glint in his eye. 'We thought you to be a true Christian and never to soil your garment. Now can you see what you have done to yourself? One big factor that determines a man's successful Christian life is the woman he marries. If he marries the wrong one, she will drag him to Hades. If he marries the right one, he will have a peaceful life and both of them can be sure of making heaven. Good luck to you,' he offered in mild rage.

'But… this lady is a pleasant person to behold. She is fair, reserved and very respectful and caring, with excellent striding steps. Above all, her moderate height and size make her seem to be admirable by most people. I think she's going to make a very good spouse,' I tried to convince them even when I knew in my mind that they were telling me nothing but the truth.

'Keep quiet!' he shouted. 'The hood doesn't make the monk. Look, the issue here, my son, is that it is not the marriage procedure in the Baptist church. You want to act according to your instinct. It will be a big shame on us for people to know that our only son is going to get a child out of a holy wedlock. Besides, if it's not God's approved, you are doomed.'

'No, Papa. I would walk her down the aisle before people get to know.'

'How much do you know about her childhood?' my mother asked.

'I don't know anything about her childhood, other than the fact that she works in a hospital,' I replied.

'I would have wished for a dignified marriage where we would freely issue out the invitation to family members and friends.'

'It's not healthy at all to go ahead of God's direction when it comes to the issue of marriage because there is always more to it than meets the eye,' my father reiterated. 'At any rate, as soon as you get back, don't forget to let the elders of the Baptist Church in Abuja know about it,' he advised.

My father rose to undress and change into more casual wear with my mother going to get some water for me to freshen up. From my perspective, they both had quickly adjusted to the reality on the ground and from their countenance, were hoping that the best would come out of it.

Two days later, I left my parents and went back to Abuja. I invited Nkem to my house. When she came, I let the news out to her that we were going to get married. She was not very sure if it was going to be pleasing news for her parents but she was as utterly thrilled as a baby would be and, I guessed, she was secretly relieved. However, she encouraged me to hurry things up so that the traditional engagement would take place before people start noticing her condition.

I was so lucky that my annual vacation had approached so that I could plan how to sort the whole issue out before it became scandalous.

When I let out the news of my impromptu marriage in my office, everyone, including my boss, ended up concluding that was what was weighing me down which apparently was showing in my behaviour. They all cheered me to be strong.

One Sunday afternoon, I went to tell the pastor of my church about my intention to get married. His name was Peter Aderemi but everyone in the church knew him as Pastor Pee. He was a middle-aged man; an outstanding, well-respected minister and church administrator of over twenty years. He was warm, affectionate and always sympathetic. He had two

93

daughters and a wife whom most church members believed had a double life, kind and peaceful in public but aggressive at home. It was like an agreement between the pastor and his wife to keep their domestic issues secret.

'That's good news, Chidi,' he said. 'Who is the lucky one and how are you planning the wedding?' he asked.

'Her name is Nkem.'

'Nkem? Nkem?' he repeated. 'I don't seem to be familiar with the name or is she not in this church branch?'

'No, sir. She is not a member of our church. I met her some months back…' Before I could finish, he interrupted me.

'You mean she is not from Baptist Church?'

'No.'

'What? Ordinarily, we don't join people together in this church if they are not both from Baptist Church.'

'I know, sir. That is why I want it in a traditional form,' I replied.

'That's all right. Whichever form is recognised by God,' he said. 'Indeed, God recognises traditional engagement, court and church wedding. Any one or combination of two out of the three would suffice. Anyway, have you prayed and be sure she is your God's chosen wife?'

'I have, sir, and I believe she is who God's chosen for me.'

'Hmm!' He blinked his eyes for some seconds and cleared his throat in such a manner that made me guess he was not pleased in the way I had gone about it. Nevertheless, he counselled me. After counselling me, he promised they were going to back me up with prayers. However, as I left him, my conscience began to prick me that I concealed what I should have disclosed to him as a man of God.

Days later, when my family went to meet Nkem's parents

and their relatives, everything went well. They were very happy to announce to their extended family members and friends that their daughter was going to be engaged to a man of her choice. I doubted it if Nkem ever disclosed to her parents that she was already carrying a baby.

We spent a long period planning for the traditional wedding because of Nkem's high expectations. She was full of the desire to make it memorable since, to her, it was a once in a lifetime event. But deep down I knew she wanted it to be the talk of the town. When I asked her for her input, she had estimated a huge sum of money for the dowry, drinks, dresses, rings, jewellery, decoration, mobility, cake and bands. I wondered why she wanted to see the wedding fitted for that of a son and daughter of presidential royalty when she knew who we were.

She kept dreaming of appearing in a flapper-inspired, full-length white gown that would also be more than five feet from the foot, without understanding the essence of the colour. And she wanted the gown to be adorned with intricate beads, and silver encrusted flower-patterned hand band attached to the veil. She demanded a sum, almost like my one-month's wages for her hair-do and recommended one of the top-rated bands for the reception. She said the cake should be nothing less than five feet in height and must be colourful. Initially, I thought that her parents or friends were behind it all but later knew that she alone was dragging us into such infinite and insane outlay. To her, if possible, we should temporarily employ staff to bring the event to life without realising that the days ahead could mean nothing but thoughtful mystifying encounters and the realities of life's instability. Moreover, if anyone asked me how much she was ready to put into it, not even a penny.

Nevertheless, we procured all that I felt were necessary, including a few gift items. And when I stood my ground, she finally echoed it over and over again to my ears, 'Our dresses must be unique and must be of golden colours, the shoes must be imported, and the food must be three course meals.' She was making all the decisions without holding the purse strings.

When she eventually went to the market with her friends to buy the clothes and shoes; they were of the highest quality and ended up costing more than we had budgeted. I was conflicted with my long-time belief that extravagant weddings were one of the social values troubling our society. Before that time, I was not only disenchanted with the political plundering; I was also upset with some of our culture and values which I felt we needed to reshape and block the holes that they were creating which were wrapping us. As for her, she viewed the ceremony as an intriguing affair and felt every onlooker must be thrilled.

On the day of the wedding, as both families seated under the large canopy mounted in front of her family compound in their village, after my family had travelled for two hours from Mbauku to Okuru, in Rivers State, a group of women led Nkem out and asked her to point to her husband-to-be. She walked very majestically to where I sat, almost unaccountably shy or perhaps because of the crowd of people watching the event. Everybody applauded as she knelt beside me to hand over to me a glass of local wine in appreciation for taking her as a wife. I collected the glass, sipped half of the content and left the remaining for her to finish.

Some of the women relations had decorated her with fine necklaces and beads common in that area and as she moved, it was with every calculated step, like one in a beauty parade.

Her attire fitted her immensely and seemed to be bringing out all her beauty to an extent that some of the members of both families were commending her, uttering it loud and clear to all and sundry that she was charming.

In the end, while everybody departed for their homes, including my parents, Nkem and I left the venue to become husband and wife.

***

On the weekend that followed, Nkem and I returned to the city and we started the journey of our marital life with a romantic dinner that night and by watching a film titled *Fireproof,* an amazing action-packed and heart-warming movie, aimed at helping to strengthen and affirm relationships.

We enjoyed each other that night until the next day when I woke up and walked from the bedroom to the living room to have a short morning prayer as had lately become my habit. As I flung the curtain that separated the bedroom and the living room, I stumbled at the centre table that Nkem had moved from where it was the previous night. The small flower jar placed on the table fell off and shattered on the floor. Some of the particles had spread near where my feet were, and I immediately stepped on them and as I made the next stride it was directly on to a piece of the broken jar. I limped, went and sat on the cushion and as I sat, I tried to pull the sharp pointed object out of my right toe. As soon as it came out, a tiny stream of blood flowed out. I managed myself to the bathroom and left the leg in a basin half-full of cold water to stop the blood. After a while, I removed my leg and wiped it off. This time the blood had ceased and I found myself again, very carefully, at one corner of the sitting room where I had my morning devotion as I had planned.

Nkem had rearranged the setting of the living room completely opposite to what it was from the beginning. When it was daybreak, the ray of the early morning sunshine was already penetrating through the windows, and the apartment was tidied up by her as she was already getting the breakfast ready. As I approached the kitchen, I was admiring her pleasant shape from behind.

'Nkem, hope you had a good night rest,' I said.

'You know of course, we both had a good time together,' she responded.

'Good. Also, I was going to ask why you moved things around in the sitting room without letting me know. I was very lucky not to have sustained a bigger injury this morning,' I said.

'Please, just leave them that way,' she responded in a strict and resonant voice that was like the tolling of a bell. The least I expected was for her to feel sorry for my injury. However, she did not utter a word in that direction. Instead, it was an expression of voiced anger, which built to a crescendo.

'Why raise your voice in that manner. Did I wrong you before?' I asked in a most gracious style.

'No. That's my voice and that's how I speak,' she reiterated, laughing gruffly.

'But I've never heard you before speak in that manner.'

'Would I be lying to you?'

'Okay, that's fine, but can you at least move back the centre table to where it was originally and also try to push the big table slightly away from the wall, and the rest would be fine by me,' I said, in an effort to reach a compromise.

'Chidi, leave things the way I have arranged them. Things are no longer about you alone. It's about two people, us, you and I. Do you understand?' she uttered with such strong authority and again at the top of her voice.

'Okay, no problem then,' I gave up and tried to calm her down. As I tried to pacify her, she only seemed to be more riled up. I looked at the wooden wall clock given to me when I was leaving the State House of Parliament; it was already past ten a.m.

'What exactly are you making for breakfast?' I asked.

'Oats and fried sweet potatoes with scramble egg.'

'That's fine but can you please remove the yoke before you fry the egg,' I requested.

'Look, Chidi, stop giving me unnecessary tasks. Men should take whatever is given to them as breakfast, lunch or dinner,' she said.

'Okay, can you just prepare yours and leave mine so that I can take care of it?' I suggested.

'You should have said that earlier, Chidi. I have already mixed the egg. Maybe next time and also be ready to prepare your meals henceforth, if that's what you want,' she muttered.

'Ha! Has it come to that, my dear, so quickly?' I asked and left the kitchen.

A few seconds after, I heard Nkem's scream from where she was still making the breakfast in the kitchen. I quickly rushed to where she was. She was holding her forehead with her left palm. She leaned slightly away from the burning gas, but in her right hand was the long spoon, which she used in turning the sweet potatoes frying in the olive oil on the fire. 'What is it?' I asked.

'I'm feeling dizzy,' she said. I gently led her trembling out of the kitchen as we crawled towards the bed in the bedroom. She pulled herself up into the bed. I advised her to lie very quietly for a while and not to allow any thoughts to creep into her head. Soon, she shouted, 'Ah! The potatoes…' She attempted to leave the bed. I pulled her back and quickly dashed back to the kitchen, and now the potatoes were as black as charcoal. I could not save any of it. I brought down the frying pan and gently removed all the burnt ones. I put the frying pan back on the fire and got the rest sorted out.

Nkem remained in bed until she fell into a restless sleep. When she woke up, she was already feeling better and she managed to have her breakfast as she felt a rumbling hunger. We spent the rest of the day very peacefully.

By the time the night came, there was thick darkness and intermittent distant thunder coming like the smell of rain. It was good for the moment. At least it would ease off the far-reaching warmth that was acute for those without good ventilation. As for us, we slept soundly like the dead.

I could not say whether the first moments Nkem and I had together was really pleasurable. Nevertheless, I became very anxious to get back to work and be with my colleagues as always. And when that finally happened, they could all see that the Chidi they used to know was the one who returned to work at last.

Everything went on very well for me in the few months that followed. Nkem also went back to work, although not finding it easy to cope with the challenges of early morning sickness. In those times, I became more or less a helper in the house, carrying out all sort of domestic work ranging from tidying up the house and ironing to cooking.

The hope of becoming a father soon and allowing my

mother to carry her first grandchild in the not too distant future energised me in living up to the expectation of a young husband.

Occasionally, Nkem's voice would trail off from the room where she lay in the bed. 'Chidi, pick up that hand fan for me, stretch your hand and pass the cotton bud to me, clean my shoes for tomorrow's work, serve my food, dust the bed, and so on and so forth. Quickly, I would often get the task accomplished. Sometimes, I would hesitate and stare at her as if I wanted my eyes to penetrate into her heart, to uncover her real intent; if her routine, actions and thoughts were necessitated by her present condition or premeditated. But, it was so difficult for me to decipher.

Around that time, Nkem would often scream my name from the front of the house on her way from work. Each time I heard it, I knew it was to collect her handbag. On the few occasions that I felt reluctant, she nagged her tongue out. I became virtually her errand boy as she idolised herself because she was carrying my baby. At night, I would not sleep unless she had found hers. Sometimes, whenever there was a power outage, she would order me to blow her with the handmade fan until she slept. She would roll from one end to the other and would occasionally blame me for not sympathising with her condition. By the time I would get up in the morning to prepare for work, she would have filled the trash placed by the side of the bed with pieces of tissue containing white and thick saliva. I must empty the basket before proceeding to do any other thing. Let me quickly own up that it was a massive pressure for me for more than seven months.

Chapter Six

By the first week of the eighth month, Nkem had begun to experience signs of early labour. That night was one of the worst and most frightening moments of my life. There was no adequate sleep for either Nkem or me. When it was some minutes to the time people usually start rushing out to their different places of work, we set out to catch a taxi to the Central General Hospital, where she once worked.

The roads were quite lonely except for one or two flashes of motorcycle lights. For us, the crisis on our hands had suddenly driven away our dread. We were lucky to find what seemed to be the only taxi on the road pulling by our side and without bargaining, we jumped on it. We got in before we realised that half of the car seat had been soaked with water. 'The seat is wet,' I told the driver.

'I'm so sorry about that,' he appealed. 'There is a part of the car roof that leaks through which rain water penetrates. I regret the discomfort,' he pleaded. We could not do anything. If we chose to get out, we could wait for a long time without catching another one. Within thirty minutes, we were at our destination and we never came across any other vehicle as we went.

The nurses and the resident doctor we met were on hand to receive us and quickly they led Nkem into the labour room. I was outside the room, sitting very isolated with all kinds of thoughts in my head, the nurses pacing the hallway every second without any word to gladden my heart. The cramp continued all day, growing in intensity. Sometimes, she managed to snooze for a few minutes.

The labour, which started at some point around 1:00 a.m., lasted for over eight hours. I could hear Nkem's voice screaming and daring me never to come near her again. 'It's natural to behave that way,' one of the nurses told me. 'Some people act worse than she is doing,' she added. 'Has she had any miscarriage before?' she asked.

'Why do you ask?'

'It looks as though she has an incompetent cervix. It is opening slightly and she is at the risk of losing the baby.' I clasped my head in my hands. She felt sorry for me. The thought of the baby's arrival had already consumed a great part of our existence. We loved him even though we had not seen his face. He had already gained our passion and care.

'Baby, don't do this to us,' I heard myself saying. 'We want you to put smiles on the faces of the doctors and nurses. We want friends and family members to wait and greet you as soon as your mum bares you on her palm to your final home. Nothing would replace the horrible pains your mum is currently passing through if you go back now. We would go home with empty hands.' I was still hypnotising when the nurse came hastening towards me.

She came with the long-awaited news but I did not know whether to say if it was good or bad one. Our first bouncing baby boy was welcomed into the world. At first, the baby refused to cry which was not a good sign by my culture. Any newly born baby should cry to indicate there is life in him. One of the nurses held him with his head pointing to the ground and gently slapped his buttocks. There was no noise still from the chubby looking boy. She then threw him up and accurately caught him by his legs with his head still pointing to the ground. My heart thumped against my chest in awe. Just then, the baby's voice went across the horizon. He looked very healthy, happy and fine. He was a squat chunky little baby, fair like the mother and hairy like me, weighing about four and a half kilograms, the highest any child had weighed in that hospital in a very long period.

A day later, Nkem and the baby left the hospital and returned home, as there was no known complication; though, the doctor wrote a prescription for some antibiotics.

Two days after, we discovered that the baby had not had his first stooling and his abdomen was rapidly swelling. We rushed him back to the hospital and following an abdominal ultrasound test, they made a confirmation that he had what the doctors called Hirschsprung's disease, which meant a blockage of the large intestine. Before anything, the baby was to live on fluids pending surgery through intravenous. Also, a nasogastric tube was inserted through his nose into the stomach to keep air out of the stomach so that the likelihood of vomiting would be less.

The doctors performed a temporary colostomy, thus creating two small openings in the child's belly, known as stoma in the abdomen. They cut through the intestines and attached the end of them to the openings. The lower part of the intestine attached to one opening and the upper part to the other. A pouch attached to the outside the body was catching his waste products. One opening lets the stool pass to a pouch attached on the outside of the body. To enable him to withstand the pains, they gave him some drugs to put him to sleep.

A month after, we took the baby back to the hospital for the full surgical operation after tendering a whopping sum that amounted to one thousand, five hundred dollars. The surgery was to detach the rectum from any other internal structure and create an anus in the normal place. The doctors advised us to bring him back after six weeks in order to stretch the anus to prevent it from narrowing. Soon after the surgery, he began to experience constipation which one of the doctors said was normal and he prescribed stool softener to relieve it.

The news of our newborn baby enchanted my parents when it got to them and my mother without giving it a second thought, offered to come over and stay with us for some time in order to assist us nurse the baby.

After our child's condition stabilised, I informed Nkem of my mother's intention to come and support us in tending the baby but before I could finish, her voice ranted from several feet away.

'Why your mother and not mine?' she bickered. 'Chidi, I ask again, why your mother?'

'Take it easy, Nkem. You know you just gave birth to a child.'

'Didn't you know that you brought up a foolish idea? You make unilateral decisions all the time without any recourse to me and expect me not to talk. If that is how you want us to live in this house, I shall give it back to you,' she added.

'Nkem, there was never a time I took any decision without involving you. Is that not why I'm now throwing it open?' I said.

'No, it's not. You have already made the decision and wanted to carry it out,' she insisted.

'Okay, no problem, I'll go ahead and contact your father to release your mother for us,' I concluded. 'Are you okay with that now?' I asked.

'Look, Chidi, I am not okay because you always like to brew arguments and, in the end, you turn around to blame me for it.'

'But now the matter is settled or what else do you want?' I asked.

'You must stop tampering with my emotions and prove to me that you love me,' she added.

'Okay, I love you very dearly and I promise this won't happen again,' I pledged.

On the seventh day, we took our baby to the church for dedication, Pastor Pee prayed for us, and gave my son the name, Chima, meaning God knows everything.

Some weeks passed without any word from Nkem's mother. Nkem kept hoping against hope, assuring me that her mother would certainly make it until one night the news got to us that Nkem's mother had taken ill and would not be able to honour our invitation. Because of that development, Nkem then consented that my mother should be the one to come.

I was so happy when my mother arrived, for she was going to relieve me, temporarily, of the numerous tasks, which were already overwhelming me, as if someone commissioned me to be doing them.

Nkem was unexpectedly nice to my mother during the first few days. My mother loved her so much as I did but she loved Chima most. Every morning, my mother would carry Chima to bathe him. She would stretch out her legs across the large white basin and place the baby on her lap as she poured warm water on him, using a very soft sponge with soap to scrub gently his tender body. Chima would scream to the extent that many passers-by would know that a newborn baby was in that house. Midway, she would throw Chima up, above her head, and afterwards she would grip his legs and, in a moment, turn his head upside down. She would then place Chima on her lap again and, with a small hand towel immersed in warm water, massage his body. Then she would open several of the bottles in the small medicine bowl to feed Chima with antibiotic, blood tonic and cod liver oil. That became my mother's regular routine, morning and night, throughout her stay with us.

Unfortunately, Nkem's initial happiness and pleasant countenance towards my mother gradually turned to hostility. Her reasons for her obnoxious behaviour remained unknown to me.

One Saturday morning, my mother woke up earlier than usual and sat by the edge of the small foldable bed in the living room after praying and reading her Bible. Nkem burst into the place, without saying a word, stared indignantly at her and walked back. Shortly after, my mother spoke out loudly from where she sat. 'Nkem, I noticed we have not greeted each other this morning.'

'Did you greet me and I failed to answer?' Nkem responded very indecently. My mother was in the interim shocked.

'Ah! So, you are waiting for me to greet you first?' my mother asked with her face somewhat beaming with her usual alluring smile. Yet, I guessed that smile at that very moment represented displeasure and not a sign of ecstasy.

'Please, I beg you to leave me alone,' Nkem said and walked away. 'All you have come to do is to look after your grandchild and not to monitor me.'

My mother who was presently stunned called me. As I stood before her, she asked, 'Did you offend your wife previously?' she enquired.

'No, Mama. Nothing like that, as far as I know,' I replied.

'Why then has she suddenly changed?' she asked.

'That's Nkem for you, Mama,' I said. Being very furious, I went to meet Nkem in the room. 'Nkem, what is the matter?' I asked.

'Nothing is the matter but just beg your mother to leave me alone and face her business,' she stated.

'Did she offend you in any way?' I asked in a very subtle manner.

'You go and find out from her and stop interrogating me like a detective,' she echoed.

'Nkem, please, I beg of you to take it easy, whatever it is,' I appealed.

'So, you have chosen to support your mother so that two of you would kill me, eh. But you won't succeed, I promise you.'

Why was Nkem being consumed by her temper? I queried in my mind. If I claim that I was not cast-down at that point, I would not be stating the obvious. I scanned through my mind to find the possible reason she was acting the way she was. There was this overwhelming feeling of fear within me. 'Nkem!' I called her very politely. 'Please, I beg you for goodness sake to calm down and try and be patient with Mama,' I persuaded. Rather than calm her down, it appeared my plea sprinkled some salt on her fresh wound.

'Chidi, if you don't have anything good to say, I ask that you shut up.'

'Nkem, please don't speak to me like that,' I said. 'To start with, I don't see what Mama has done to you. She has very diligently taken good care of Chima and has not at any time neglected to tidy the house.'

'I know you will be on her side because you are a very dishonest husband,' she bawled out.

'Now outline one after the other the wrongs she has done to you since she came into this house, to warrant the disrespect she's beginning to get from you?'

'She knows, so you go and ask her.'

'I want you to tell me so that I can take it up with her,' I beseeched.

'Chidi, please get out of my sight and stop pestering my life!' she yelled.

Nkem walked out on me only to return a few minutes after to instruct that she does not want to see my mother in the kitchen from then on. 'Okay, I'll tell her,' I responded. It now became obvious that Nkem meant something more sinister than I had ever imagined when she served my mother her dinner that evening. She came into the room and requested me to inform my mother to go to the kitchen to get her food. 'Why won't you bring the food to the dining table for her as you had done since she came?' I asked.

'She is not sick,' she responded, sharply. 'The game has changed,' she added.

I walked to the kitchen to carry the food for my mother. The portion of the food by all standards was small for even a young infant and was not by any description decent to behold. She must have deliberately added some water to the soup she served her compared to the one she dished out for both of us, I was sure.

I decided to call Nkem out to the kitchen. 'Why are you taking such deliberate repugnant moves?' I queried. She was dumbstruck, so I demanded that she serve a fresh portion of soup for my mother.

She blew up, shouting, 'Your mother should look for something else to eat if she is not going to have what I served her.' Realising that Nkem was adamant and not prepared to cooperate, I went, collected another plate and began to dish out a fresh portion of soup for my mother to have with her yam flour. Nkem came, pushed me away and stood between the pot of soup and I. 'You can't do that, Chidi; you can't dunk the spoon in my pot of soup. You didn't prepare it, I did, so you can't touch it,' she insisted. Just then, I heard my mother call my name and I went to her.

'Tell your wife to serve my dinner, or she doesn't want me to eat tonight,' she said. She was very unaware of what was going on between Nkem and I.

'That is what we are trying to sort out, Mama,' I said. 'Besides, it's like the soup is soured so we are trying to look for something else for dinner until tomorrow when she would make fresh soup,' I responded being as diplomatic as I could possibly be. 'Would you like bread and a cup of tea?' I asked.

'Just anything would do,' she responded. I then set the water on the fire for the tea and dashed out to get some bread. As soon as I left, Nkem served her the same food that was in contention.

'Chidi told me the soup is sour and that you are going to serve me with bread and a cup of tea and is like my appetite has centred on that,' she stated.

'That is not true, Mama. I have already dished out your food and I wouldn't know why Chidi doesn't want you to take your usual yam flour,' she argued. As Nkem bent with squeezed face to carry away the tray containing the food, I came in.

'What were you trying to do, Nkem?' I asked. She looked the other way and pretended not to have heard me as she walked away with the tray. I felt she was acting funny so I followed her.

'Why are you beginning to be callous? What has come upon you?' I queried. I became agitated all of a sudden. That night, after we had all had our dinner, I laid in my bed deeply depressed, wondering if I had made the worst mistake of my life in deciding to take Nkem as my better half. My mouth went sour, my teeth cracked. As I leaned my cheek on the pillow, I could hear the sound of my palpitating heart. My thoughts completely encased in negative emotions.

I struggled to come to terms with Nkem's fearless current demeanour as against her initial soft-spoken voice, that gentle touch with which she guided me through on the day I had my interview for the job I was still doing. I was lost in thoughts.

The door of my memory yet opened as I remembered when I asked Nkem the day of our wedlock if truly she loves me and she responded, "Yes, I do." *Did something take over?* I queried angrily. I rolled in my bed repeatedly, cuddling my pillow as though I was deriving the comfort I was searching for, unable to soothe my nerves.

Suddenly, I came to my consciousness by the cry of Chima. His voice buzzed like the sound of a bee from a distance. I went to where he lay in the cot. He halted his cry as I stood beside him but kept flipping his eyes as if he had seen a scary object. My mother now came into the room and carried him away. After a little while, he was calm again, thus acquitting my mother who soon after that went back to sleep.

Chapter Seven

The next morning, my mother was eager to return to her own home. 'I'm considering going back to the village earlier than I initially proposed,' my mother exclaimed. 'I had a terrible dream last night and I'm having some feelings that my husband is not in good health.'

I was very unhappy to hear that. But the truth was that she'd had enough of Nkem's spiteful behaviour. The good news was that she promised to assist us search for a housemaid as soon as she gets back to the village. Later that evening, I called Nkem and informed her of my mother's decision. 'She can even go today if she wants to, I don't care,' she roared.

'Nkem, when you speak, do you ever listen to yourself?'

'Please don't slight my person this evening,' she wailed.

'Is this the voice of a woman? Women are renowned for their tender spoken manner, gentle behaviour and support. Where is that voice with which you responded to me that first day I met you? Where is it Nkem? Anyway, she has made a promise to assist us get a maid,' I added.

'No!' her voice went up again and she got up. I held her and she tried to resist but I had a firm grip of her arm. 'Where do you think you are going?' I asked.

'To go and tell your mother myself that she should stay away from looking for any housemaid,' she stated.

'So how do you intend to cope with nursing Chima and going to work by the time you resume and Mama is gone?'

'I have sent a message to my mother already that she should organise a helper for us. That is better than allowing your mum to, perhaps, get us a girl who might be possessed with the evil spirit.'

'Why didn't you first discuss that with me?' I asked.

'Why? Must I obtain permission from you before I talk to my own mother?' she asked.

'Okay. It's all right. Has she seen someone?'

'Yes, she has.'

'So, when is the person going to come?'

'Not quite sure but I would suggest your mother doesn't leave until the maid arrives,' she submitted.

'So, she should remain with us, in an atmosphere of animosity and contempt, even if it takes a century for the maid to arrive?' I asked.

'It's all about her grandson. Isn't it?

Both Nkem and I remained at odds, and the bond between us continued to detioriate as we were constantly snapping at each and neighbours were beginning to hear raised voices even at night as they lay in their beds.

***

The next Sunday, I asked Nkem if she was going to come with me to the church but she would never consent. She had never agreed to come except that Sunday we all went for the dedication of Chima, eight days after his birth. So, I went with my mother who also put Chima on her back.

That day, I decided I was going to see our pastor and make known to him the early difficulties I was experiencing in my marriage. Before that service ended, the pastor had sent for me. I felt an unusual mixture of trembling and fear swirling in my stomach. Has anyone revealed to him that Nkem took in before our traditional wedding? I wondered. I made up my mind to tell him the whole truth and nothing but the truth, if he ventured to talk about it. My conscience continued to trouble me as I blamed myself repeatedly, for not opening the whole matter at the beginning. Could this secret, which I failed to divulge, be the reason I was getting intractable behaviour from Nkem? Maybe it was the law of retribution following me, I speculated.

As soon as I entered the office, he gave me a warm, glowing, smile as if he was congratulating me for an award he was about to give to me for meritorious service. 'Chidi, I have been watching your consistency ever since you started coming to this church branch and I also got interested in you when you told me your parents are both senior workers in the Baptist church,' he said forcefully as soon as I sat in front of him. 'Therefore, we have decided to make you the Youth Leader of this Church branch and, in fact, one of the young ministers too,' he said. The former Youth Leader left the country last night for further studies and we don't want to leave any vacuum.'

I did not know how to react to the matter he put before me. I was silent and still for a while except that my lips were visibly unsteady as I was creaming them with my saliva and was winding my eyes all over that office. I gaped at him, peeping directly into his eyes, thinking he would discover the hidden truth in me which I had kept away from him but was now radiating through my eyes.

I paused for a long while, perplexed whether to say yes or no. I did not know so much then about Christian leadership, but I knew that a true minister of God must be above board, a man capable of taking care and control of his own immediate family. Could I have said that was true of me? I marvelled.

'Well, I do not expect you to say anything. God will help you in working in His vineyard,' he interfered with my silence.

That day, I left not knowing whether I should be happy or sad. How could I function effectively as a youth minister when my wife was constantly at loggerheads with me and would never consent to come with me to the church? How could I assert that my life was above reproach both in and outside my home with that kind of squabble taking place daily in my home? How could God have chosen me to work for Him when my conscience continued to convict me of one lie that I succeeded in concealing? It might be that I still had value in God's eyes, I felt. From that moment, I became conscious of everything I said and did both in and outside my home.

On the evening of the day that followed, after I had returned from work, I was walking down the road to pick one or two things up from the shop behind our street, when a vehicle pulled by my side. It had a registration number DS 836 AA and an inscription "The more you look, the less you see." I thought over that inscription for a long time trying to uncover its actual meaning, but I could not. I had seen more interesting inscriptions carved over the bodies of some vehicles, that were clear and conveyed inspiring messages like, "Nobody knows tomorrow; the young shall grow; slow and steady wins the race," and so on. But with the white coated paint and a green stripe, six inches below the window, I could confirm it was not an Abuja municipality cab. I noticed an elderly man who was sitting in the front along with the driver and two other women behind.

'Please, sir, we are trying to locate number eight Elijah Close,' the driver enquired.

'What a coincidence,' I replied very quickly. 'That's where I live,' I stated.

'That's very good then. I have a young girl in the car who I want to drop with one Madam Nkem,' he said.

'Which girl is that?' I replied.

'The girl at the rear seat,' he answered. It was only then I realised there was a third row and the girl in that row had spread herself on the whole of the seat, fatigued as it were, making herself invisible to passers-by.

'Well, I am Chidi, the husband of Nkem,' I said. 'We have been expecting her. I will take you home then but you have to make a U-turn in front and meet me up over there,' I pointed. 'You will drive slowly behind me and will turn in front of that kiosk over there to the street behind. That is where we have Elijah Close.'

As soon as we got to the front of our house, the driver pulled by the side and came down to open the door from outside as the inside handle of the door had broken. The house cleaner's name was Mary who alighted and headed towards the boot to get out her luggage. It was just a medium size rubber travelling bag containing few of her clothes and other minor personal belongings. 'I was told to collect the fare when I get here,' the driver stated.

'That's no problem,' I told him. 'How much is the fare?' I asked.

'Two thousand and five hundred.'

'Okay, give me a few minutes,' I told the driver and went inside to get the money. As soon as I entered, I announced to my mother and Nkem that the house helper just arrived.

'Where is she?' my mother enquired, feeling a bit emancipated. I looked behind me and did not see Mary.

'I thought she was coming behind me as I left the driver to get her fare. It may be that she does not want to leave the driver until I have settled him.' As soon as I came out, I handed the money to the driver and he drove away with the other passengers. He was also going to drop them off at their final destinations.

'Why are you still standing there?' I asked Mary, who was now our maid. 'Come with me and let's go inside,' I said. She followed me and as soon as we entered the house, she knelt down in front of my mother and greeted, 'Good evening, Mama.'

'Nkem!' I called. There was no answer. She might be busy breastfeeding our little baby, I thought.

Mary was about the age of fifteen or so and was extremely dark in complexion with light lips but plump-cheeked. She was short and likely not to be anything more than half an inch above five feet. She had a very small stature and would perhaps not be weighing more than thirty-five kilograms at that time which I considered too small for her age, yet tiny stature did not hinder her agility.

She bore very noticeable traditional tribal marks on the two sides of her cheeks, which would make it so easy for anybody to know she was from the shoreline area of the country. She appeared to be very shy but later I got to realise she spoke very eloquently and had a sharp memory. When she wore a sleeveless top, one could effortlessly see circles of faint tattoos, which she claimed were fading scars of inoculation given to her when she first started her primary school. Though she carried an unattractive and hostile looking face that could make people not want to associate with her, but spending a little moment with her would prove she was such a pleasant little teenager with good disposition.

Soon Nkem came out from the room and Mary quickly went on her knees again. 'Good evening, Aunty,' she greeted. Nkem responded with a wave of her hand and again went back into the room where our little baby lay. My mother then took it up upon herself to take Mary through what would soon become her daily housework.

'Every morning, as soon as you wake up, you have to sweep everywhere, the living room, the room, the kitchen and the corridors. You have to dust the tables, chairs, the bookshelf, the windows and the doors. After that, you have to mop the floors of the room and the living room as well as the kitchen. You have to clean every day and ensure you do not leave any unwashed plates in the kitchen sink overnight. You should always endeavour to wake up on time and neither your uncle nor your aunty must wake before you. Make sure you look after the baby very well. Anything you do not understand, always ask them, they will explain to you. Try to be a good girl, okay. In the long future, you would not regret staying here with them. Do you understand?'

'Yes, Mama,' she answered. 'Would I be bathing the baby?' she enquired.

'No. Not until the baby is grown up. The mother would have to be doing that for the time being, before going to work.'

I thought it too hasty of my mother introducing Mary to

the routine of the house, so quickly, without allowing her some moment of rest or the opportunity of being acquainted with her new home. But I said nothing.

Not long before Nkem's voice came from the room, 'Mary!'

'Yes, Aunty,' she answered and ran into the room.

'You don't have to run inside this apartment because it's not safe to do so.'

'Yes, Aunty.'

'What did the big mama tell you?'

'She explained to me all the housework I have to do on a daily basis.'

'Don't mind her. It's not her duty to do that, okay.'

'Yes, Aunty.'

'I'll let you know what work has to be done at the appropriate time. Do you understand?'

'Yes, Aunty.'

'Where is your bag?'

'It is still in the living room.'

'Go and get it and keep it at that corner of the room,' she said now pointing. 'And whenever you need to take your dress, you should come in and take it and go into the bathing room to dress up. Okay?'

'Okay, Aunty.'

'Now go to the laundry basket in the kitchen and wash all the clothes in there. The clothes are for the baby.'

'Yes, Aunty,' she ran towards the kitchen.

'Come back here, Mary,' Nkem ordered her back. 'What did I tell you a few moments ago?' Mary stood gaping, unable to answer. Fear gripped her and her lips were shaking, her eyelids blinked many times within a second. 'I say what did I tell you minutes ago?' Nkem repeated.

'I'm very sorry, Aunty,' Mary finally uttered.

'Come nearer me, you have an empty head and I am sorry for you,' Nkem said. She gripped her left ear and twisted it until it turned red, yet she still held on to it. Mary screamed.

'Shut your dirty mouth. Didn't I tell you never to run while you are inside this apartment? Didn't I? Answer me.'

'You did, Aunty,' she answered with a distorted and crumbling voice. Her eyes dipped and she gradually struggled to rescue her ear from those sharp pains, which were now spreading beyond the left ear. She must be careful or else she would inflict on herself a more severe sore. 'Aunty, please, I won't do that again,' she entreated.

'You better be sorry.' Nkem pushed her away and she fell on a nylon bag containing some of the baby's toys. 'If any of those toys get damaged, I will pull out your teeth and rub pepper in your eyes.' Mary staggered away from the bag and went to the kitchen to carry out her first assignment in that house.

'Nkem, please you have to be very patient with her until she gets used to her routine,' my mother persuaded.

'No, no, Mama. Leave her with me. It's me she will give troubles when nobody is at home. Afterwards, she was brought for my supervision.'

'What a foul temper?' my mother uttered, inaudibly. She could not speak further as she could then confirm that Nkem's temperamental behaviour was not something anyone could cure immediately.

The next morning, I rose very early to get ready for work. As soon as Mary heard my movement, she got up and was about to begin the house cleaning when I persuaded her to go

121

back to bed and wait a little as the only reason I woke so early was to be in the office on time that day because of a special assignment I was given.

I had become very much excited over my work because of the recent letter of commendation I had received with a recommendation for an international two weeks training. Besides, it seemed that I had redeemed my initial bad image before my colleagues since I officially got married to Nkem coupled with the arrival of our new baby.

Later, I discovered it was a very busy and challenging day for me at work, but I was full of hope that as soon as I got back home, I would enjoy enough rest.

My mother was the first person to welcome me and she hardly allowed me to change my dress when she informed me it was about time she left for the village. 'Has my wife upset you again?' I enquired.

'No, all is well. Just that I have been away for so long and have left only your father to cater for himself.'

'Yes, I know, Mama, but I beg of you to stay a little while, at least for Mary to get used to the domestic routine. I will expect you to guide her through. Remember that when you first arrived you assured me you were going to stay with us until Chima starts walking.'

'Your thoughts are very good and right but Nkem, your wife, doesn't seem to want my presence any more. I'm fine once you are both happy with each other. However, I must tell you the truth as my son. You have to be on your knees at all times for God in heaven to soften her heart and make her a virtuous woman.'

'Yes, I know, Mama. You and my father owe me that special prayer on this matter.'

'You spoke well of her prior to your marriage; so, what has gone wrong? I would have suggested you immediately return her, if she was to be something you purchased in the market. Because if one purchased a product that does not meet specification, what does one do?'

'He or she has to return it, of course,' I answered.

'Sadly, this case is very different. You know quite well what Christian principles are about marriage. God's law has decreed from the outset, that only death of one of the partners can dissolve the marriage union. Was that not why your father and I warned you beforehand not to entangle yourself with the city women until you have prayed and be convinced that God wanted you to go ahead. You didn't pray, and you didn't listen. You didn't seek counsel of the elders in the church. You just went with your guts and listened to your emotions, focusing on the physical appearance. Nevertheless, God allowed that to happen and He knows how to handle all the difficult situations if we repose our trust in Him. Don't worry.'

'I thank you very much, Mama. Just continue to pray for me. Now, talking about your returning to the village, can we leave it for next week Saturday? It's only about nine days from now.'

'I've heard you, Chidi.' She gave her concurrence.

When I finally entered the room, I prepared a long list of items, of the things she would need when she gets back to the village. I handed over the list with some cash to Nkem to arrange to buy all the items. Nkem glanced through them and counted the money. 'Would it be late if I buy them in three days' time?' she asked.

'That will be fine. You know Mama still has nine more days to go.'

As time went by, every time I got back from work, I would scan through every nook and cranny of the apartment, hoping to see the bag containing the items I asked Nkem to buy for my mother. I never did.

When it remained only three more days for my mother to go back, I called Nkem, 'Mama has only three days to go and I haven't seen any of those items I asked you to buy.'

'The list is on top of the fridge, you can have it back.' Nkem responded, abruptly.

'Ah! Why?'

'Because I have got no time to turn to the market.'

'You should have said so all this while.'

'It's still not late.'

'Okay, let me have the money.'

'Which money?'

'The one I gave you to buy the stuffs.'

'Well, I've used the money for something else.'

'What?'

'You heard me.'

'Why are you doing this to me, Nkem?' I asked. 'Tell me where have I gone wrong?'

'Please, just don't start this evening, I beg of you. Otherwise we shall attract neighbours into this apartment right now.'

'I know that this is not Nkem who took my hand that fateful day and proclaimed, "Yes, I do". Who did this to you? Even the dew and the wind can smell my love for you. Now the sun is roasting my head and the enemies are rejoicing. Who shall redeem me from this marital tragedy? Who shall remove the shackles that have so quickly bound my hands and twisted my legs together? Who shall reclaim my love for me?' I took my face away from her as I began to fight back tears. My eyes were red, my hair and eyelashes, all fluttering and standing in their places. To say that I was greatly troubled was to say the least. I turned away, walking towards the kitchen, I called 'Mary!'

'Please leave her alone. I have instructed her not to leave the kitchen until she has finished what I asked her to do.'

'I want her to buy some articles down the street.' As we exchanged words, Mary appeared, 'Yes, Uncle, I'm here,' she said.

'Come here, Mary. Didn't I tell you not to leave until you have finished the washing?' Nkem queried.

'Yes, Aunty, you told me so.'

'So why did you leave?'

'Uncle called me.'

'You are very silly.' She got hold of Mary's right ear and twisted it brutally. She let go of the ear and went for a piece of wooden spoon. She hit her legs several times with the spoon. Then I went and held the spoon, pleading that it was enough. She pushed me away with all the strength in her and I stumbled. If I were to be a woman like her, I must say that I would have found myself on the floor. Yet, I was so determined not to let her have her way. I took the wooden spoon again and felt like hitting her. Just then, I remembered I was a young minister in the church, so I restrained myself.

'This is not how to bring up a child,' I said.

'Have you trained one before in your life?' she replied. 'As for you, Mary, there is no dinner tonight because of your stubborness,' she boasted.

'You can't do that after you have beaten her with the wooden spoon.'

'Look, Chidi, Mary is a young teenage girl and only a woman can bring up a girl. Therefore, it's my duty and not yours to bring her up.'

The next day, I went to the market after work and came back with all the items I needed for my mother towards her trip back home. I bought her fine wrapper, half sandals, flat shoes, towel and toiletries. I also got my father some jumpers. I wanted them to have happy memories despite my mother's horrid experience in my home. Before this time, she had gathered all her stuffs ready for departure first thing the following day.

Chapter Eight

The day broke very slowly as if it was wintertime. My mother hardly slept a wink as she was very thrilled to go back and I could perceive her spirit was already kilometres away. She must have spent the last hours packing and unpacking and then packing again, all her clothes including the recently tailor-made, the head ties, the old sandals and the waist purse, all securely crammed together in what now appeared like an undersized leather bag.

Before the cock crowed three times, she had taken her bath and was already putting on her travelling outfit. She now sat in the living room, making every effort to spend the remaining moments reading her Bible written out in our native dialect, and waiting for when I would come out from the room to announce it was time to take her to the motor park.

In a few moments, she could no longer contain her anxiousness. For her, time seemed to be at a standstill. Initially, she was willing to allow me to sleep as long as I desired but not again. She made her way to the door leading to the room and gently knocked at it, whispering my name a number of times. My eyes were, by that time, opened although I was still feeling very lazy getting up. I quickly answered before Nkem turned round to accuse her of interrupting her sleep.

'Mama, are you ready to go?' I asked.

'I've been ready a long time ago,' she responded.

I went to brush my teeth and freshen up a bit, but there was no time for bathing. I spent less than ten minutes and came out calling Nkem. When she did not answer, I proceeded to where she was still lying and tapped her. I felt she heard me but chose to give me a cold shoulder on purpose.

After some moments, she shifted her position and uttered very sluggishly, 'What?'

'My mother is ready to leave,' I said.

Unlike her, she quickly got up and came out of the room. 'Mama, thank you very much for everything and when you get to the village, give my greetings to everyone and especially Papa.'

'I'll definitely do so,' my mother said. She went into the room where Chima lay in his cot. She touched him on his forehead. 'May God continue to be with you, my son,' she prayed.

Nkem sighted where Mary was still lying at the corner of the living room. She became exasperated. She reached out to her and kicked her several times. Mary jumped up and in a great bewilderment ran towards the door leading to outside. 'Where are you running to?' Nkem queried. 'Didn't you hear the noises we were making all this while and you are still lying on your mat like a lizard with bellyache.' Still not able to overcome her disorientation, she stood, staring at everyone. She was, perhaps waiting for Nkem to tell her what exactly to do. 'Will you go to the kitchen and start your routine work,' Nkem ordered. Nkem then went back to lie in her bed. I went to meet Mary in the kitchen and asked her to accompany me with my mother to the motor park.

'Ah! You have to tell my aunty first,' she uttered, terrifyingly.

'Don't worry, I will,' I assured her. She now wiped her hands already soaked in the cold soapy water and followed me. I went to where Nkem was and informed her that Mary was to come with us to the motor park. She kept mum, though I did not need her response. Mary carried the medium sized leather bag while I went with the small one containing some of the items I bought for my mother.

The bus going straight to my village was already half full by the time we got to the motor park. While waiting for the last passenger to arrive, my mother started encouraging me to be patient with Nkem and take everything to God in prayer. She reminded me that there is no alternative solution to her problem than prayer, emphasising that God's way is to stick to our wives whether good or bad. She appealed to me to do all I could to protect Mary from her violent reaction. She turned to Mary. 'Don't mind all the nasty things your aunty is doing to you.'

'Yes, Mama,' she responded.

'With time, she will get to cool down.'

'Yes, Mama.' As soon as the bus was ready to depart, Mary and I bade my mother goodbye.

As Mary and I walked back home, I could sense that she was already beginning to show her nervousness. 'What's making you apprehensive?' I asked.

'Is because of Aunty,' she replied. 'I don't know what she would say when we get back,' she added.

'Don't worry, she won't say anything,' I encouraged her. Not up to a month since Mary had joined us, she had mastered the behaviour of my wife and knew what she was capable of doing. She knew I had the muscle to protect her at any time but not from the cruel hands of Nkem.

The moment we entered the house, I went into the bathroom to have my shower while Mary went to the kitchen to continue with her work. I was still in the bathroom when I heard Nkem's voice calling Mary who, from the kitchen, hurried to the room.

'How long did it take you to get to the motor park and come back?' she interrogated.

'Uncle asked me to wait until Mama departed,' she said. She seemed to have made her case worse by that defence, especially by bringing my name into it. She hardly ever believed her, anyway. She grabbed her right ear and twisted it until tears began to flow down her cheeks. She released the ear, went for her shoe and started hitting her with the heel. Mary screamed but managed to run away. Nkem flung her shoe at her, which hit the edge of her eyelid. It would appear she was gaining the utmost pleasure seeing Mary weep. I then rushed out of the bathroom, almost half-naked, struggling to knot properly my medium size cream towel around my waist.

'Leave this poor girl alone, Nkem,' I stated, glaring at her with fierce rage.

'I hope you don't have anything to do with her,' she asked. 'Do you know her before? I'm now beginning to get worried why you have become so protective of her.'

'Should I therefore watch you deform her because she is not my blood relation?'

'Chidi, please I beg you to stay away completely from this girl. I'm the one accountable for her and not you.'

'But I won't stay and watch you dehumanise her as if she

is an illegitimate child, for even the sea monsters cuddle their little ones and draw out their breast to feed them.' And in fairness to Mary, the short time she had stayed with us proved that she was the daughter of anyone's desire. Nevertheless, there was Nkem wanting always to cause her the maximum harm.

I remembered turning to Mary and recoiled when I noticed the indication of blood on her head. The heel of Nkem's shoe had done some havoc. A little while after, a sudden shiver came upon her and I asked her to go and have a warm bath so she could calm herself down. She was so scared and would not move an inch until Nkem shouted, 'Filthy pig and senseless beast, get out of my sight.'

She sobbed and used the edge of her skirt to wipe off the tears that had covered her eyes. She was touching her forehead at intervals, trying to check out the gravity of her injury. I could imagine, she had almost become half-sick as words completely ceased from her and for days, she was left still grappling with her wounds.

**

It was now obvious that peace and harmony had become very distant from my home. Nkem had not wasted any time at all in showing her true colours soon after she became my legitimate wife and she never spared Mary for a day, before Mary began to face her wrath.

The way and manner in which Nkem was relentlessly abusing Mary was ceaselessly hurting my feelings. I wished Nkem could come with me to the church one of the Sundays so that both of us could seek counsel from the elders. But that would be the last thing she would agree to do.

Friends were beginning to think that either I was weak as a man and lacked the slightest ability to control my wife or it was a magic spell. But both notions were wrong. It was too early to start washing our dirty linen in public. I wanted the matrimony to work. I wanted to prove the world wrong.

For Mary, what would have been a sweet home had become Guantanamo Bay Detention Camp in the United States of America, where heartless strong military men and women torment offenders beyond measure.

What Nkem represented to Mary was nothing else but horror and dread, and I was sharing Mary's moments and emotions.

The quiet movement of any living object could make Mary drop whatever thing she was holding with the belief that Nkem, who was like the queen of a general in the army, was approaching her. Every assignment given to her by Nkem always ended with nagging, chastening and beating.

Despite Mary's quandary, she exhibited true love and care towards Chima, our son. Often, she would cuddle and pet him to sleep when Nkem or I could not. She was up and doing all tasks that were needed to be done by her. She swept, dusted, mopped, washed and cleaned anything worthy of that task, repeatedly, until I would interject and compel her to take her rest. More often than not, she would choose to displease me in order to please my wife only to come back secretly to make it up. She was not naive. She had a mind of her own and was determined to succeed, yet there was neither freedom nor liberty in the home she found herself.

One day, when I returned from work, I met Mary bound to the window iron with a dog chain. Only Nkem could tell where she picked up that chain. I could see bitterness etching lines on her face, ready to mete out the worse abuse on Mary. It was a tug of war between her and I as I struggled, using my superior strength to loosen the chain. When the chain was finally unfastened, Mary's hands were already numb that it took the grace of God to bring them back to normal. Only a person with a beast's heart could treat a fellow human being with such cruelty.

As soon as I untied Mary, I called her aside and asked, 'Will you want to go back to your parents?'

'No, Uncle,' she responded without thinking over it twice.

'But you are not happy,' I stated. She knew what that meant. She was mute as if she was drowsed away; her eyes gleamed as she gazed nervously at me, eyeball to eyeball. I could read from her face that she was recounting every past ugly encounter with Nkem.

'I'm happy, Uncle,' she finally voiced out with fabricated courage.

Any presumption that she was not willing to risk reposing her confidence on me could be right. The conversation suddenly opened the window of her mind and she became terrified. I could imagine that the regular twisting of her ears, the high pitch tone of my wife, the clattering of her footsteps each time she approached were all rehearsing in Mary's mind.

So far, Nkem had not demonstrated any warm regard or encouragement towards Mary. Nkem's expectation of Mary was too high. No doubt, such high hopes about Mary's abilities and strength were unrealistically misplaced and that influenced the regular punishment meted out to her. Nkem totally forgot, or perhaps deliberately ignored, Mary's needs particularly those of emotional warmth, praise, encouragement and some level of allowance to make mistakes without the consequence of beating for failures. All that Nkem had done was using physical force to enforce the desired behaviour. Mary had therefore experienced tight boundaries that left little room for errors. She had rapidly developed values and an understanding of rules which were dependent on Nkem's use of violence rather than talking in order to allow for learning without fearful compliance.

Over time Nkem would hit Mary, shove, pinch, slap, bruise, kick, stab her with a pencil or pen and scratch her; knowing full well that the consequences would be physical injury and pain.

At one time, Nkem took a hammer with the intent of removing one of Mary's teeth. It was not surprising that Mary often looked as if she was seeing evil all around her, constantly afraid as if something nearby was trying to harm her. As a teenager, she wanted Nkem to be her mother and I, her unfaltering mentor but all of that did not happen.

'Uncle, let me go,' she begged and turned to leave without asking for any supplementary permission.

'Mary! Come back here,' I commanded but with a compassionate expression, feeling extremely sorry for her.

'Yes, Uncle,' she responded. She delayed before walking back, this time she was cuddling Chima on her shoulder, who, in turn, clasped on to his toy. Just then, both of us could hear the footsteps of my wife coming out from the rest room and without a second thought, Mary bolted. She knew that my wife hated to see both of us engaging in any conversation. In her haste to avoid my wife catching her, Chima hit his head on the frame of the door. He cried as if the building was about to collapse and Mary used her palm to cover his mouth. She knew my wife must not meet Chima in a bad mood, let alone find tears in his face. For my wife to meet both of us conversing was far better than what was now on the ground. I decided to take Chima from her, at least to relieve her from any beating that evening. As I stretched my hands, my wife walked in. It was not a time to say anything.

'Mary!' she barked as she came closer. 'So, this is how you make this baby cry all day when I'm not around?' she questioned.

She flung the napkin in her hand aside and went for Mary's ear. She twisted it so hard that this time Mary had no choice but to bellow for help, 'Uncle, please rescue me.'

I came and tried to push Nkem away from her, but she would not yield. The more I tried, the more Mary was yelling because Nkem held the ear very firmly. I then went inside the room and put Chima in his cot, who at that time had stopped crying as his pains all of a sudden disappeared.

I returned and pulled Nkem by her hand with a careful force, ensuring that Mary did not by that get hurt even more. Ultimately, I succeeded. On a normal day, Nkem would push back but she must have been worn-out from her constant visit to the rest room because of her troubling stomach coupled with the previous day's overwork in her workplace. She had already narrated how the previous day was so busy for her and some other nurses who delivered some women with different level of complication of their babies.

Nkem went into the room to undress while Mary returned to the kitchen. Afterwards, her voice came as if from an empty auditorium, full of echoes. It repeated the dread and disgust which Mary usually pay attention to her name. Mary hastened to meet her.

'You have stained my work dress,' she alleged. 'It was

previously immaculate with no spot of any form but now you have smeared it.'

Mary began to shiver because she had hardly recovered from the last encounter with Nkem.

'I'm so sorry, Aunty,' Mary admitted and pleaded.

'Don't be sorry, you beast,' she cursed. She flung the dress at her. 'Take it and I don't care what you do to it to make it ultra-clean again.'

I came into the room and requested to have a look at the dress. As I tried to examine it repeatedly, I could not spot any stain.

'Nkem, can you point at the exact spot of the stain because I can't see any,' I said.

'Mr Advocate, I know you won't see it. Always wanting to come into matters, no one invited you. Anyway, it isn't your dress so you won't find it. I know where the stains are hidden.'

'Could you please show me so that I can see too?'

'Okay, hand it over to me and let me show you.' I handed over the dress to her.

'Doubting Thomas, look at this,' she pointed, 'and that.' I bent my head to close the gap between my eyes and the dress in order to capture the stain. There was nothing whatsoever that I saw. Meanwhile, Mary was standing, almost changing her position at every second, temporarily relieved of any harassment, watching all the episodes of the drama between Nkem and myself, waiting for when Nkem might call her in to act her part. As I turned to the other side of the dress to take another closer look, Nkem quickly removed it from my hands and threw it back at Mary.

I walked away quietly but not without a warning to Nkem. 'If you like, slaughter her, but just take note that I won't participate in her burial.'

Mary felt disenchanted as, I, her only witness seemed to be throwing in the towel and turning my back.

'Should I soak it with bleach?' Mary asked.

'Imbecile! Have you ever seen me soak it with bleach?'

Mary became even more perplexed like a fish in the dishwasher.

'Get out of my sight,' Nkem uttered. 'Go and light the gas cooker and boil water to prepare the baby's food. After that, boil some rice for my husband and I. That is what we shall have for dinner. As for you, you will eat the remaining beans.'

'Ah!' Mary exclaimed. 'I tied it in a small nylon bag and threw it away yesterday because it was just a very small portion that remained and it seemed some ants had got inside it.'

'What do you mean? Where did you throw it?'

'The general dustbin stationed down the street.'

'In your own interest, go and fetch it because that is going to be your dinner tonight.' Mary hurried out without any hindrance. The dustbin was a six by six inches metal drum with height approximately the same dimension like the width and breadth. Not only the nearly three dozen families within the neighbourhood had the privilege of dumping their waste in that drum but people from across the other side of the area also had. The drum was evacuated a day before and was barely empty in the morning but by the time Mary got there, it was already overflowing again. Mary realised that it was better she came back with any knotted nylon of anything than returned empty handed. She knew exactly where she stood as she flung the beans into the garbage drum the previous night. She could not recollect how far her hand stretched but she resolved to try her luck.

It was already dark but one could still see oncoming objects at close range so she looked in all directions to be sure no one was near the drum. Then as she attempted to climb it, she noticed two people coming from the opposite side. She then held her peace and waited even though she was conscious of the fast-moving time and would not want my wife to rebuke her for spending all the moments outside. As they drew very close, she hid herself from their sight; otherwise, they could become suspicious of her. As soon as they passed, she quickly climbed and stood on top of the heap of garbage. It was a great risk for her for there were many disused tins, some fully cut into two others half cut. There were also cans and other waste with possibly human excreta, oozing out odours. As she stepped on the bin, she noticed several rats running helter-skelter. As soon as the coast cleared, she quickly bent searching for the knotted beans, opening and smelling every object she could lay her hands on, digging the entire place. After several attempts, she then came up with what she felt was the same-knotted beans she threw away the previous night.

Now she tried to make her way down but holding the nylon compounded her efforts so she cast the nylon on the ground, pushed herself to the edge of the drum and dropped down. She then picked up her nylon.

As soon as she entered the house, she stretched out her hand, showing the nylon containing the stinking beans to the warder of my home.

'Very good,' my wife said, covering her nose and squeezing her face. 'Now go and warm it on the fire and take it with the small bread in the fridge. Note that you have to eat it under my watchful eyes. Next time you will learn how to preserve food, no matter how small.'

'Yes, Aunty,' Mary replied. She was still standing as if she was somehow disorganised.

Nkem went close, threatening to hit her, without a sting of conscience, she pushed her away, shouting, 'Leave my sight.'

Mary fell on the brightly coloured medium sized clay pot holding some of my beautiful flowers positioned adjacent to the bookshelf. The pot shattered into pieces. The only thing left were the flowers. It was the previous week I had brought the pot and the flowers into our sitting room and since then it changed the beauty of the whole place; every day I came in from the office, it was the very first spot my eyes went to and it made me feel so good. I suffered so much that day I brought it into the house. I had to contract a taxi driver to bring it all the way from the Island. It cost me a fortune. Now it was broken owing to Nkem's temper. And when I called her attention to it, she gave me a quick and horrible reply of, 'Is it finished in the market? Go back to where you bought it and get another one.'

I had thought of remaining passive for the rest of the night but with what I was observing, I could not bear it any more. I remembered that my mother had entreated me to always rise for the poor girl whenever the need arises and not allow Nkem to assault her at will. On the other hand, Mary had always looked up to me to come to her rescue whenever Nkem was descending on her. That I did occasionally and cautiously without undermining my own interest. I walked straight to Nkem. 'Nkem, you can't do that to that girl,' I said.

'Do what?' she asked, pompously.

'Compel her to feed on that putrid smell of rotten beans

she picked from the public trash. How do you think that felt?'

'Why don't you mind your own business for once?'

'And if you insist, I would call out neighbours to come and see the inhuman treatment you are delivering to your blood cousin.'

'I'm glad you said my cousin and not yours. If anything ever happens to her, they will ask me and not you. Anyway, if you like, you can invite the social workers or even the Human Rights Organisation here, I don't care.'

'Mary!' I called with an unusual tone. Shouting was not my nature but I used such a high pitch in an attempt to let Nkem realise that this time around I meant serious business. I wanted her to know that every person possesses both the good and the ugly sides. It was up to one to choose which side one wants to show to others.

Mary quickly appeared before two of us in her almost oversized gown that was so transparent and exhibiting her groins. She was very uncomfortable with her teeth gleamed white against the tanned cloudy face and it broke my heart when I realised to my shock, that her show of naivety was giving Nkem some measure of pleasure. I saw the satisfaction in her eyes. 'Where is the portion of beans my wife asked you to heat on the fire?' I asked. Before she could answer, Nkem sent out a long hiss like the sound of escaping gas from the cylinder. She eyed Mary with profound resentment.

Nobody dared remind Mary that Nkem had become such a vindictive woman she would never forget. Mary stared at me very systematically and gradually brought down her face as if some creeping objects caught her attention. Her fears were boundless and visible.

'It's in the kitchen and I'm already warming it. Don't

worry, Uncle, I am fine with it.'

Until that time, I had never given any thought to the practical aspect of marriage as a prison environment with the wife being the chief warden.

Soon, my wife began to make a song and dance of Mary's submission, humming victory hymns over the fact the Mary voluntarily accepted to comply with her hateful directive.

I walked away disappointed and feeling pity for Mary as the end of her agony was not in sight. I sensed she had her mind made up to subject herself to my wife's will and cruelty. She was ready to endure the constant beatings, maltreatment and so many unthinkable acts of callousness. From that moment, I made up my mind, for my own peace, never to intervene again in matters between her and Nkem even if it meant that Nkem would sniff the life out of her.

Chapter Nine

I went to the living room and lay dozing until a whistling air started penetrating heavily through the windows that I had left opened. I was in no way in the mood of going to meet Nkem in bed but stretched myself across the double sofa. The crumb of affection towards the woman I called my wife had steadily diminished through no fault of mine and similarly, I no longer saw or felt even an ounce of love from her. The whole relationship had been one long battle.

Mary was on her mat at the other end. Not long and she was already snoring and if not for that, one would think she was lifeless. She must have overworked herself. She did not deserve the treatment she was getting, I had thought. She was invariably an obedient and reserved teenage girl, faithful to the core.

I knew that Nkem could not find her asleep in time and was envisaging that I should come over to the room but I snubbed her that night. I was still on the sofa until the alarm woke me up in the morning. I prepared and left for work.

At work, I struggled to hide my story and made every effort to accomplish all my tasks without allowing the domestic ordeals to gain access into my heart. Yet, Caroline, a senior human resources officer, who came to see my boss, caught me reciting some scriptural verses in the Bible when she stopped by at my office to see how I was doing. She stood quietly by the corner as I went over those verses:

'He that dwelleth in the secret place of the most High shall abide under the shadow of the Almighty. I will say of the LORD; He is my refuge and my fortress: my God; in him will I trust.

'Surely, he shall deliver thee from the snare of the fowler, and from the noisome pestilence. He shall cover thee with his feathers, and under his wings shalt thou trust: His truth shall be thy shield and buckler. Thou shalt not be afraid for the terror by night; nor for the arrow that flieth by day. Nor for the pestilence that walketh in darkness; nor for the destruction that wasteth at noonday. A thousand shall fall at thy side, and ten thousand at thy right hand; but it shall not come near thee. Only with thine eyes shall thou behold and see the reward of the wicked. Because thou hast made the LORD, which is my refuge, even the most High, thy habitation.'

'Chidi!' she suddenly called, and I looked up almost perplexed. The stanzas she had heard me recite immediately set flame on her psychological mind, convincing her that I must be passing through some troubles. We did not talk about it rather we talked about company challenges and goals and later briefly delved into some social matters.

Caroline was married with two children and she appeared like someone utterly below my age. Yet, all her actions and behaviour would leave one with no alternative conclusion than to say she was an advanced woman. I was so much attracted to her happy countenance and it interested me amply when I noticed that she was without cosmetics, jewels, necklaces or armlets. She had a natural appearance without any artificial attachment to her hair. Nature endowed her so much with long and dark hair, enough to cover her head without any scarf. She was quite elated to hear that I was a Christian and a member of the Baptist Church. She was a member of the Orthodox Methodist. It was then I realised the reasons behind her constant full-length, well-rounded blouses that rode up the neckline, which deprived others from seeing what they should not.

Later that day, we met at the lunch desk, sitting side by side. I could rely on her at that time, knowing that we shared the same principles and faith. I told her all that I was undergoing at the hand of my wife. She saw me that very moment, downcast and dispirited and I too realised for the first time that I was slightly pale in the way the muscles in my stretched-out arms stuck out like thin wire. She felt very sorry and I saw sympathy lodged heavily in her two eyes. I kept looking down as she glanced intermittently at me, taking her eyes away every second even though I knew she acknowledged my pains. Suddenly, as I looked up, my eyes clashed with her white naturally coloured eyeballs, bright, and filled with compassion and tame. 'There is a solution to the problem,' she whispered.

'What is the solution?' I enquired with some measure of curiosity mixed with cynicism.

'Will you like to come with me to our church next Sunday so that you will receive special counselling?' she asked. I pondered and felt confused for a few minutes.

'Well, I am a young minister in my church and I have great responsibility in that church, especially on Sundays.'

'It doesn't matter, Chidi. You have to have yourself

excused just once and I assure you that you will be pacified in the end.'

'If that is the case, I can seek for the same counselling in my church.'

'I know, even with that, still come. The man of God you will see is so much experienced and gifted with family conflict and mediation.'

'Okay, I will prefer you work it out for any other day, leaving Sunday out of it and I'll try and show up. It won't be easy for me anyways.'

'Good, then, Wednesday will be ideal, after our Bible studies.'

'Okay, then.' We went back to our desks after we had had our lunch.

The Wednesday that followed, I made my way to the Methodist church venue, which was closer to where we lived compared to where the Baptist Church was located. It took me only about ten minutes on public transport to get there. It was on a considerable large piece of land, about eight plots, with two structures squeezed on one-third of the space. The rest was garden. While one of the structures was for the adult services, the smaller one was for the little children. Each would not house more than one hundred and fifty worshippers but they often filled up all the seats in both halls at every service. It was a well-arrayed premises, dissimilar to the Baptist church. There were different species of flowers, bird of paradise, bottle brush, camellias, primrose, hibiscus, lavender, lilies, roses, just to mention but a few. From what I read in the Bible, the garden seemed to be a replica of the Garden of Eden. It had different plants ranging from guava, grape, oranges, pawpaw, mangoes, to coconut. Everything about the church was quite appealing.

The mode of worship, the songs, the admonition, the entire environment—all spoke of harmony and optimism.

The entire environment and all the things I met ignited my hope that a special miracle was eminent for me. As the Bible Study began, Caroline, who invited me, sat by my side. She was tapping my leg when the choir sang words of faith and assurances to confirm what she had told me, to build my trust on nothing else but the God Almighty. I heard songs like, *Go tell it on the mountain*, and *Come Thou Redeemer on Earth*, both arranged by David Wilcocks, and *Behold the Star*, composed by William Dawson, *Violin Concerto No. 5*, by W.A. Mozart and *Andante,* by G.F. Handel, amongst others.

As soon as the service ended, there was shuffling of feet to the altar, people so eager to kneel and pray, all pushing their heads down on a number of benches lining up in several rows across the breadth of the building. Suddenly, I saw a man in his eighties also limping towards the altar but before he reached, both the young men and older ones had covered the whole of the benches, their heads bent on them and their voices rising to heaven. The aged man moved straight to the altar rail and knelt before it. He dropped his chest on the rail to make his weight less pushing to his knees and his lips parting soundlessly, in such a way that made me believe he was emptying his mind of all his wrong actions and pleading for mercy. I wished I could pray like that.

At the end, Caroline led me to their pastor, who looked aged, in my own verdict. For such an old man to be at the helm of affairs in a church like that was a misfit. I guess he would not be less than eighty-six years old. He was lanky and sat hunched over his desk like a person with a humpback, though he looked nourished and full of agility. Later, I got to realise he was hard of hearing in his right ear, a condition that dated to his days as a bank worker and no doubt worsened because of the beating he received on the day gang men raided the bank for five hours, close to the week he retired.

'You are welcome to our church,' he said. 'How did you find our service?'

'The service was quite interesting, sir,' I replied.

'I hope you have been blessed?'

'So much, sir.'

'Is there anything special we can do for you?'

'Yes, sir.'

'Can I hear you then as there is nothing God can't do if we put all our trust in Him?'

'I have some family challenges. Ever since I got married, I have not been getting on well with my wife. It has been a very tough relationship. Her character is such that not even an angel can put up with it. She nags and curses all day and physically abuses the teenage girl staying with us. The worst is that nobody can ever make her own up to the fact that she is abusive. She has learnt no other expression but anger, always anxious and willing to act out her vision of cruelty. And she seems to be enjoying every bit of her pugnacity.'

'Every morning, she wakes up with fresh energy for her belligerent attitude. In the past, I had reacted by talking back, persuading or keeping silent. Sometimes, I have left the house in order to get rid of that ugly feeling but nothing has so far worked. She relates with me with absolute disregard to my person and I seem to be fed-up.'

'God will overcome for you,' the pastor responded after pausing for a while. He stared at the ceiling as if the solutions to all that I have narrated were carved-up there. 'You see, according to the scriptures, there is no circumstance that permits a man to put away his wife except when someone catches the woman in the act of adultery. Even with that, the Bible enjoins us to forgive whether she begs for forgiveness or not. I encourage you to intensify your prayers and before long, you will be an overcomer. For God to give you victory, you must consecrate your life deeper and abolish those things, which hinder love. You need special help and God provides that help when we give up ourselves to do the right thing. If you allow God to be in perfect control, the problem may seem to be there but you will have peace of mind. My brother, don't worry. God is a specialist and He will handle your case. My final advice is that you should continue to show her your love. I pray that God will give you the strength to do that.' He kept silent and focused his eyes on mine in a way that was conveying the message to me that he had finished.

If I say that I was not frustrated the more when I left that pastor's office, I would be lying. His approach was more devastating to me. I was expecting that he would hand down a particular formula for dealing with my situation or at least ask me to kneel before him while he lay his hands on me, and probably input in me the power of forbearance and long-suffering.

I told Caroline how disheartened I was, but she continued to assure me that God would not neglect me, as she too would join me in prayers.

The good news was that in the weeks that immediately followed, I realised that God had dealt with my heart and I learnt to pray for my wife on daily basis. I spent many agonising hours in prayers and fasting, seeking to pursue the demon in her.

After every prayer, I would rise up and put more pressure on her to come with me to church but I never succeeded as she often left me with her customary reply of, "When I got married to you, you were not seriously going to church." My thoughts were more like, *Nkem can you ever lay off?* However, for fear of her erratic reaction, I never uttered those thoughts. Occasionally, I would cajole her, and she would look me right in the eye and say, "Leave me alone, young man."

***

All went very quiet for a few weeks after I had gone to see the pastor for counselling. There was no outrageous fall-out in my relationship with my wife, neither did I stumble at her again spanking or punching Mary as she usually desired. But when I was in some way beginning to be comforted that my troubles were miraculously ending, something that shocked me beyond imagination happened.

I woke up that beautiful bright Monday morning and was hurrying down the road that led to the point where I would catch the staff bus to my office. It was roughly half past six in the morning and the atmosphere was still very blurred. The staff bus was only about ten minutes away from me. I was walking as fast as I could so that I would not miss the bus. Missing the bus meant that I would have to go on public transportation. That also entailed I would have to change commercial buses three times before getting to my office. No staff would want to miss his or her staff bus in the nation's capital because apart from the hassles, it would take that person a longer time getting to destination.

As I looked back, I could see my wife running after me

like a cat after the rat. She was still in her nightgown save that she covered half of her body with a single piece of wrapper, without any feelings of loss of dignity. Housewives who wanted to earn respect would never appear like that even at the front house where they live. As she moved closer, I could hear her calling my name, 'Chidi! Chidi!' Her voice came down the line as clear as a bell. I turned and started walking back towards her as I was almost at the bus stop where many other commuters were standing, waiting for their private buses or the commercial ones. I made the right decision when I suddenly decided to walk back towards her in order to divert the attention of possible onlookers away from the looming drama that was bound to take place. She was holding a nylon bag and in it was an empty can of baby food.

'What's the matter?' I asked in a haste but gentle manner.

'Didn't I tell you yesterday that the baby food got finished and you sneaked out this morning without dropping some money? Didn't I?' she chanted.

'I can't remember if you mentioned it. Nevertheless, you could have waited until I come back or at least use part of your money and get the refund as soon as I return.'

'You must be out of your senses, Chidi.'

'Take it easy, Nkem. This is serious embarrassment for we are in the public arena.' I dipped my hand in my pocket and took out some money. 'Okay, have this money and go back quickly.'

'Thank you, useless man.' She stretched her hand and collected the money, counting it. She frequently uses filthy, disgusting language and caring was the least part of her. There was no indication she realised that her actions and habits were bringing mental pains to me. With every possible opportunity, she was tearing me apart; she was attacking and hammering me verbally. She appeared to be enjoying what she was doing to me. She prided herself in people referring to her as a tough woman and I was paying the price, silently. There was hardly anything she did which was not an enticement and appeal to strike her. But stronger than before, I felt called to be a missionary to her, my so-called, dear wife, the mindless and boorish woman I had married. In-between my thoughts, I was also anxiously wishing that she should initiate a divorce. I knew the marriage had not lasted long at all, but I did not care anymore. I did not want it to come from me because I knew it was not right before God.

'The money won't be enough,' she argued.

'How much is there?'

'I don't know. All I know is that it can't buy one tin of the baby food.' As I turned to leave with only two minutes before my bus arrived, she rushed at me, plunged her left hand into my pocket and collected all that was on me and left. Just then, I sighted my bus and I ran in order to get on it as quickly as possible.

While on the bus, I remembered the exact words of the Methodist Church Pastor I had gone to see. 'There's no circumstance that allows a man to put away his wife...' That thought made my head spin and I felt like jumping off the bridge when we got to the short distant flyover of the OBJ Lagoon, linking the mainland and the island.

Those words of admonition were now bringing pains to me rather than relief. The initial anguish I thought I had overcome returned. The next moment, I recalled the pastor's final consolation, 'God is a specialist and He will handle your case,' he had told me. But when, when would that happened?

I now began to query within me. Yet, I made up my mind to let that be the only thing that will keep ringing out in my head. I struggled never to allow the growing tension in my brain to weigh me down in order to avert any psychological disorder.

Constantly, returning home from work was like walking into a self-made hell on earth. That day, I was ready for the worst but instead of that, I received a surprise. 'Welcome, my sweetheart,' Nkem greeted as soon as I entered. She had never greeted me like that before.

'Thank you very much and how are you doing?' I'd asked feeling very elated but suspicious.

'Hope Chima did not disturb much today?' I enquired.

'Not at all except that he doesn't seem to like the tin food I bought for him in the morning. I had felt like trying out a new one in the market. Maybe I'll go back to the original one he's used to. In that case, I shall require additional money.'

I declined to make any comments and went inside to undress and refresh myself.

On coming out, I met Mary sobbing uncontrollably as she was bleeding from the head. She was dabbing the blood with a piece of rag she took from her many clothes that were no longer her size. 'What happened to you?' I enquired.

'My aunty hit me with a piece of iron.'

I went closer and removed her palm from the glued piece of cloth on her head to blot the blood from the injured part. As I removed the rag, *poom*, the blood gushed out. Not only that, her left eye burned darkly, had swollen up like a golf ball, and there was a soft peeled skin, about three quarter of an inch wide. With only my light towel on my waist, I walked straight to the kitchen where Nkem was. 'Nkem, do you want to kill this girl?'

'Why should I kill her?'

'Then why is your body always itching to hurt her?'

'Hurt her?'

'You go and see the havoc you have inflicted on her.'

'Hope she's not dead?'

Immediately, I felt a certain heat in the depth of my stomach and my lips parted out in disbelief. She was carrying on like a crazy woman, without any fear of hurting the poor girl. I came back, took some spirit and applied on the wounds. But the blood would not stop easily, so I went with her to a pharmacy down the street where she was given appropriate first aid. She had to carry some bandages for many days. She was now beginning to feel vulnerable as Nkem's cruelty struck home. For the fact that I had attended to her with care, Nkem was upset and waited till about the midnight when she sent her out for the night after I had slept. In addition, for seven days she compelled her to sleep on the bare floor and without dinner for those days.

Chapter Ten

A couple of weeks after, as I was on my way back from work, I could notice from a distance, some people, including an elderly woman with fine wrinkles around her eyes, standing and talking in front of the compound. They were very close to the entrance leading to my flat.

As I approached them, I noticed my wife was there too. She had on a transparent top, and skin-tight short chinos. The whole of her hips were showing to the disgust of some of the people who knew that that was not the proper way for a dependable married woman to dress outside her apartment. I remember thinking how inappropriate she always dressed, even when showing herself to the public. I could hear her voice chirping like the sound night crickets and other cacophony of voices. It was a hot argument but others who were there seemed to be attacking her verbally. One was inches aside, shrugging her shoulders and spewing out air from her mouth. Another was making every effort in a cultured manner to prevail upon her, to see some reason in what they were saying. The rest were reprimanding her for what they felt was a wrong action of hers.

'What's the matter?' I enquired as I reached them. I held

her by the hand and tried to march her into our apartment, but she flung away my hand.

'Go and refresh and I'll sort it out with this unruly woman,' she uttered.

'Is he the husband?' One of the women pointed at me, asking.

'Yes, I am,' I cut in.

I was already tired and so eager to go in, refresh and have some rest. I only managed to unknot the tie on my neck but still holding my laptop bag. With the circumstances I met on the ground, I would not be able to leave the scene as quickly as I desired.

The woman who seemed to be interested in making peace began to explain, 'I'm a tailor and I live two streets behind. Your wife brought some cloth to me to sew a blouse for her. I measured the cloth and took her measurements too. We agreed on the style she wanted me to sew but I told her that with that style, the material she brought would not be sufficient. I told her to buy additional material and bring it to me but she insisted that I should buy whatever additional materials needed and pass the cost to her. That was exactly what I did only to bring the blouse on completion and she said she would not pay for the extra material used because she doesn't like the texture.'

'Nkem, is she correct?' I asked as I turned to my wife.

'Don't ask me stupid questions,' she responded, grumpily. She had never been half as enraged as she was when I tried to establish the truth from her. I was speechless. Some of the people looked at one another. The expression on their faces spoke volumes. Some were shocked and others were upset to think that a married woman could be acting in such a brash manner.

'Is this how you talk to your husband?' one of them asked.

'Do you talk better to your husband than me, stupid woman. By the way, is that any business of yours? Hopeless idiot who is not fit to kiss the ground I walk on.'

'This woman is sick,' one of them opined.

'It's you, your husband and the whole members of your family who are sick,' my wife reacted crossly, exposing her usual surge of bitter hatred. She was now conducting herself like a lunatic, without any feelings of loss of dignity. No one admires a nagging and impertinent housewife.

Now the people began to leave one after the other with the presumption that I would handle the matter. I quickly turned to the tailor, 'How much does she owe you?'

'Three thousand, two hundred and fifty only. One thousand, seven hundred and fifty for the additional material, and one thousand five hundred only for the cost of labour. It was three thousand, two hundred and fifty in total.'

I opened my bag, brought out my purse and counted the sum. As I stretched my hand, to hand over the money to the tailor, my wife got hold of it, insisting it was not right for me to give the money directly to the woman. I pleaded with her to pay the woman but she would not yield.

'Go and come at the month end. That is when I shall be ready to pay the money. Go! I say, go!' Nkem roared, demonstrating like someone who was tipsy.

'Where is your shop located?' I asked the woman. She described the place to me, in a way I would never miss it. 'Okay, you can take your leave and I promise to pay you a visit by the weekend,' I persuaded. Without a second thought, she thanked me and left.

Nkem kept shouting at her as she walked away, 'You'll not get the money soon, I assure you!'

How would I explain it if any of the worshippers in my church came to see my wife, the wife of a young minster, in a shouting mood? I felt grossly agitated.

Having spent over an hour now in front of the house, I was fatigued, so much that I barely fought to lift my step. As I got in, I jumped in the bed, having lost my appetite, only to wake up at midnight to have my bath. By five a.m., I was up again for my morning devotion and the preparation for yet another day's work.

I did not talk about the incident of the previous day until two days later when I returned from work. 'Nkem, please tell me why you choose to bring my person into disrepute?' I asked in a most friendly manner, grinning as much as possible with my arm stretched across her shoulders.

'Please take your hands off me and get straight to the point,' she responded, glowering at me.

I insisted, leaving my arms as they were but she flung them off and looked at me dispassionately. I stared back amorously, hoping to calm her down.

'I'm referring particularly to the incident that happened between you and the tailor.'

'What about it?'

'Was it appropriate to have acted the way you did before those elderly men and women?'

'Why do you always choose to take medication for another person's ailment? I'm not a coward like you, who doesn't fight for his right; and I don't know why you always want me to be defrauded.'

'You are the person wanting to swindle the poor woman.'

'That's your opinion, as you don't know what we both agreed.'

'May I again beg that you should endeavour to pay off that debt and save yourself from an unnecessary disagreement?'

'Never! I have told her she can only get the money at the end of the month and that's the price she has to pay for her idiocy.'

'Nkem, I want you to think over all your negative behaviour? I see no reason you should punish that woman.'

'That's the way I want it.'

I knew that nothing made sense to her once she decided on what to do. After I had my shower, I called for my dinner. She requested that I give some money to Mary to go and get some bread. 'Nkem, you know quite well that I don't like bread and egg for dinner. I love my yam flour with okra soup every evening.'

'Sorry, I forgot to get the soup out from the freezer and it's so frozen that it will take hours to defrost and I'm too tired for all that now.'

'I better go without dinner then.'

'That's fine with me. You are very difficult and never wanting to see some reasons.'

I felt exhausted, emotionally hurt and drained, and now, for the first time, longing seriously for a real woman's warmth and comfort.

***

A week after, I returned from work to be told by Nkem that Chima was having teething problem. His temperature had risen beyond normal. 'Let's hurry and take him to the clinic,' I said.

'No, that won't be necessary as I know what to do. Give me some money and I'll go to the pharmacy and get a combination of drugs and he'll be all right,' Nkem maintained.

'You know I don't support any medication without a doctor's prescription,' I reiterated.

'The symptoms are minor.'

'Okay, make use of the money meant for the tailor and I'll refund it later.'

'I've used the money for something else.'

'It can't be.'

'Well, if you turn down my request, we shall both watch Chima's condition get worse.'

I found Nkem's position very disquieting. I now felt a stench of real despair as my heart was frozen and I thought I was going to break down. In the midst of my anguish, Nkem raised her face, looking at me as though we were strangers to each other, or perhaps she was expressing her hidden joy, that my spirit was being knocked-down. Her weird actions continued to expand my judgement. Anyone who was acquainted with our family would very quickly admit that there was something eccentric about Nkem. I knew she was not ready to budge. If I reacted based on her affectionately detached behaviour, then our son was going to bear the brunt. The feeling that I was being held hostage by the woman I brought into my home at my own volition started increasing fast. With no sensible option left, I provided some money for Chima's treatment and yet again, that endorsed Nkem's thinking that she gave the orders.

***

Around that time, no week passed without having to manage a boiling contention. After about six months, I was amazed to learn from Mary that Nkem had stopped going to work a few weeks before. How it all happened without my knowledge was a mystery to me. She made that decision soon after she ended her maternity vacation. 'How was work today?' I asked her one day even though I knew her circumstance had changed.

'Which work?' she asked.

'Your engagement by Saint Michael General Hospital, of course.'

'Well, I've stopped the work for some time now.'

'Why?'

'Because I chose not to work again. I want to start a special business of my own.'

'Nkem! So, you resigned without discussing the challenges you were having?'

'Why should I discuss it with you? Do you know the stress I go through to get to work or to come back home? I couldn't cope any more. That's it.'

I shook my head in disbelief and left her.

The next day, I returned very late. The traffic was heavy. When I got home, I struggled to have my rest. Much later, I set my alarm as usual and went to bed after skipping my night prayer in exasperation. Suddenly, I felt a gentle hand touching me. I woke and raised my head only to see the twisted face of Nkem showing under the blue light in the room.

'What is it again this time?' I enquired.

'Please get up, I want to make a request and I hope you will oblige me.'

'By this time? Check the time and see for yourself. It's already past midnight, can we discuss it tomorrow? I came back late from work today and sat briefly in the living room. You should have come to meet me by then. We should have talked before now.'

'I'm sorry, please hear me out,' she begged. Yet I knew that her smooth speech never lasted longer than few seconds.

'Okay, what is it?'

'I'll need you to raise some money for me to start the business.'

'Which business?'

'The one I just told you of.'

'You want me to give you money to start business when you never told me before you left your job?'

'Chidi, I am sorry.'

'I've heard but give me till the weekend to think over it,' I cut her off.

'That has been your usual habit, never wanting to hear me out, not for once ready that we should both sit down and discuss like husband and wife,' her voice very quickly accelerated.

'Do you want to wake the neighbourhood up?'

'It's good they wake up so that they can see how you are manipulating me.'

'You are the direct opposite of your name and I'm greatly disappointed in you.'

'You must listen to me and give me positive response,' she insisted. She pushed me and I could have fallen off from the bed if not that I anticipated it. By this time, the sleep had gone and an unfamiliar throbbing headache was beginning to build up. I went into the bathroom to have a cold shower, my head still pounding and I was unable to sleep again until daybreak. Surprisingly, she did not follow me.

The following day was a Saturday. The night had passed by in the blink of an eye. Nkem woke earlier than usual and sat on the double sofa in the living room as if she was keeping vigil on me so that I would not bolt away. After holding her fire for a long time while I was still in bed, she came back into the room and tapped me. 'You have slept enough, Chidi,' she said. After stretching over and over again, I got up knowing there was no hiding place for me that morning. I felt like someone caged me with a fence barbwire. 'Can we conclude our discussion?' she uttered, giving me a little half smile.

'What discussion?' I asked, stretching and yawning at the same time to sway her to believe she interfered with my rest.

'Is this not the reason I'm always upset with you?' she said.

'All right,' I said and stood up. I went into the rest room and sat on the toilet seat. I was not really doing what I went in there to do yet wished I could remain there and not come out, thinking on how best to deal with the present circumstance. I began to paraphrase and practise my response in advance. Soon, I was already overstaying, and I realised she could come over to bang the door of the restroom if I failed to show up within the next few seconds. Finally, I came out and sat very close to her. 'Yes, I heard your proposal, but you have to give me time to raise some money for you,' I yielded. 'By the way, which business are you thinking of?'

'Buying and selling of clothes.'

'So, how much are you looking at?'

'Two million.'

'What! How will I get that?'

'What's two million that you can't get?'

'Nkem, you really have to give me time to work things out.'

'So how long do you want me to wait?'

'Nkem, be patient and give me some time.'

She rose in anger, not pleased, not satisfied. She did not get the answer she was looking for at that moment.

Minutes later, she returned with another demand. 'Can I

get five thousand to go to the salon?' she requested.

'Okay,' I responded.

'But should I not have my breakfast before you come up with another request,' I put across to her.

'I have already instructed Mary to prepare your breakfast and when it's ready, she would serve you.'

'Why not serve the breakfast now?'

'In a few minutes, I shall be going out.'

'Going to where?'

'Why are you asking? So, you still want to retain your control over me when you can't satisfy my wants? That won't happen.'

Moments later, we heard a knock coming at the door. Nkem went to identify the person. It was a neighbour in one of the other flats. We barely knew each other though we had met on the staircase sometime in the past, during one of the early morning bustling.

It was obvious Nkem had not seen him before, though they exchanged greetings as if they knew each other somewhere. 'Where is your husband?' the man enquired.

'Chidi!' my wife called.

The man raised an eyebrow, wondering why Nkem was calling me by my first name, in his presence, a stranger. He was not at all happy with it as if he had any stake in it. That was not the culture of our people, he probably thought. I stepped out to have a view of the man. We greeted and I requested that he come inside and have his seat. But he had only come to leave a message from the landlord. The property owner would want to see all the tenants by the weekend so that he would explain a new development about the house. It was most likely that he wanted all of us to know that the house had been put up for sale and once the sale is consummated, terms and conditions of the rent would change.

'Thank you very much for that piece of information,' I said to the man when he finished, and he turned his back to leave.

'Sorry to bother you, sir,' my wife called him back. 'Before you go, may I make an enquiry from you?'

The young man was quite pleased. 'I guess you are married?' she asked.

He was astonished, the question came unpredictably, but very reluctantly, he nodded his head. 'In that case, please be kind enough to help me talk to my husband to support me with some money to start my personal business?'

There was an unmistakably expression of shock on the man's face and he appeared to be indifferent. He was silent for a while before he said, 'Okay, madam, I'll talk to him.'

I followed the young man to see him off a bit but before then the balance of my composure had vanished and I was so much ashamed of Nkem or perhaps, myself, that I could not say a word to the gentleman I was seeing off. He would not be anywhere near my age. He was very young and could possibly not have been married for more than a year. He was new in the premises. He could notice how discredited I felt. He tried to comfort me and help me suppress my emotions.

'Look, my brother, women are the same. Just try and see how you can be managing her,' he advised without the slightest understanding of the level of my hurt and anger. He was a complete guest to my world of psychological misery.

How, on earth could a woman see another man for the first time and begin to wash her dirty linen before him. That was abnormal as far as I was concerned.

When I came back, it was with a sad spirit that I shouted Nkem's name, 'Nkem! Nkem!' but I did not hear her voice. I stormed the room only to find Chima playing in his cot with his favourite toy.

As soon as Nkem realised I had come into the room, her voice came from behind the toilet door. 'What have I done wrong this time around?'

'You know what you have done.' I replied.

'Oh! For the fact that I requested our neighbour to talk to you, your head is swinging. I haven't started. Just wait. Tomorrow you are going to see me in your office. I have to report you to your boss. He must know how uncaring you are.'

I did not take Nkem seriously until the next day when I received an intercommunication call from the receptionist that my wife would like to see me. I felt a bit of dizziness. Before I could utter any word, the receptionist told me that she observed she was in a fighting mood but promised to deal with the situation. So, she quickly told her something I was not sure of. She did not tell me. 'Does he know you will be coming to see him?' the receptionist further interrogated her.

'Must I inform my husband that I shall be coming to see him before I am let in; my own husband? So, if I have an emergency situation, will you still expect me to follow your nonsense protocol?' she queried. 'Okay, madam, can I see his boss?'

'That would not be possible without any previous appointment,' the lady said to her.

'Anyway, I'll wait until either of them has a window to attend to me.'

The receptionist did all she could to discourage her from waiting but to no avail. The receptionist then called me on the phone to tell me what the situation was. I could not believe it myself. I became cold from my head to my toes and was almost shivering until I went for a cup of coffee.

Meanwhile, Nkem sat on the only single iron chair at the reception. It was the most comfortable chair in that room and first comers usually prefer to sit on it. It had a wide arm and backrest, with fat legs that stationed very well on the floor. It had four rollers that made it almost impossible for the chair to remain stable on the sparkling brownish tiles. To avoid having to roll around, one must rest one's feet on the tiles.

Nkem experienced some difficulties maintaining a steady position for a long time without having to adjust herself. Maybe because she was restless or perhaps, she was building up her usual anger. She would cross her legs for one minute and in another, she would bring them down.

She waited for hours at the reception until it was a few minutes to the close of work. By the time the receptionist looked up to take note of her, she had vanished. Even with that, I dared not come out of my office unless I was prepared to encounter her outrageous mood, not when I knew what she was capable of doing.

From that day, I realised that whenever Nkem said she was going to do something, she was not mixing words. That day, I discovered that there was so much about Nkem which I did not know. For hours, I felt as if I was in a sort of spiral of gloom. Would these feelings ever go away? It was such a bleak path for me, which no one could ever understand.

The only reason I stayed in that marriage was my belief that God was capable of changing Nkem and making her a good homemaker, because He had changed me too, so much.

For the first time in many months, the serious thoughts of

separating from her came. Again, I wondered if it really mattered. When I thought over it, I felt whether I was separated from her or not, it made no difference. As far as I was concerned the marriage seemed dead, and an official separation or even divorce was merely a ceremonial acknowledgement of the reality. I was won over by my conscience in thinking that God Himself must have brought the union under the judgement of nonexistence.

But how would the church look at me? In as much as I would want to uphold the Christian family values as a sense of my religious duty, yet it was my neck and not theirs, that the woman I love so much was squeezing. Still, how would I make people feel the same way I was feeling, all the mental torture I had gone through? How?

Thoughts continued to run amok in my head, yet ending up floating without result. Now my heart throbbed against my chest and I began to feel breathless. Was I going to have a heart attack? I became afraid and remembered one of the things the First Aiders taught us in school about preventing a heart attack. I took a deep breath, hit my chest very gently and gradually released some air through my mouth until the rhythm of my heart regularised itself. I waited until everyone had left the office, before I finally slipped away.

Chapter Eleven

When I returned home that day, I felt like taking my turn by physically battering Nkem. There was perfect silence in the house that evening. Every one of us was carrying cloudy faces. This time, Nkem knew she had crossed the red line and was apprehensively anticipating the consequence. I waited. We all had our dinner.

As soon as she was in bed, the entrance door already bolted, I approached her by surprise and quickly seized her by the neck, and threw her on the floor. I sat on her back; with one hand, I clipped her head to the ground and with the other seized her hands. The sound when she landed would have awoken some of the neighbours but I did not bother myself with that this time around. It was the least she expected to happen at that very moment. She made steady effort to release herself but I had exerted tremendous level of energy to meet every resistance. As I pinned her to the ground, I tried to extract her commitment that from that day onwards, she would uphold an atmosphere of peace.

'I need a break from you, Nkem,' I screeched, repeatedly. 'You must assure me that you will give me peace of mind before I let you go.'

She remained adamant, only struggling to discharge herself. I completely subdued her but was mindful not to raise my hands on her when I remembered I was a young minister in the church.

Soon, I heard on knock at the door. 'Is everything all right?' the voice asked and the tone was quite sharp. I quickly turned her face upwards and stocked her mouth with my palm.

Even though I was yet to determine who that person was, I uttered, 'All is well.'

I continued to screw her to the ground and made sure I did not release myself from sitting on her back, until finally she stopped her resistance. When I felt I had entirely overcome her, I got up, expecting her to react, though I was yet ready for any surprise. To my amazement, she walked away quietly but gasping very audibly. A few seconds later, I saw her lying in bed, exhausted yet without any evidence of penitence. I believed she realised she had transgressed a boundary that no man could tolerate it.

The next morning, she woke up with swelling on her neck, which she nursed for many days. That weekend, I received a call from the pastor of our church that it was urgent I come down to the church without procrastination. Nkem had gone to him to make a complaint against me.

'Your wife came here to report that you beat her up during the week,' was the first statement the Pastor confronted me with as soon as I went into his office. He looked displeased and shocked. 'And I saw the proof all over her when she came,' he continued. 'You are a big disappointment to the entire congregation of the church and especially the youths. Well, for your information, we have decided that you cannot continue to be a worker in this church under that circumstance. Therefore, you are to cease officiating as the youth leader and minister with immediate effect. So, hand over whatever material that is in your possession to the assistant youth minister, Brother Kenneth. Meanwhile, you have to continue to pray that God should restore you.'

I could see cloud of anger billowing out from his voice and it did not seem as though he was ready to hear my own side.

'Sir, but I thought it would have been imperative and fair to ask for my own side of the story,' I submitted.

'Why should I ask when I saw her with swollen neck? What other evidence would one look out for? God will help you.'

'Amen!'

'Please leave my office,' he ordered with a twisted face. I got up and left. When I got back home, Nkem knew I was coming from the church and she needed no oracle to guess what the outcome was. She knew that no worker in that church would ever lay hands on his wife and went scorch free. She felt she had delivered the worst blow on me. She would be satisfied to weaken my zeal for the service of the Lord but I got determined never to be discouraged. She later discovered that my spirit was not in any way dampened as she had envisaged and I never missed any of the church activities. She was surprised.

After the incident, I would sit in my study where I wept each night, remembering what my parents had warned me against during my early years. I now felt caged, like a bird full of energy yet without the freedom to fly.

More than ever before, it became obvious that there was nothing I did, that pleased Nkem any longer. Despite what had happened, I continued my resolution to raise the money she needed for her business. At least that would keep her occupied. Nevertheless, her subsequent actions were very unhelpful. Her demands for money to meet her personal needs increased on a daily basis. They were unwarranted and careless. Household items that were supposed to last for several weeks were to my amazement getting finished before the middle of the anticipated period.

Each time I provided money for home needs, she diverted it for her personal needs and turned around to request for additional funds. Even with that, the worth of our meals diminished in both quality and quantity. It was too apparent that her actions were premeditated.

One day, while in the living room, reading an article titled 'Found the Right Way to Live' which was in the latest edition of our church bulletin I received the previous Sunday, I noticed a big object crippled down from the side of the window. It was such a rocket speed. Soon all was quiet again. I stood up and moved towards the direction that object ran to. All I could lay my hands on was a three-hundred-and-eighty-page hard cover general studies textbook I used in year one of my university days. With it, I was ready for that little nasty object. I got to the spot and held the hard book up, ready for it. There was no longer any sign of movement but I remained in my position. When I became tired, I tried to make some noise, so that in fear, the foolish object would run out. All was quiet and I became frustrated and impatient. When I could not hear any sound, I started doubting whether indeed I saw an object.

Suddenly, a thought came to me, *Ransack the entire area to be sure*. As I bent to begin the process of clearing the area, I noticed something. At last, it was a long-tailed tiny rodent.

Quickly, it climbed the leg of the stool and hid behind it, elevating itself from the floor to avoid anyone seeing it. As soon as our eyes caught each other again, it descended and raced with all the energy in it. I was smarter, so I followed very fast. I was not going to let it escape. We both ran from one corner of the sitting room to the other until it sneaked into the room and disappeared. I had seen the direction it took so I dropped the hard cover book I was holding and went for a broom. When I came back, I started tumbling anything my eyes saw. There were heaps of different stuff at one corner and that was where I suspected it must have been hiding. There were some newspapers and magazines kept on top of two cartons, which I initially thought were empty. With one hand, I held firmly the broom and with the other, I was clearing the spot. After unloading the papers, as I shifted the cartons, there was the tiny callous object, staring desperately and calculating its next move. Its eyes shone like that of the moonlight. Without wasting further time, I wedged it with the cartons and hit it with the broom, using my left heel to press its head against the floor, without giving it the slightest chance to break away. It was all over.

I nearly felt let down that it was not worth the efforts when I lifted it up by its tail, looking as flat and small as a household pest until I found the destruction it had inflicted inside those cartons. It carried out a massive demolition inside the cartons. I began to unpack the content of each of the cartons. To my greatest amazement, there were several sachets of sugar and beverages torn nearly to pieces, with their content littered inside the cartons. Only the items in tins such as milk, sardine, tinned tomatoes and beverages were safe. Alas, those were some of the many provisions previously purchased by my wife even though she often claimed they were exhausted in order to extort money from me.

Later, I discovered that many a time she would bring out some of those old stocks and maintain that she purchased them newly with the money handed over to her. I was initially slightly upset but became infuriated when I discovered at the bottom of the carton a thick brown envelope. The envelope was tucked in-between an old magazine which would have made it so difficult to stumble on if not that the cartons were combed. The rats had eaten a great part of the magazine and nearly got to the brown envelop and its content.

When I opened the envelope, I saw notes of high denomination currency neatly arranged. Some bore marks, which I clearly recognised were part of the money I had given to Nkem in the past as a feeding allowance. At the end of the exercise, I left the envelope where I found it. I remained composed and did not mention my discovery to her. I guess she knew what I had found given the massive house cleaning that took place that day because of the ugly tiny rat.

The next day as I was approaching my house from work, I noticed that the tailor was seated in front of the house, waiting. As she sighted me, she started walking towards me to collect my bag. My heart flipped. I remembered that we still owed her for the job she did and felt terribly bad. She must be a very nice woman. She did not come to make any trouble. What she needed was her money. 'Please forgive me. I did promise to bring the money myself,' I said as soon as she got to me.

'I understand,' she responded. 'I know you are busy with work.' As we proceeded, I observed she was retreating. She did not want to go beyond the door. 'Come right inside,' I said to her as I entered.

'I am fine,' she replied. I did not blame her. No woman would crave to receive some abuse from another woman who was far less than her age.

'Nkem!' I called. Without hesitation, she walked out calmly and greeted me cordially in the most unusual manner. But I knew her very well, that whenever she acted that way, I had better be very careful. 'Thank you very much,' I said. 'The tailor is here to collect her money. It's over a month now and you still have not paid her. Why?'

'I told you earlier that I have used the money for something else. Didn't I?' I gave her a mad look at that moment. That was not the first time or second or even third, she would be acting like that. For a second time, I felt like pounding her but I had resolved within me never to raise my hands on her. I went into the room, counted yet another sum of money and gave it to the tailor who departed with much gratitude.

***

One day, very near the end of the year, when I felt I had a reasonable amount in my account, I called Nkem to find out the nature and details of the business she intended to do. 'It's wholesale fresh fish distribution,' she mentioned. 'I remember you told me is clothes business? How come you have suddenly switched?' I queried.

'I changed my mind,' she replied.

'Have you done enough research?' I enquired, but in her usual characteristic way, she flared up and changed her mood. 'Give me the money for goodness sake and stop interrogating me as if I'm in police custody.'

'You need to carry out a feasibility study to know how

viable the business is and also the cost implication.'

'It will require a gigantic refrigerator and a standby generator amongst other things. In fact, it might require up to two and a half million cash to start with.'

'I remember you mentioned two million at the outset and not two and a half.'

'Yes, I know, but from the look of things that amount may not cover all the items that would be needed.'

'Okay, I've heard you but still give me time to conduct my own research.'

'So, you know you have to conduct a research when you called me out here for a pointless cross-examination,' she stated impolitely, raising her voice nearly to a shout. 'Go ahead, Mr Researcher!'

Weeks later, I came up with a proposal. It was my ardent desire that she kick off without any further waste of time.

'I would first give you the money for the rent of the space and a week after, we shall go out together to procure the refrigerator and the generator. When these are ready, we shall then go to the suppliers to arrange for the frozen fish…' I was still talking when she interrupted in a very discourteous manner, yelling at me.

'It's me that wants to run the business and not you. So, if you want to assist me, hand in the money and I know how best to apply it.' I knew that if I wanted peace, it had to be her decision and not mine, so I made up my mind to hand over the money to her as she demanded, thinking I would find respite in doing so.

Nevertheless, the business started some days after I gave her the money worth nearly half of my annual income.

Nkem became virtually missing from the home from the

very first day she started the business, returning nearly every day close to midnight. Gradually, Chima, our only child, was losing the familiarity of his mother. The nursing and bringing up of an only child, day and night, became Mary's sole responsibility.

Every day, before Nkem returned, Chima would have been deep asleep. Mary would have bathed and fed him as well as pet him to sleep.

As soon as Nkem stepped in each time, no matter how late, she would walk straight to where Chima was lying in the cot, swung the cot a couple of times and said, 'Hey, my baby, hope you are all right today?'

Often, I would frown at her saying, 'Please, Nkem, don't wake up that little boy.' She would never listen.

'Won't I say hello to my baby again?' she would always ask.

'Then you have to make it a point of duty to be home early,' I would argue.

Sometimes, following my complaints, she would leave him and only to wake up the next morning without the little boy sighting her. Some other times, she would ignore my objection and go ahead to lift him up and shook him until he opened his eyes. 'I miss you my baby,' she would often say.

Whenever I was in the disposition, I would remind her of how she had abdicated her responsibilities of not taking care of the baby and serving the food.

'Please… please,' she would often cut in. 'Don't just raise that point. Go out there and find out for yourself how serious the traffic is all the time. Do you want me to spoon-feed you? There are all kinds of food in the fridge. All it takes is to bring them out, dish and put them in the microwave. Besides, Mary is there to serve you, if you want.'

'That apart, how would Chima get used to his mother?'

'He's no longer breastfeeding so he can do without the mother. Can't he?' I could not help but grieve over the circumstances I found myself. Often, I would kneel beside the bed, pray and would wish that I would one day sleep never to wake up again.

As days went by, my fears grew as to whether I would still be able to hold on. Sometimes, tears would push out of my eyes for minutes, yet it would not turn my pains away. I kept on reminding myself that I was a man and must be strong, hoping that one day, I would wake up with all the troubles rolled away.

At a point, I started to believe that other homes could be like mine, where clashes consistently took place between my wife and I as if it was what the legislature required. I seemed to be consoling myself that I could not have been the only victim; maybe others were covering up.

The more I comported myself, the more arrogantly Nkem exhibited her flagrant abusive behaviour. I was sure that every woman desired peace in her home but rather than that, Nkem seemed to be working against it and baking hostility all the time. A part of me kept clamouring for a walk-away. But God forbids it. Then the thought of taking her to a mental health clinic crept in. Maybe her behaviour has something to do with her mental state, I thought. It was going to be a big task to convince her to leave her business for something she might not consider important.

Joyfully, three months after, the opportunity came when she woke up one morning and began to scream that her stomach was hurting her badly. Her face created a picture of serious agony and pain and it was an indisputable fact she needed immediate relief. I offered to take her to the hospital and she quickly consented. I led the way out of the house and pushed towards the main road where we could get a cab. We waited until a cab pulled up.

After a test at the hospital, it was only a typhoid fever. We both walked into the doctor's room for her prescription. After that, I asked her to sit at the waiting area in order for me to collect her drugs from the pharmacist. I had something else in mind. I went again to have a word with the doctor. He appeared like one of the youngest doctors I had ever come across. He dressed quite casually in a way that made me doubt if he was the doctor on duty. He must have rushed to the premises because of an emergency or perhaps he lived nearby. From his looks, my spirit told me that he would very much understand any young man's predicament. He had a surname that made me believe we were both from the same state. Therefore, that boosted my confidence. 'Please, Doctor, I have another case I want to mention to you.'

'Sure, call your wife in.'

'That is not necessary, Doctor.'

'Okay go ahead then.'

'I would appreciate it if you can refer us to a mental health specialist where she could be examined because I have seen in her signs of mental illness.'

'Really?' The doctor asked with a twisted face, very anxious to hear more. 'What gives you that impression?'

'My wife has a worrying unstable behaviour and I would want a specialist to examine her but I don't want her to know about it.' The doctor hesitated for a while, thinking. 'Call her in,' he later said.

'Remember, I don't want her to know.'

'Don't worry.'

I stepped out and beckoned Nkem over with a wave. It took her several minutes to cover the short distance that would have taken not more than five seconds.

'Sit down, madam,' the doctor said to her. 'You see, I took another look at your case file and there is something else I found out. However, I don't want to pre-empt the result, therefore, I'll give you a note for a special test at the general hospital.' He wrote, stamped the referral and handed it over to me and we left. I was glad.

'What else could be the doctor's suspicion?' my wife asked soon after we got on our way home that morning.

'How would I know?' I replied.

Surprisingly, she kept quiet. Normally, she would have confronted me with one of the most ferocious arguments. Not this time around, she was weak and tired. Everyone we came across on the road before we boarded the cab felt so sorry for her. For many days, she was indoors and unable to open her store.

If physical indisposition were something of esteem, I would have gladly chosen that my wife remained in that condition for many months. For the whole of that period, I had my peace and was able to converse with her freely without any heartbreak. She would stay in the warmth all day, quiet and relaxed and when we served her lunch or dinner, she would have it gladly and was able to show a little tenderness and love towards Mary who she distasted so much.

Rather than grow thinner in her illness, she blossomed as if restriction on a sick bed was a moment for gaining weight. I was then able to understand so clearly what nagging and ill temper do to the body. For the first time, my home was void of verbal clashes, noise and incessant abuse of an innocent little girl, Mary. Throughout that time, when she spoke, her voice was smooth and friendly, even when I raised a subject that many times in the past made her respond with emotions. It was as if those inflamed feelings had vanished from her. Yet, I could not stop worrying that one day she would explode again with her customary barking and fury.

Before this time, most people within our vicinity knew that Nkem had earned herself a reputation of cruelty and violent behaviour. Those in the apartment blocks where we lived knew she had the loudest voice. I will never forget how I intensified my prayers to God that He should never allow her relapse into her past.

After we had visited the General Hospital for Nkem's mental test, we were both eagerly awaiting the result. To my greatest shock, when it came, everything was normal. Some days after, I rang the doctor to inform him of the result. When I enquired from him on what could have possibly accounted for her irrational and inconsistent conduct, the doctor stated that it could be her nature, resulting from her upbringing.

In those times, I would pray and pray until sleep caught up with me like rapture and when I woke, I would feel better as if my nightmare had finally died out. Afterwards, I would realise that my bad feelings remained with me whenever Nkem acted up.

At that time, Mary, who had been greatly weighed-down and broken aside could smile occasionally and sang choruses aloud to the enjoyment of our little boy. She would bounce from the kitchen to the living room and then into the room in her anxiety to accomplish her task without having to be scared of being punished unjustifiably. For her, it was a great independence. It must have been her keen desire for the relaxed ambiance of the home to remain.

Apparently, for those three weeks that Nkem stayed at home, every object in our apartment knew that something had happened to the chief warden of my home.

Chapter Twelve

They say nothing lasts forever. Nkem recovered and had to resume her business. After not too long, we realised that there was no notable distinction in her comportments. It became evident one morning, towards the beginning of September when it was time for Chima to start kindergarten.

That day was going to be Chima's first time at school and I woke up, ready to leave for work but requested Nkem to take Chima to the school for the necessary registration before leaving for her work. Her response was the shock of the season.

'I don't have time for that,' were her exact words. 'You don't want to leave your work but you want me to leave mine,' she stressed. 'Anyway, I'll instruct Mary to take him if you don't have the time.'

'Aunty, I don't know the school,' Mary chirped in from quite a distance.

'Who called you into the matter?' Nkem asked, aggressively.

'Anyway, do whatever pleases you,' I said and left.

'Okay, what about the fees?' Nkem asked.

'I'll appreciate it if you can use the money in your hand

and I'll reimburse you as soon as I come back,' I responded.

'In that case, we better postpone it until you make the money available because I'm not ready to use part of my money. After all, he does not bear my father's name but yours.'

'Nkem, trust me. I'll give whatever amount you will spend back to you as soon as I return,' I persuaded.

'I've told you my mind. Take it or leave it.'

'Nkem, I'm surprised you could utter such a statement.'

I left with the hope that Nkem would sway her mind. By the time I came back, she had not arrived. I enquired from Mary if all went well with Chima's school. 'No, Uncle,' she responded.

'What happened?'

'I don't know, Uncle. I even reminded Aunty but she shouted me down.'

Now it was already midnight yet Nkem was still on the road, so I picked up my phone and called her. 'Please don't pressure me,' she replied, sarcastically. 'Or didn't you witness the heavy traffic on your way back?' She cut off the phone. It was not until one hour later that she entered and when she did, I could see temper in her eyes. It was as if she was waiting for the least words from me so that she would detonate her bomb. As far as she was concerned, she was not at the tender mercies of anyone.

'Mary!' she called even before she dropped her handbag, not minding that it was already bedtime for most people. Mary knew for sure that the next session with her would be hot. In her usual over-zealousness and awe, she appeared before her like the Queen's house cleaner before the princess. She threw her shoes before Mary and ordered her to polish them. But unfortunately, one of the shoes had hit Mary's toe and she was gently massaging the toe. 'Get up,' she charged. She would stop at nothing to make her feel some pains.

'Yes, Aunty,' Mary replied. Yet, she could feel that she was badly hurt but dared not vent it. I could tell from her aura that she was incredibly frightful.

'Did I hit you with the shoes?'

'No, Aunty, one fell on my toe,' Mary responded.

'So, get on your feet immediately and if you like, don't polish them well and you will see what I would do to you.' She gave her a gloated look.

After she had taken her bath, and what was supposed to be dinner, I called her in a very mild manner. 'Nkem! Come over here and sit by my side.' Without hesitation, she obeyed. 'Why don't you always want us to reason together?'

'What are you talking about?' she asked.

'You know what I'm inferring. You certainly know that I am talking about your refusal to take Chima to the school and get him registered. Or is it proper to leave him in the hand of Mary or the school bus driver this first time?' She stood up, exhibiting her usual hostility to the subject matter.

'I thought you had something good to say? If you don't have time to take him it means you don't want him to begin school,' she uttered in a warring voice. I realised that in Chima's interest I had better attend to his needs. She was fool-headed, I knew. I called my boss the following morning that I would get to the office late in order to ensure that Chima got started in school.

Things went as planned and, in the end, I felt a massive overriding sense of accomplishment. Shockingly, when Nkem and I both met each other at home later that day, Nkem did not raise any discussion about Chima's first day at school. Instead, it was another row with Mary. I met Nkem and Mary facing each other with Mary receiving a hot slap from Nkem. Even as I stepped in, without any procrastination, Nkem slapped her again. As Mary stood stunned, another slap landed. Yet another. Mary lay dazed. Seeing no end to the beating, suddenly, she curled herself into a ball, sticking her head in-between her lap, trying to protect her cheeks. 'What has she done again?' I asked with concern, pushing Mary away from her. It had not been a joyful experience for her just as Nkem had not been the easiest of people to get along with.

'She stared at me with narrowed eyes and seemed to hesitate in answering when I called her,' Nkem alleged. She made for Mary again and started dragging her over to the kitchen. I tried to stop her but she was defiant. I followed calmly waiting and watching to see what would happen. She got to the burning cooker and placed Mary's palms on the ring of it, holding them down for some seconds before releasing her. Mary screamed with such a terrible agony. It was unimaginable. Her arms felt stiff from the shoulders down. She burst into a fresh wave of crying. Tears started flowing from her eyes, which she kept wiping away with the back of her hand. She had never cried so bitterly like that before.

'Whatever is your reason for doing all this, you are definitely overreacting,' I said.

Nkem pushed herself in-between Mary and I and went into the room, with a throttling cough.

I lifted Mary's hands. They had turned red and swollen. I went to the refrigerator and collected one raw egg, broke it and poured it on her palms, spreading it all over, from the wrist to the palms of the hands. It would help them not to swell further. That was what my mother taught me.

I went into the room to ask Nkem why she went too far but she would not even utter a word. Then I switched the topic and talked about her not being bothered about Chima's school. But it was as if I had touched the snake on its tail.

'Please spare me this moment,' she muttered. Indeed, I had just turned the wrong channel. 'I've told you that Chima is your son and bears your name and not mine.' From that moment, I began to wish that my life would be over rather than continue to live with her.

***

A few days to Christmas, when every family was nursing the hope of a good Christmas celebration, something terrible happened that was to inaugurate a completely new chapter of misery in my life. It was also about two weeks to Chima's birthday and only one year after Nkem started her business.

On that chilly night, Nkem woke me up. It was long past midnight. I would not say it was unprecedented but this time I was nervous and unsure what to expect. 'Can we go to the living room?' she urged.

'Okay, take the lead,' I said.

As soon as we sat, she started, 'I've got something important to tell you and I hope you would not show your customary refusal this time around.'

The expression on my face was very unstable. 'I'm listening,' I told her, though still very anxious to continue with my sleep.

She took a very deep breath, pausing for a long while. It was obvious she was encountering difficulties on how to put across the matter. In a moment, I closed my eyes and tripped towards my right shoulder. She pushed me. 'Are you sleeping?' she asked.

'No,' I answered nonchalantly.

'Well, I've decided to close down my business in order to travel to South Africa for a greener pasture.'

'What?' I asked, almost shocked to my marrow. All traces of sleep departed from my eyes immediately. Instantly, I had a feeling of overwhelming chilliness enveloping me right from inside my stomach as if I had suddenly caught influenza. I imagined I saw lightning that must have been because of a sudden throbbing headache in one part of my head. I constantly experienced the headache any time I got upset. I became completely weak and it was as if my bladder could no longer hold my urine, as, without much ado, I hurried to the rest room. I stayed there for a long time not knowing what to do, thinking. 'Please can you make me understand better what you said earlier,' I asked as soon as I came out.

'Chidi, you heard me very well.'

'If I heard you well, I won't demand that you repeat yourself. Please recap it one more time,' I besought her.

'I want to travel to South Africa. I understand the nursing profession over there is in great demand. My intention is to be there for a year or two, make some money and then come back and set up a bigger business.' I declined to contribute to that topic. My refusal was intentional though I pretended I was slightly delighted, my face wreathed in superficial smiles, even though I was gazing at her like an ape.

'Say something, Chidi,' she shoved me.

'Okay, I have heard you. I'll think over it and let you know what I feel in a couple of days.'

'This is not about thinking over it for days. The matter is

urgent for me. I need you to say something now.' She pushed herself closer and tapped my shoulder a number of times. I felt like strangulating her or at least spitting in her face but for some reason, I held my peace. I now looked away as if I was scanning the horizon, nodding my head repeatedly in a manner that left her not sure what my real intentions were. With no further opinion, she got up, went into the room and returned with her handbag. Still wondering what she intended to do next, she plunged her hand in the bag, pulled out an A4 white envelope and threw it at me, in her bid to alter my feelings.

'What is in it?' I asked.

'Open it and see for yourself,' she responded. Wondering what joke she had for me, I felt the envelope and I could finger a hard object, which I guessed was a small booklet. I was scared to unseal it. 'Open it and look at it,' she persuaded. Very reluctantly, I turned the envelope upside down and the contents fell out.

'What! An international passport!' I flipped through it and I could see the greenish background visa with South African coat of arms emblazoned in gold at the top left-hand side with the bold print of Republic of South Africa in the centre. 'So, you processed a two-year visa in this house without telling me? Ah! Nkem, you are such a treacherous partner,' I uttered. 'You can murder someone. So, where do you intend to throw Chima? How about all the money I spent for you to start the fish business which has barely lasted a year?'

'As for that, the money is not lost. I have already sold off the store with its content to a colleague of mine. Mary would continue to look after Chima or what do you think?'

'I think you have gone off your senses? I can now confirm you are mentally deranged.'

'I didn't expect any reaction different to what you are showing now,' she responded with a high-pitched yelping sound. 'This was why I could not tell you when I was processing the visa because I knew you wouldn't support it. You have always gone against my desire. You are continually selfish and tight-fisted, caring more about yourself. Heaven would judge you.'

I did not say a word, but she continued her attack. I let her nasty comments wash over me like cold water over a rock. I tried to look away from her and threw down my face but I could not help turning to her. In anger, she grabbed the passport and went away, moving in a way to attest she was ready for the worst.

I got respect anywhere I went except in my house where my wife incessantly trampled on me with her actions and strings of profanities coming from her lips. I was not perfect but I knew I was far better than she was. I was always passive and more absorbed. I loved peace and harmony and never exhibited two types of character. I was zealous in pursuing my goals and did not envisage any hindrance. I valued challenges but not the type that would defy my spirit. I thought I could rise and fight for what I believed in but now the actions of my better half had shaken and drained me. Outside my home, I gladdened the hearts of my colleagues and friends with humour but inside, everything looked blue all the time. All along, I thought I was borne without the ability to hold grudges against anyone but now I understood myself better.

Again, my chest ached and I was beginning to yelp in excruciating pains. It seemed as if hot metal heated several times in the furnace pieced through my heart. I struggled to make an utterance at that point, but could not. A few seconds later, it was just on my lips to tell her of my conviction that she was probably under the influence of a strange spirit that wouldn't allow her to have a happy home when I started throwing up. She looked at me, turned her back and walked away. I called on Mary to clear the mess.

Shortly after, I heard the sound of Nkem's silent sobs and when I went and opened the curtain and peeped, she was jiggling her head and shaking her legs as she moaned, like someone who was plotting another scam.

I sat for a very long time on the sofa. In the end, sleep came slowly and I dozed off only to be awakened by the noise of the alarm coming from the clock that hung over my head, sounding, 'Ding-dong, ding-dong, ding-dong,' to remind me it was time to prepare for another day's work.

**

There was no single moment I found an outsider to sympathise with me nor did I ever gain the support of any of my friends, both within the church and my neighbourhood. Not even one person encouraged me. Except my bosom friend, Matthias, who knew a little of my dilemma and who, because of it, began lately to visit me frequently. He lived a stone's throw across the road with his slothful and languid wife. He was a devout Christian and very famous old member of the Baptist church in Abuja municipality. He was working on a full-time basis in the church, as the treasurer. He was a very handsome man, with the looks of elegance and a grandee. Apart from being a straightforward fellow, he believed in the Christian teachings of "for better and for worse", and would do everything possible to dissuade couples from separating. But he too had suffered significant set-backs in his relationship. He and his wife, Sarah, had been without any child in their nearly eleven years of marriage, though they were both already in their late forties.

Matthias once told me that his only hope was to die serving the Lord. It was obvious he was a deeply unhappy man, yet he kept the horror of his family life secret, not wanting anyone to know, acting anywhere he went as if all was well in his life. He was resolved to uphold the Christian family values as a sense of religious duty, yet his wife was suppressing his life. Unlike others, he had so much courage and determination and would not just do anything but wait for a miracle to happen. Indeed, he was a saintly character.

One of those times, I went to see him, very close to Easter, when families were supposed to be planning on how to make the event extraordinary. I witnessed what I considered dereliction of responsibility by his wife, severer than what I had to endure.

Matthias had knelt with one knee, sweat littered on his face like splashes of bubbles as he kept crushing the fresh onions on the hand-made grinder. He was himself preparing his dinner based on dietary advice. His madam had no time for the patience required to get the meal ready. Meanwhile, she stretched her legs across the small stool under the avocado pear tree, cutting her nails. She was dressed in an immaculate white lace as if she was expecting a special guest. That was how she usually dressed during the weekends. She was acting very awkwardly despite the fact that Matthias would take care of all her laundries, which usually included her panties and bras, even without any exception to ironing. Sometimes, he would show her some gestures like making her tea or buying some special gifts. She would throw them at him, saying, 'That's not what your colleagues buy for their wives.' Often, she was stubborn and ungrateful. Matthias accepted all of this in order to allow peace to reign. They never meant anything to him as he felt he was carrying his own cross.

'The only way to live peacefully with any woman is to obey the woman, always,' he often would admonish people. 'It's not for the man to question the woman, it's for the man to cooperate with her all the time,' he further would postulate.

I could understand Matthias' special circumstance. In eleven years of their marriage, his wife was pregnant seven times. The last one nearly took away her life. Once, I did not hide my feelings by openly disagreeing with him totally. 'I don't accept your concept of relationships,' I had told him.

To pacify me, he recounted a popular story he said he read in a book called *The Amadi Kingdom* while he was still in primary school. 'It was a very small kingdom,' he said. 'And every member of that kingdom was going through one form of harsh conditions or the other. It was more like hell on earth for them. One day, the king of that kingdom, seeing that their problems were too much, gathered all the people to deliberate on how to lessen their pains. As the people sat in the open air, not caring about the scorching sun, their seats already arranged in a circle so they could behold one another's faces. They were anxiously anticipating that on that day, all their adversity would end. They did not know the magic their king was going to perform but they were not undermining him. Some of them had taken their seats before the sun arose, almost all without food yet. After they had spent a long time deliberating and bringing up ideas upon ideas, with no lasting solution, then came their king with what they all felt would be an excellent one. They were all ears to hear what their king had to say. Finally, he told them that they were all going to exchange their problems among themselves. There were people suffering from terminal diseases, impotency, acute poverty, brain tumours, children imbecility or deformity, hearing challenged, blindness, spouse witchcraft and barrenness. Then, a man stood, who was to be the one to lead the crusade by exchanging his troubles with that of another person among them. And which was this man's problem? He had a nagging and abusive companion, as your case, and he felt that he could no longer cope. The man took his time in evaluating every other person's problems, one after the other. After assessing them carefully, he ended up, very reluctantly preferring his, just as the rest of them later did, too. So, the king advised all of them to go home and continue managing their issues, emphasising that God has given every man the grace to wade through whatever comes his way.' he narrated.

'Chide! The God who has helped me to endure will be your solace,' he concluded.

From then on, I made up my mind never to miss any of the church prayer meetings, with the hope that God would make me be like Matthias. Yet some members of the church who knew about my melancholic conjugal affairs were passing judgement, blaming me for my failures in not praying and putting out a fleece like Gideon in the Bible did, to be sure that my will and God's will be matched.

Chapter Thirteen

When I got to work the next day, everybody knew that I had quickly relapsed into the bad time old days as almost all who came across me noticed that there was something wrong again going on with my life. I still had a clear and conscious memory that in those times, my doctor expressed his fears that my blood pressure was gradually moving towards an alarming side. I remembered him saying one hundred and sixty systolic over ninety-five diastolic was not a good testimony. I had shared with him what could probably be the cause of it and he ended up telling me what, on a number of occasions, others had told me in the past. 'Take it easy and do not allow it to bother your mind.' Yet, could one ever be in a house engulfed by fire and not feel the heat? Could one be in the deep sea and not be frightened?

Some of my colleagues had occasion to complain about my declining output, which nobody, except me, knew why it was happening. I so much disliked what was taking place at that time.

About six months later, while I was returning from work, I stumbled on one of my old-time friends during my secondary school days. We had not seen each other ever since we left junior secondary school. That would be thirteen years before this time. Then, he was popularly called Alaska, which was his nickname, because his first name was a seventeen-letter word which nobody could pronounce because it was not only just too long but sounded so hard. If anyone asked me then, I had forgotten the name. Even the teachers at that time were also calling him by his nickname because they too could not remember his real name. He was so popular with the nickname that he later started using it officially and requested that it be included in his certificate.

Alaska was so tall even as a young teenage boy that everybody feared he was going to be the tallest man on earth. We were all humorously calling him, Shorty, at that time. He always carried a very strong face and would never put up a smile even under the most hilarious circumstances. None of us ever messed with him as his height alone earned him all the respect a strong young man could deserve.

We had stood side by side without noticing each other, at one popular bus stop called Tripled-C near the national stadium where hundreds of passengers were waiting for the low-cost state government buses. The buses had all delayed their services after a heavy downpour and the number of passengers had grown beyond expectation. That evening, everyone was anxious to board any bus that would arrive first. The obvious signs in the sky that the rain had not yet finished its business made the already bad weather worse. Almost all the passengers pointed their eyes in one direction, the direction where the next bus would eventually emerge. As people noticed a red light from afar, pointing its parking light that showed it was coming to pick some passengers, everyone started hurrying towards it even though if we all had stood, it would meet us where we were. It was all because it would not take one tenth of who were waiting. It was going to be a scramble.

As Alaska made an unexpected move to catch the bus like many other people, someone hit his hand unknowingly and the flat file jacket he was holding fell and many of the papers in that file flew everywhere. I bent to pick some with one or two other persons who felt sorry for him. At the point of handing in the documents to him, our eyes caught each other. 'Chidi!' he shouted with a loud voice filled with excitement.

'Ah! Alaska!' I could not believe it was him. 'It has been ages.' He paid no heed to the papers I was handing over to him. He hugged me, holding me very tightly to his body, and not wanting to let go. 'Do you live in Abuja?' I asked.

'No, I don't. I just came in two weeks back. I left the country eight years ago soon after my high school to further my education. After I finished, I was thinking of returning to Nigeria to look for a job when I found an opening at the university where I graduated. I showed interest, applied for it and luckily, I got it. That was how I changed my mind and remained in the United Kingdom after the university authority assisted me to obtain a Working Permit.'

'You are very lucky then. You must be married by now and how many children do you have?'

'Ah! Chidi… you remind me of my pains which were already gradually disappearing. I try not to talk about it because I am not proud about what happened. Do you know that two years after I got that job, I came to Nigeria and was wedded to my old-time school girlfriend with the assistance of my parents? Initially, I was quite pleased with the young woman because when I looked into her eyes, I saw what seemed to be irresistible affection. She appeared very caring with lots of understanding. She stayed with my parents for a while soon after the marriage until I decided she should come over and be with me. They confirmed she was hardworking and respectful. She did all the cleaning for them, the cooking and ironing. She also polished their shoes and served the food, which my father could at times reject, if he was not pleased with it. My wife never picked offence. My parents commended her so much to the extent that my father said she was an angel sent to me.'

If Alaska was smart, he could have easily seen envy in my eyes as he related his story to me. I began to wish I were in his shoes for I had longed for such a wonderful woman. Unlike me, it must have been a great accomplishment for him.

As Alaska went on, he could perceive that his life story was having an effect on me, which he could not exactly picture why. I sensed he deliberately decided to jump to the conclusion. 'Like I said, in the end, I decided to arrange for her to join me in the United Kingdom. Unfortunately, it wasn't long she joined me,' Alaska continued. 'She got herself amalgamated with bad friends who misled her, and she started acting in a way that beat my imagination. They taught her how she could swindle money from me and soon she danced to their tune. Do you know that surprisingly, she changed and became arrogant and uncompromising? She would leave the house and come in so late, expecting me never to utter a word. Her initial love and care suddenly disappeared. We started having rows almost every night until one day, after she came home so late that I became so cross with her and I hit her with my bare hand. In anger, she immediately reported the matter to the Social Workers who came into the matter and made a big case out of it. Do you know that, in the end, the British authority asked me to leave my own apartment for her, with everything I had acquired before she joined me? The one that pained me most was my giant television screen and its stand that was finished with American made Formica.

'Later, the authority ordered me to maintain always a distance of two kilometres away from that vicinity. They only allowed me to pick up my clothes, shoes and a few of my personal belongings, including my certificates. My dear friend, as I speak to you, I'm back to where I was eight years ago, trying to gather my life back. Anyway, the good thing is that I have recently remarried; to a young, amazing, lady whom I later met in the United Kingdom and have forgotten all about Agnes, my first wife. I can tell you that divorce brings peace and what other people think of me is not my business.'

After Alaska ended his story, there was silence between the two of us. He sounded very excited and happy without any iota of regret in the way he had chosen to address his challenges. He was carrying on with life the way he saw life and wished everybody would be like him. To him, that was how to survive what could have turned in to a mental health issue. After a long pause, he then asked, 'How about you?'

'Well...' before I could begin to speak, I noticed the red light of an oncoming bus. It was a Mega Bus. 'We are lucky!' I shouted looking at the direction of the bus. 'Three buses are approaching at the same time. We can't afford to miss this because darkness is around the corner.'

'That's true. Let me have your telephone number then so we can talk later.'

'07405867580,' I read out as we both ran towards the bus, now flashing its full light. People were already beginning to jump in and before it could come to a complete stop, it was half-filled. No one was ready to comply with the government rule that passengers must always be in a straight line and follow the order of, 'First to come, first to board'.

As I got on the bus, I discovered it was the wrong one. I should have entered the one behind, which by now was having some people hanging on its door. Alaska who was ahead of me was already sitting comfortably on one of the seats in the middle row. He entered the right bus. Slowly, slowly, the bus was beginning to take off. I quickly jumped out only to sight Alaska waving at me. I waved back. 'Please endeavour to call me so that we can talk before I return to United Kingdom,' he shouted to the irritation of the other passengers.

By the time I checked my wristwatch, it was already past seven p.m. but it was so dark that one would think it was past nine p.m. It was still cloudy, and I was now praying that another rainfall should not catch up with me. Not long after, another bus came, and yet another and another.

The rushing had eased off and passengers were now boarding very casually, willingly obeying the government order of embarking as there were less people to stampede down the bus entrance.

It was not quite an hour before I got home; the roads, which were usually busy, were very free. I would have been very surprised if I had met Nkem at home. I could count the number of times she got home before me. Now, the mere thought of her weakened me once again as I felt so irked having to bear the fact that she was still living with me as my other half. I remained deeply unhappy throughout the weeks that followed.

Chapter Fourteen

Finally, one day, as soon as I arrived from work there was another turn of events. Nkem told me that it was time for her to fulfil her dreams of traveling to South Africa. Sometimes, it was very difficult to distinguish between her bluffs and rare moments of honesty. I ignored her and walked into the room to change. She followed me. 'Did you hear me, Chidi?' she asked, spitefully.

'Are you pulling my legs or what?' I enquired.

'Pulling your legs, how? Have we not discussed this matter before now? I'm leaving tomorrow morning, for your information.'

I seemed lost in thought for some minutes. The price of remaining in the marriage was climbing higher and higher on a daily basis. It might be fatal if allowed it to run its course.

Meanwhile, the room was messy with dirty woolly jumpers and bits of shredded papers covering every available surface. As she gathered her belongings, she flung things where they did not belong. I dared not switch the discussion to the mucky condition of the room, unless I was wishing that hailstones fell on me.

'Nkem, do you mean you have not backed down on this

absurd idea of traveling and leaving us all alone in Nigeria?' I queried.

She hissed, like the escaping sound from a leaking tyre, and stared at me like a hungry cat. She then came very close to me to whisper into my ear in a very offensive manner, 'For once, try and show understanding, young man.'

Her breath stank with a strong alcoholic drink and I recoiled from that horrible stink. *Where must she have gone to be in that messy condition?* I asked within me. I had never smelt any drink in her mouth ever since we got married. *What could be happening?* I asked myself gruffly, screwing up my face. She was going farther and farther away from me. I hated her passionately at that moment, and she made me wish briefly that we were not married. Somehow, I managed to ask, 'Who lured you into drinking, Nkem?'

'Is that any business of yours?' She now turned to leave, but she staggered, walking with weak and unsteady steps, as if to confirm my fears. Who would, on earth, believe that Nkem was the woman of a young minister in a famous church? Tears stung my eyes. I could hardly see because of the water now slowly spilling down my cheeks. I, alone, knew what all this meant for me as a man, and the pain was excruciating. This was that same woman whom when I met many years before, appeared so innocent and calm that any man would have wished to marry her.

As I looked around, I could see she had already packed her important belongings in her giant portmanteau and medium-sized travelling bag. It was evident nothing would induce her to change her mind at that time, not even if an angel came down from heaven. Her decision to tell me must have been probably not because she was asking for my clearance but merely out of courtesy, just for information purposes.

'Now, Nkem, listen,' I said. 'If I give you the promise to make a sum of two million available to you, to improve your business, would you agree to shelve your plans?' I asked.

'Why not if only you hand the money over to me right now?'

'If you accept, I shall apply for a loan at my place of work,' I offered.

'It shows you are never serious, as you can see,' she stated.

'How?'

'Because I'm talking of now while you are talking of later.'

'Nkem, please don't yield to the devil. Remember all the recent stories in the newspapers and the ones we heard over the radio, that the people of South Africa have a strong feeling of dislike and fear of people from other African countries, especially, those of us from West African.'

'Which story?'

'Story of their apartheid and democracy and now xenophobic violence in its biggest city. Scores of people were recently reported injured and hundreds of Nigerian stores looted.'

'Don't worry, I shall be fine. It doesn't change the fact that it is still a land of gold, making it an attraction to other African countries.'

I went to where she dropped her heavy loaded luggage. She had not zipped it off completely so I tried to open the box, initially fiddling with the zip. 'Chidi, stop that!' she shouted.

I flouted her instruction and went ahead. The next thing she did was to hasten to the kitchen. I became worried of what was coming next. I was yet to work out what she intended but I panicked. So, I stood up, in order not to be caught unawares. In a matter of seconds, she appeared, pointing a kitchen knife at me. 'Chidi! If you ever try to stop me, I will stab you, bet it.' I gave up.

What happened next came as a rude shock. The next day, before I returned from work, Nkem had hauled her luggage and all that was important to her and went away. I did not know whether to feel relieved and rejoice or feel bad. I was between the devil and the Dead Sea. I supposed I should have felt relief but instead a huge wave of sadness washed over me.

Mary recounted how Nkem woke up as soon as I left the house, got prepared and for the first time, got Chima ready for his school. 'Before I guided Chima to the school bus which arrived a little bit late that morning, she curdled him, tossed him up several times and, in the end, presented a song to him,' Mary stated.

'Hmm.'

'And the song goes like this:

My little boy, my little boy,
I'm going to a faraway city,
To fetch you some bread and butter,
And many other good things I can't mention,
When I return, you shall be proud of your mother,
Goodbye, my boy, until we meet again.

'Before she could finish singing that song, a young man, with overgrown hair and whiskers, in a saloon car, was already pressing the horn for her to come down,' Mary recounted.

I could not lift my feet from the doormat where I stood as

Mary narrated the story. Many thoughts filled my mind and I was more than ever before downcast and it looked like I was not going to survive a breakdown this time around. I must admit that at first, it seemed I could not manage without her, despite all the snags, but as time went by, I found out that life for me was better without her.

The next Sunday, I got to church and went to explain the development to the pastor of our church, who did nothing to offer a relief but simply admonished me to intensify my prayers, emphasising that God was chiselling me.

It was exactly one year since the then pastor stepped me down from being a worker in the church. That time I went with the premonition that he would ask me to resume my activities because I would love to occupy myself in order to forget all about Nkem but to my dismay, the pastor never made any comment about that.

Days, weeks and months passed and there were no words from Nkem. It took six months before I received a voice message from her. 'Hello, Chidi, sorry I have not been able to reach you all this while,' she stated. 'I was trying to settle down and get used to the system here. I hope Chima and Mary are both fine? I miss you all.'

I was marvelled especially when there was no number that could enable me return her call. She must have called from a public telephone, I believed. Different thoughts hovered in my head. I likened her to salt that is essential in every household but had lost its value, would be thrown away and not even be used as sand to build a house. I wished that someone would rewrite the Bible to give me the will and liberty to do away with her forever since I was not getting any benefit a woman usually gives to her husband. One thing I was sure of was that

God knows all things more than any man does, and I had to clinch on the promise that, "All things would work together for good, for them that fear Him."

What happened next would shock anyone. One day, I returned from work and met Mary weeping profusely. That was after about one year and two months since my wife had left. She narrated how the same man, who picked my wife the day she left for South Africa, came to say that my wife had asked him to get Chima.

'I trusted the man when he again told me that Aunty said I should give him her small purple purse she kept on top of the refrigerator,' Mary further related. 'Since the man had never come into our apartment before to know there is a purple purse on top of the refrigerator, I believed him. Again, in a little boy's mind, Chima was filled with jubilation when the mention of going to see his mum came up,' she added.

For the first time, I felt upset with Mary and thought of skinning her. Yet, I could read confusion and remorse from her eyes. She was terrified but was somehow confident that if I ever chastised her, it would be for good and not with any kind of animosity, like what she used to go through in the hands of Nkem.

The next day, I received a telephone call in the night, this time I was on time to pick up the call. It was Nkem. She confirmed to me that it was she who arranged for Chima to be picked up and who was already in her custody. How all that happened was still a mystery to me. 'I know you won't consent to it but I have to do it for his sake because life is far better over here,' she claimed. Years back, a fraction of Nigerian currency was the same with that of South Africa, but the reverse is the case now. Any wonder why more and more

Nigerians are trooping to South Africa? I shall talk to you again as soon as I'm able to get him into a school,' she concluded. I was dumbfounded as that was not what she suggested when she first expressed her wish to travel.

One evening, after I returned early from work, I decided to go and see our pastor once again, to update him on the latest development in my home. He nodded that I should sit down on the chair opposite him as soon as I entered his office. As usual, he gave me his traditional advice of "You need to intensify your prayers". However, he felt it was time to resume my normal activities in the church as a worker and the youth leader. He said it was the adversary engaging me in a spiritual welfare emphasising that the trial of our faith would work out patience. He did not fail to remind me that as a worker in the church I must not do anything that would embarrass the church, encouraging me to, instead, suffer the pains in silence with unwavering hope that God will intervene, no matter how long.

I felt temporarily relieved and went home that day feeling lighter. I found fresh energy to push ahead and not allow the situation to cast me down any more. How easy that was going to be, I could not tell. Every night I would glue to my pillows after each prayer, and snoozed like a little baby, with every moment void of hot wrangling over nothing, incessantly initiated by my so-called wife. I was left with Mary, who though was still a little girl, became everything to me. She went to the market, cooked and served my meals. She nursed me in periods of fatigue and indisposition and we became so much attached to each other. I could often read from her expression that she had the greatest sympathy for my circumstance. Her thoughts were more like, 'Can things ever be the same again in this home?' A home she now called hers. She never spoke those thoughts because she was not so sure if I would like to hear them.

One day, I called her and asked if she would like to go back to school. I thought it would make her feel excited but she puckered up her brows. Her entire aura changed straight away, in a manner that kept me wondering. 'Don't you like to go back to school?' I asked again. She stood still, looking away from me. 'Can't you talk any more, Mary?' I probed further.

After wasting some time, she then responded, 'I'd like it but my aunty had warned me that I'm not in this house to go to school but to take care of Chima. She said that after I might have spent some years, I'll then become a tailoring apprentice.'

'Don't worry. Your aunty is not here now so if you want to go to school, I'll put you in school, okay.'

'Okay, Uncle.' She slowly nodded her head as if it was against her will. During the school session that followed, I got her enrolled in a private school, even though she had out-grown everyone in her class, she was very enthusiastic and optimistic too that at last she would attain her goal.

After some weeks, when I came back from work, I noticed she was not in her usual happy mood for the first time since my wife left me. 'What's the matter with you, Mary?' I had asked.

'I don't think I will like to continue with the school,' she said.

'Why? Don't say that again,' I told her.

'I'm the biggest in the class you put me in and my mates often make jest of me.'

'Don't worry, Mary,' I persuaded. 'Keep ignoring them.

With time, they will be tired. Focus on the result, in the end. Very soon, you would be through and won't see them any more. So, don't ever think of not continuing, okay.'

'Okay, Uncle.'

***

For a very long time, Nkem did not call me neither had I any details of how to contact her if I had wished to. Her initial plan was to work for a year, save some money and come to Nigeria but now it was two complete years. Nevertheless, it would seem that I was now accustomed to living my life without her.

Incidentally, the event of my existence turned more dramatic on the fourth year of my wife being away, when I woke up and went to the office that beautiful Monday morning only to receive a recorded delivery parcel correctly addressed to me. If anyone had asked me to guess where the parcel was coming from, I would never have been right. When I opened the parcel, it was a long letter from the South African City of Cape Town Council. It read:

'Dear Mr. Chidi,

Please be advised as follows:

A court in South Africa has decided that your son, Chima, and one other child whose age was not determined as at the time of writing this letter, named Jude be made the subject of a full care order to the City of Cape Town Council. This means that the Cape Town City Council now has the right and duties of a parent over them. These rights are shared with you and your wife. Furthermore, because of the making of the full Care Order, your son and Jude cannot leave South Africa without the agreement of the local authority or in the absence of such an agreement with the permission of the Court.

As your son and the other boy found in the custody of your wife, are the subject of a full Care Order, if they were to decide to come back to another person's care in the future, the only basis on which that could happen would be if the Care Order were discharged by the Court. In order to discharge a Care Order, the Local Authority would have to apply to the Court giving reason why the Care Order should be discharged. This is a complicated process and if you or Jude's parents were to consider such an application in the future, I would strongly advise you or them to seek legal advice and representation.

If you have any query from what I have stated above, please feel free to contact me by e-mail or letter if you so wish.

Yours sincerely,

Johnson Makapolo,

Solicitor for Community Services for Cape Town Borough'

After going through the letter, the spit in my mouth dried up and I was holding myself not to fall into a coma. My eyelids began to blink faster than usual, and the temperature of my body went up. I was praying that it would not result into a long-lasting ailment. Was I right in my decision to continue to hold on until the end or could I have harkened to the voice of some of my colleagues who felt that the best way out was to call the bluff and give the idea of divorce a consideration? That would certainly be a stench in the nostrils of the church.

The greatest challenge at that time was how to reach out to Nkem so that she could explain to me what exactly was happening. The telephone line that I had reached her once on in the recent past was no longer going through.

Using the e-mail address included in the letter to me, I sent a mail requesting clear details of what led to my son and the other child, whose exact identity I had not ascertained, to become a subject of a full care order and I got an immediate response, which read:

'*Your son and the other child, Jude, came to the attention of South African Social Services on the 8th of October when their School informed Social Services that Jude had told his teacher he was unhappy at home as he was regularly beaten on his head, arms, hands and legs by your wife. He said your wife used her hand as well as metal and wood implements to hit him. Further, he said your wife disallowed him from going to school for two weeks. On that day, the police took out Police Protection orders in respect of Jude and your son. They have been in foster care since then. A week after, the Police interviewed Jude and your son who claimed your wife systematically beat Jude with wood and metal objects for the preceding three months. A police search conducted in their home some days after, when the local authority instituted Protective arrangements revealed the object that Jude described. Jude, as well as your son, were suffering and were likely to suffer significant harm if the order was not made. Furthermore, it was understood that your son and Jude were left alone at night while your wife worked as a health care assistant.*

It was believed your wife was arrested by the County Police but granted bail and that she was due to return to the Police Station in four weeks' time. Your wife was yet to be informed if there would be any criminal prosecution against her for assault, neglect or immigration offences. They believed she was an illegal worker or had over stayed. Consequently, on the 9th of December, the City Family Proceedings Court made Jude and your son the subject of an interim Care Order to the City of Cap Town Council. The City Family Proceedings decided to transfer the matter to the Principal Registry of the Family Division because of its complexity and the international dimension of the case. The matter has been listed for an allocation hearing at the Principal Registry on the 15th of February, at one p.m. Your son and Jude remain in their foster placement. The local authority intends to promote contact between your son and the mother and between Jude and his parents.

It was understood that your son has experienced a lack of emotional warmth from his mother and has lived in an environment of fear and submission with his mother often shouting at him and hitting him. The mother has failed to provide him with a nurturing and protective environment. As a consequence of the above, your son has suffered emotional and physical harm in his mother's care. If he were to be returned to his mother's care, he would be at risk of suffering further harm in the future. However, in view of the allegation against your wife, such contact will be supervised. The local authority will refer your wife for a parenting assessment by Cape Town Court Family Assessment Services. The local authority will also assess the viability of returning your son to your care in Nigeria.

Lawyer—Community Services
For the Borough Solicitor.'

I had no reason to doubt whether those allegations happened.

Nkem had carried out such unbelievable acts against Mary who was her cousin. She could hit Mary with a broom, metal rod, shoes, plank of wood and anything hard. She was used to striking her as many times as she wanted until she became satisfied. Occasionally, she smacked Mary for no reason at all, for things she did not do. At one time, she spanked her with a plank because her hair was messy. She could hit Mary several times a day, especially at weekends, even on her birthday. Once, Mary had an injury in one of her toes and Nkem aimed at it and hit her right there with a piece of wood so that she would be hurt the more, and the injury stayed for over a month. Mary would be scared to say if she was ill or wanted to ease herself if Nkem gave her any work to do in the kitchen. She would never let anyone know when she was very hungry or go to pick her meal without Nkem asking her to do so. Whenever Mary was not feeling fine, maybe she was down with fever or malaria, she would wait until I stumbled at her in a corner and at such a time, Nkem would not notice her, to hint to me of her state of health. Nkem might beat her to a state of stupor, if she dared utter such a complaint.

Before Nkem left for South Africa, Mary had turned skinny because she would never eat owing to too much work and the beatings. One morning, she could not rise from her mat where she slept. She curled herself under a duvet, dehydrated and could hardly lift her head until I came to take her to the hospital. At another time, I took a critical look at her, as she walked past me with one single wrapper knotted from her chest down and I saw two hyper-pigmented marks on her left forearm, up to twenty millimetres by ten millimetres caused when she was hit with an iron by Nkem. Similarly, there was a small spherical mark on the front of her left knee, caused when Nkem hit her with a horsewhip. Another dark, oval scar was on her right shin caused when she was hit with a metal pole. All of those marks were of a shape and in a position specifically not suggestive of accidental injuries. There were many other unclear marks and bruises on her forearm, right thigh and shins also not suggestive of accidental injuries. The poor girl had none of those ugly marks when she came to our house for the first time. One could only accept that such maltreatment happened because Mary was a distant relative. Now to think that Nkem could inflict such damage on her own son and a little boy kept in her custody was mindboggling.

How could a relationship between mother and son lack the warmth and affection that was necessary for a positive attachment and bond? For even the mentally sick mothers draw out their breast to feed their babies, how much more a woman who was well. At no time in my life did I bargain for what I was getting.

Not too long after, the police investigating the case again arrested Nkem. They released her on bail, some hours later, through the efforts of a lawyer. They made her report to the local police station and instantly debarred her from seeing my son, pending the determination of the case. In addition, they stopped her from working anywhere in that country.

Then, I got another huge surprise. One hot afternoon, I was in the office when my telephone rang like the last time. When I found it was a foreign number, I crept out as quietly as I could into the restroom to receive the call. 'Hello, Chidi,' I hesitated as the "hello" came repeatedly. My suspicion was right and I recognised her voice. It was Nkem. I was somehow confused whether to go ahead with the conversation or to cut off the call, for in my opinion, I had enough.

After dilly-dallying, I later return the same "hello" and she knew immediately I was the one speaking.

'Chidi, I'm absolutely sorry for all that I have caused you,' she said. 'I know I've hurt you so much. I had no reason to have done what I did…' I was mute as her voice went on and on like a radio presenter, now gentle and not in her usual manner of quacking liking a duck. 'Are you listening?' she asked when she could not hear anything from my end. I was very hesitant to speak. Sometimes, her voice could be deceptive, as smooth as butter, yet war in her heart.

'Yes, I am.' I replied to her very reluctantly. Now dozens of questions were buzzing in my head. I instantly abhorred her with anger even though I realised that was not going to help me spiritually.

'I was pushed by an instinct I couldn't control,' she claimed.

'What do you want from me?' I asked as the urge to respond to her came quietly. 'You have separated into three what used to be one family. Here, I'm in Nigeria, our son is in a foster home in a faraway land and you, only heaven knows where.'

'Stop, Chidi, I said I'm sorry.' I could hear her sob. 'Who told you Chima is in a foster home. It's a big lie,' she denied.

'Why are you denying? There is nothing hidden under the face of the earth. For your information, I received a letter from the South African City of Cape Town Council explaining to me, in detail, the events that had taken place between you, him and one, Jude. Who is Jude and how did the South African authority get my details?' She became dumb with that revelation.

'I'm very sorry,' she repeated rather than answer my

questions. Instead of her usual voice of baritone blended with fluctuating echoes with which she often spoke, she had suddenly become a woman with an alluring persuasive tone.

'Who is Jude and how did you come across him?' I asked again.

'I'll explain to you later,' she entreated.

'Now what would you want me do?' I asked.

'I need you to help me, please,' she stated.

'In what way?'

'I have been stopped from working and I need some money to keep myself.'

'If a woman discovers her folly, the woman ought to retrace her steps back and do the right thing. Isn't it? It's your choice anyway,' I advised.

'You know it's not going to be possible to leave Chima in the hand of a foster carer and come back to Nigeria at this time. 'Okay, if that is the case, I'll write to the South African authority to appeal to them to hand over Chima to me…'

Before I could finish, she interjected. 'Ah! No! Please don't do that yet.'

'Why?'

'It would jeopardise my present application for asylum.'

'So, why do you want to remain in South Africa?'

'Chidi, you won't understand, just help me.' The initially manifested blurred hope departed. Her determination like a lion-hearted opponent drained out the balance of my patience and I could no longer hold my vexation. I banged the phone. It appeared as if the whole air where I was had been sucked out and I was beginning to feel choked. She rang back and I left the phone ringing without picking up.

As soon as I returned from work, I went to see my pastor

215

to explain the situation. 'You have to continue to do whatever that is possible to be of assistance to her as she remained your wife, pending when God would touch her,' the pastor admonished. That idea burnt my heart, I must confess.

'I have a friend whose name is Jacob and who, after ten years of getting married to his wife, the wife moved out of the house, only to remarry in the year that followed. That did not stop Jacob from holding on to the Christian principles of no remarriage. He lived like a bachelor for ten years until the women reconciled with him, after giving another man two children. Jacob was trying to live by the example of that Biblical injunction that says, 'It's better for such couples to reconcile and come together again. Can't you see, Chidi, that you are lucky your case has not reached that stage?

'Another case is that of Sister Theresa, the head of our children department,' the pastor continued. 'Her husband drove her out for no just cause and married another woman. After five years of separation, the husband started chasing her to come back and when she decided to join the husband, the man had married two wives and she was to join them as the third wife. She chose to join the husband just to sustain her Christian belief. Chidi, there is hope for you. You are blessed,' he concluded.

I must admit that I left him being in great despair instead of optimism. I moved from disliking Nkem for all that she had caused me to hating to hear someone mention her name. I felt I would never get rid of that feeling for the rest of my life.

Despite being counselled by my pastor, I had my mind made up that I was not going to render any assistance to Nkem, against the pastor's advice. I wanted her to learn her lessons.

By the time I went to the church the next Sunday, the

pastor sent for me. 'Have you attended to Nkem's request?' he enquired.

'Not yet, sir.' Instantly, he asked me to stop whatever service I was rendering to the church for the second time. I begged him to allow me to continue my services with the sanitation group even if I had to stop my involvement in the youth activities and teaching services. I still had great respect for and pleasure working with the sanitation group. I remembered how I used to join those responsible for cleaning the male toilets, to make sure the toilets did not run out of water and tissue papers. We were also involved in the most unpleasant task of flushing the toilets for those who were not careful enough to ensure the waste went down the sucker. Sometimes, after flushing, there were streaks of brownish or perhaps yellowy particles encrusted on the edges of the toilet seats. Many a time, they glued as if they had been there for ages and it required a hard brush and some quantity of soapy water to scrub away the stain. Hardly would one bear the acid stench of the urine that splashed everywhere as one cleaned those toilets. Meanwhile, the head of the sanitation group would from time to time go around the toilets and could at any time order those who were permanently roistered for the job to appear before her. 'Why are some of the toilet floors wet all the time?' she would scream as if it was all their fault. 'It's your duty to ensure the toilets are pleasant to users and if you are in need of any material that would enable you carry out your work, you should come forward to request. I won't take it kindly with any of you if I receive any query from the District Head,' she would add.

When I was not busy in the toilet routine, I would find myself among the group who went into the neighbourhood to collect children who were willing to come to our Sunday school. And it was always our duty to return them at the end of the service.

The pastor did not succumb to my request, instead he directed me to sit among the congregation anytime I come to church from that time onwards, emphasising that I was disobedient to the church authority.

Within a few seconds, there was a revolting pain in my stomach as I was still listening to him. I held it with my two hands and was massaging it, not sure if that would help ease off the inflammation. The pastor splashed his two eyes at me, wondering what the matter was. He stood up and I sensed he was coming to hold me and probably get me first aid, but I waved at him that there was no need. 'Please sir, can I go to the rest room?' I requested.

'Sure,' he said. As I headed towards the exit door, he uttered. 'Don't go out, you can use my toilet.' He then stood up to assist me open his toilet door.

When I got into the toilet, I had a feeling of wanting to throw up of which nothing was forthcoming. I waited and waited but there was nothing still. Later, I came out to meet him. 'I hope you are fine?' he asked.

'Yes, sir.'

'God will touch your body.'

'Amen,' I responded.

'Sit down, let me lay my hand on your head and pray for you.' He went for the anointing oil; he opened it and bent it towards one of his fingers. He dabbed my forehead with the oil at the tip of his finger and laid his two hands on my head. He then prayed.

'Back to what I was saying,' he continued after he

finished. 'You have to step aside from all church activities and focus yourself at a prevailing prayer.'

'I've heard you, sir,' I replied with no attempt to wriggle out of it. How I survived that day and was able to reach my house without losing my mind was a mystery. I blamed myself again, for following my unction and not my parents' advice, in my decision to marry Nkem. It was one of the biggest mistakes, I would ever live to remember. Then a silent voice came asking if I would want to deny my faith and satisfy my carnal desire or keep holding on until heaven opens up a way of escape. At that time, my spirit was still willing to hold on but my flesh was completely weak.

From then on until the next few months, I made a deliberate effort to block Nkem from contacting me again. I focused more on my job and that year, I had a double promotion at my place of work with a number of overseas training programmes. Also, I remember that I won two awards that year at my company's end of the year award-giving events. The first was for the overall best employee while the second award was the Managing Director's Award given to the employee judged as having added the greatest value to the company. The first award came with an opportunity to travel to any European country of my choice with free accommodation and the second one provided a cash equivalent of two thousand United States dollars.

I would not forget the cold side of that end of the year event. There had not been any party during the previous two years due to recession. Many companies had cut down on their costs due to the economic downturn, which the government declared to be the worst in twenty years. According to the radio announcement, the National Bureau of Statistics had confirmed that the economy had slumped and was due to the inability of past administration to save the country's over-dependence on foreign products coupled with the existence of wasteful and abuse-prone subsidies as well as the activities of the militant groups. Any wonder why my company decided not to organise the party in the previous two years but instead paid some money into every employee's account as end of the year gifts.

As things became better the following year, the director of the company issued a circular that the end of the year party would hold that time around. We were all expected to come with our spouses and that was when my once clouded world manifested itself again. It was obvious I was going to walk into the venue as a single person.

On that faithful evening, all employees were in their best outfit and marched into the hall with their spouses by their sides. There were lots of introductions that went on and people clustered near the double door entrance, some saying to one another, 'Meet my madam or this is my husband.'

I got fagged out of repeatedly answering the same questions of "Chidi, did you come along with madam?" or "Where is your wife?" I walked in not accompanied by any one and was just as lonely as a patient in a private hospital ward would be. I stepped into the hall where the couples had already filled the tables. Two couples sat at each, pleasantly decorated with flowers and wine. It was emphatically awkward for any staff who came alone, as such persons faced the perplexity of not knowing which table to go to. The few unmarried staff somehow distorted the entire sitting setting. Those of us who were single were allowed to come with any opposite sex, whether relation or friend, yet I had no one to accompany me.

Indeed, it was such an uneasy moment for me, especially when I saw the way and manner some of my colleagues caressed their wives, the intimacy with which they discussed and cuddled each other and the smiles on their faces denoting their solitary delight and contentment. Envy and jealousy embraced my thoughts as I recollected all the scuffles I had endured with Nkem. Though it was not impossible that for some, their relationship would also be suffering some hindrances but there they were, looking perfect on the outside so much that no one could ever construe that any form of dispute or abuse ever took place in their homes.

Some of the couples were charming and happy looking; others were too possessive of their spouses, especially the men, and extremely guiding them with the greatest fear and hope that no man could entice them. With all of that, I saw myself degenerating into yet another phase of low self-esteem and I began to struggle with how I could assert myself and retain my earlier momentary joy. It was a chilly psychological condition for me.

Gradually, people filled the hall and at a point, no seat was empty. There was surplus food, both local and European dishes. There were assorted drinks too with cold and hot chocolates as well as baileys, pure orange, grape and pineapple drinks. It was extraordinary. There were two high life musicians to entertain the audience. Each of them was taking their turns to amuse the attendees. For someone like me, it was quite unfortunate that the musicians dwelt so much on love songs, using some of the couple's names to manipulate the songs. The mere mention of love was making me feel sick because nobody had ever shown me deep affection other than the period I lived with my parents, not even by my so-called wife. I felt like leaving the venue if not that I was yet anticipating the award of the best employee for that year. The song that brought people up on the dance floor was *Elizabeth, My Love* and it went like this:

> *Eliza, Eliza, my love,*
> *Who would love me as you do?*
> *Whom would I cherish like you?*
> *Where you go, I must go with you,*
> *Where you die, I will die with you,*
> *People say I am blind,*
> *But, my Love, I don't mind,*
> *My friends say I am crazy for you,*
> *Yet I don't mind,*
> *Eliza, Eliza, my love,*
> *If this is a dream,*
> *I don't want to wake up,*
> *We must be together for ever.*

Both the young and old couples were drawing each other up to the dance floor. It was a momentarily emotional love song that seemed to have ignited the affections of many who were really moved. When the music later stopped, couples were embracing each other, some pecking, others kissing.

For me, it was a sad moment because I had never felt like any of my colleagues. I was very desolate. Yet, I was convinced within myself that none of them had made the kind of sacrifices close to the ones I had made in order to have a happy home, which had eluded me, so far. Yet, I was certain that there were some who were staying in their unhappy marriages, and most times were covering up and making other arrangements to enable them to fulfil their heart needs.

I recalled when I had my traditional wedding, people were well fed and gifts that people would remember for a long time were given out. It was a wedding, which left many talking about it some months after. Afterwards, the guests disappeared leaving me to manage my home that soon turned into a family with so little to talk about, other than my wife being a very good cook in my eyes.

I could still recall how I was so fatigued that I could not get myself many days after. I continued to feel guilty and ashamed of myself that I did not heed to my parents' advice. I remember my father sounding a clear note of warning when he saw the huge amount I budgeted for the wedding, that wedding does not have to cost so much money. It does not have to have too many people in attendance, because they would soon after disappear and never to be seen anywhere near us. "Big or small weddings, the husband and wife would still be couples," he had told me. I wished I had listened to him; I would not have been a loser at both sides.

Chapter Fifteen

Back in South Africa, the borough solicitor had informed me in one of his letters that the police went to search my wife's apartment after establishing what they felt was a mountain of evidence of child abuse. Her home was a two bedroomed flat, located towards the outskirts of Soweto. It was in a block of fifteen flats and my wife was on the ground floor. Also, living in the same flat was a male neighbour who stayed in one of the rooms and my wife, Chima, and Jude occupying the second room.

Jude was the son of woman of Nigerian descent, his mother was a close friend to my wife and who also stayed in that flat briefly until she travelled to Cape Town to market her business products which were principally African handmade wrappers of multiple designs and colours, usually brought in from the neighbouring country, Botswana.

Jude thought his mother would be returning immediately but it was over two months then and the twist started as soon as she left. My wife became friends with Jude's mother at one of the shopping malls shortly after the arrival of my wife in Soweto fourteen months before. My wife was desperately looking for any Nigerian she could make friends with at that time.

Chima was in year four while Jude was in year six at the Margaret Gwele Primary School in Dobsonville, which they both said they liked. They were both doing well in their classes and were neither bullied nor abused.

Both Chima and Jude appeared neatly dressed when the police got there. Jude weighed an average of twenty-nine kilograms and Chima, twenty-seven. Their heights were nearly the same, one hundred and fifty-one centimetres.

During the investigation and interview with Jude, he alleged that my wife was fond of hitting him with a broom, metal rods, shoes, two types of canes, one short and fat, the other, very long and skinny, a plank of wood and anything hard. He said that my wife hit him as many times as she wanted until she was satisfied, alleging that had been happening for the previous two months since his mother brought him to live with my wife and Chima. He said she would hit him at times for no reason or for things he did not do. According to him, he was last hit two days before. He said he had an injury at the top of his leg from where my wife constantly hit him with a metal rod. He said the mark usually stayed for many days.

According to Jude, my wife would shout for no reason, cursed him and had banned him from watching television. He claimed they were not going out nor had fun outside. They just stayed in the parlour. He stated he was always scared to say he was hungry, insisting he did not want to continue to stay in that house any more.

Jude was an intelligent and articulate little boy who was able to express his wishes and feelings. The investigative police established that he, like Chima, was born in Nigeria where his father was still working in a small private textile firm.

My wife told the police that she was of the Christian faith and it was her wish to raise Chima within that faith, and that was what she wished for Jude too. Despite Chima being her son, he too had suffered physical and emotional abuse whilst in her care. Notwithstanding Chima's experiences, he impressed as a confident young boy who had a positive image of himself. He exuded a mature attitude and spoke openly about the abuse they suffered while in my wife's care. He was academically sound in his own way and very focused, and had remained so irrespective of the recent upheaval and changes he had undergone in the past months. He was also thinking that my wife was not his birth mother due to the way she had treated and abused him.

Following the investigation and interview, my wife was arrested and taken to the police station for interrogation while the Social Services department was contacted to take custody of the two lads.

My wife was availed with the service of a lawyer who happened to be from Ghana. His name was Thompson Kobi from a small town near the capital city of Accra. He looked young but when he spoke, he sounded like an experienced and versatile lawyer, though he was unmarried.

The police took my wife straight into interview room four, at Soweto central police station. And as she sat in front of a large desk, in the fully air-conditioned room with no other object in sight, Detective Constable Nkuru Miyala introduced himself as the officer attached to the Child Protection Investigation Command with another officer present who did not bother to introduce himself. My wife's lawyer was also present.

'The time by my watch is six fifteen p.m.,' Constable Miyala said.

'I know you have a harsh voice, but could you please try to speak gently and slowly?' Barrister Thompson Kobi advised her.

'Do you understand what your solicitor said to you?' Constable Miyala asked.

'Yes,' she replied.

'Whilst you are in police custody, you are entitled to free and independent legal advice and that is why you have your legal representative, Barrister Thompson Kobi, with us. You have the opportunity to have a consultation in private and prior to that consultation, we would continue with the interview. Are you happy you have had sufficient time to speak and liaise with your solicitor?'

'Yes,' she answered, inaudibly.

'I need you to speak up,' Detective Constable Miyala stated.

'Yes,' she answered, now a bit louder.

'Your right to free and independent legal advice remains the whole time you are here. Any time during this interview you want to have a further chat with him, I'm sure he wants to have a chat with you; you need to let me know so that we'll stop the interview to enable you to do that. Do you understand that?'

'Yes.'

'Please, you have to tell us the truth and nothing but the truth. Do you understand the caution?'

'No.'

'Okay. I'll explain this to you in three stages and then I'll invite you to explain your understanding back to me. All right?

First part is, you don't have to say anything, so it is your right not to answer any of our questions put to you today. The middle part is a slight warning if you like. It may harm your defence if I ask you a question today and you choose not to answer, or you give me an answer that later on will change. On the other hand, if you produce an account of events, such that if this matter was to go to trial, an inference could be drawn as to why you didn't explain that to the officers in the first instance. The last bit is that anything you say may be given in evidence, in the court. I hope you witnessed that in the beginning I put in two tapes in the machine.'

'Yes.'

'They are tapes recording this interview and these microphones around the room can pick up what we're saying right from those tapes and that is why I said it can be used as evidence on full potential proceedings. Do you understand that?'

'Yes.'

'Can you now explain back to me how you understand that caution, please?' Nkem responded a bit inaudibly. She seemed to have understood the caution.

'Nkem, I'm little bit worried because you don't seem to be hundred per cent with me. Are you really feeling all right?'

'Yes.'

'Are you sure you do not need to see a doctor?

'No.'

'If at any time during this session you don't feel well, can you please let me know? Also, if you would like us to reduce the air condition, please do let me know. Okay.

'This evening, I attended your home address at about five p.m., I knocked at your door and you opened it. We went into your apartment and later, at about six p.m., we arrested you on suspicion of assault occasioning actual bodily harm on Jude and neglect of those two children. Because of that arrest, we cautioned you at about six twenty p.m., originally. When we got there, we started searching the room. Then, we were specifically told that we were going to be looking out for weapons or items that the children alleged you used to beat them with, specifically: pieces of wood; sticks; metal rods; and so on. We told you where we were told they might be which is by the refrigerator in your room. Do you remember me coming to your house this evening and asking for those weapons?'

'Yes.'

'Do you remember all of what I just said to you happened?'

She kept quiet, staring kind of angrily.

'Your room is a very small one and it is very packed with computers, lots of bags, suitcases, wardrobes, etc. Do you remember that when I asked for those weapons, you said you got rid of the piece of metal and wood? You claimed they were broken so you got rid of them last week.'

'I said I don't keep things and didn't say I got rid of them.'

'So, you are saying you didn't make that comment?'

'No.'

'Later you said it wasn't a piece of wood but a piece of white plastic. Is that correct?'

'No comment.'

'What I'm trying to do is to do this interview in stages. The conversation we are referring to now is the conversation we were explaining initially about looking for the piece of wood that the children had said you used in beating them. And in the course of my other colleague looking for that wood you explained to him that you haven't hit them with a piece of wood but it was with a piece of white plastic and you showed us the plastic?'

'That was last month.'

'Yeah, but do you remember the comment about the white plastic?'

'No.'

'I have written down so far my account of what happened this evening. So, we are clear that we did have this conversation and that you said to me that it wasn't a piece of wood but a piece of plastic. And by that, you are saying you meant that was what you hit Jude with? Is that what you are saying?'

'I said I can't remember when I hit Jude.'

'I'm going to remind you and advise you but I'm not going to force you to do anything against your will but it is my advice that you tell us the truth. It's your choice. Do you understand what I've just said?'

She kept quiet.

'My colleague found a piece of broken wood from underneath the refrigerator in the bedroom. Well, you know your room and the layout. You have the table, the bed, the wardrobe and much stuff, and he put his hand right down the back of it and he found the wood that has been broken. That is the piece of wood we found and you said that is the bit of the wood from the stick you threw away last week and you referred to Chima playing with it. Is that comment true?'

'No comment.'

'We then found documents relating to immigration that you are an over-stayer and have no permission to remain in South Africa so I had to carry out further enquiries. When I showed you that piece of wood which was a table leg, you said to me, "I never hit the children with that, come, I'll show you what I used". Was that correct?'

'No comment.'

'And lastly, one of the allegations was that you also used a metal rod to beat them. Jude described the rod and mentioned that we could find it in the kitchen. He said that sometimes you will heat up the rod and place it on his hands. Again, I'm not saying this is that item. This is an item that fits the description so it's an item that I have taken and when you saw it, you got very upset and said, "Why do you think I'd use that on the children, am I a monster".' Is that a comment you made?'

'No comment.'

'And you tidied yourself up and collected your belongings, and while we were still in your flat and during the search you complained of a headache and told me that you had taken some paracetamol. Later, we brought that to the notice of the custody sergeant and while here you had seen the police doctor. Is that correct?'

'Yes.'

'And he has given you some more paracetamol. Have you taken that?'

'Yes.'

'How are you feeling right now?'

'Better.'

'Sorry.'

'Thank you.'

'Are you happy to continue?'

'Yes.'

'So, that is my account and my notes of what happened this evening. Therefore, what I want to do is start by asking you what your family composition is. Obviously, I know there is you and there is your son, Chima, who is seven or eight?'

'Seven.'

'Do you have other children in this country or in Nigeria?'

'No.'

'Who else lives in that house with you?

'Mr John.'

'What about Jude?'

'Yes.'

'Is there anybody else?'

'No.'

'You work as a nurse or is it a care assistant?'

'Care Assistant.'

'And I noticed when we were going through stuff, it is geared to that sort of work. Is it? Are you qualified to do that sort of work?'

'No comment.'

'What sort of hours do you work?'

'Nights.'

'What time, for example, do you leave home to get to work?'

'Eight p.m.'

'Eight p.m. at night and you would be back at seven thirty a.m. before they go to school? So, when you go to work in the evening and you leave about eight p.m., who is looking after the children?'

'Mr John.'

'You are closing your eyes, are you sleeping?'

'No.'

'Are you all right?'

'Yes.'

'Do you remember what day of the week was Chima's birthday and did you beat Chima with a piece of wood?'

'No.'

'Did you beat any one of them on that day with any instrument?'

'No.'

'Now, let me stick to Jude for a moment. He's not your son, is he?'

'No.'

'Where is his mother?'

'Cape Town.'

'How well do you know her?'

'She's a friend.'

'So, what's the circumstance of her leaving Jude with you?'

'She travelled to Cape Town on business.'

'Do you remember how long he has been staying with you?'

'Who?'

'Jude.'

'Three months.'

'Jude has described a number of incidents where he states that he has been beaten. He says that he gets into trouble sometimes, in fact, sorry, I don't have transcripts for this so I've to do it from memory. Refer to an incident where he said Chima took something of his and then he lost it and because it got lost, he got the blame and you beat him with the stick. He said you hit him across his back and his arm and his head. Can you comment anything on that? Have you ever beaten or smacked him for anything?'

'I can't remember.'

'Have you ever smacked Chima?'

'No comment.'

'Have you ever used implements, like the piece of wood I showed you to smack the children?'

'Never.'

'Did you ever leave the children at home to be on their own?'

'No.'

'Jude describes that he sleeps on the floor and Chima sleeps in the chair with duvet and pillows. And he describes how he gets himself up in the morning and he will cook himself various things he has for breakfast. Quite often, he has tea. Sometimes, he has bread and tea; sometimes, he has bacon. I asked him to tell me how he cooked the bacon and he described a big pot and drew it for me. Similar to a lot of pots and he describes a big saucepan with a lid, he drew the gas flame and said, "I light the gas and I put the bacon down on the bottom of the saucepan and that is how I cook the bacon".'

'He doesn't cook bacon.'

'Does he ever cook his own breakfast?'

'Who?'

'Either of them?'

'They don't cook anything. They often take cornflakes or cake for breakfast and they are not cooked?'

'And how do they go to school?'

'I walk them down the road to the school.'

'You take them to school? Because Jude told me they walk to school on their own.'

'No.'

'The children have described a number of incidents and, in fairness to them, and until the transcripts are done, they weren't able to give specific dates and times which is normal with children. They claim they do all the housework, they sweep the floor, they wash the plates, they clean the toilets, and they clean your shoes and do all the tidying up.'

'No comment.'

'Sorry, are you saying no comment to it or it is not true?'

'It's not true.'

'I'm sorry to keep juggling my questions. Jude alleged specifically that you have beaten him with a metal iron and banned him from school. Is that true?'

'He was ill so I called the school.'

'Do you know who you spoke to at the school?'

'The secretary to the head tutor.'

'What Jude told me was that it was because you said he had been naughty and had returned from school very late and that you beat him, causing some marks on his hands. He also said there was a time that you had thrown red pepper in his eyes and then suggested that sometimes you mixed the red pepper with water and that you have poured pepper and water in his eyes. Jude is saying you, Nkem, did these things.'

'No comment. Maybe he was talking about his mum, I don't know.'

'I can only put to you what I've been told.'

'If I can't do that to my own child why would I do it to somebody else's child?'

'So, you are saying you did not do that?'

'I didn't.'

'Chima told the police that he was very upset and distraught about what he saw happening to Jude. Any comment on that? That is your son telling me that.'

'No comment.'

'Chima, your son, said that sometimes you used to pinch and twist their ears if they had been naughty, and you have said it yourself that sometimes, they are naughty. How would you punish them if they were naughty?'

'I always ask them to stand by the wall.'

'Is there any other punishment?'

'Jump up.'

'Anything else?'

'No.'

'Chima describes you as a mother with a hot temper and that you shout, beat and abuse them. Would you say you are a woman who has a hot temper?'

'No comment.'

'What the children are saying is that whenever they came in and you were in a bad mood that you would shout, scream at them and beat them?'

'Why would I be in a bad mood? What would make me be in a bad mood?'

'I'm asking you, would you be in a bad mood and react by beating the children and shouting and screaming at them?'

'No.'

'Can you think of any reason the children would make these very serious allegations against you?'

'I think they are not happy that I do ask them to wash their pants?'

'So, you are saying it's for that reason alone they have made all this up?'

'Yes.'

'Now I want to give you one final opportunity to tell me the truth. From the items I took from your house this evening, that's the stick my colleague took from your bedroom this evening,' Constable Miyala pointed. 'That's the stick you recognised this evening and said that was part of the stick you had got rid of...'

'I didn't say so.'

'Can you tell me what that is then and where has it come from?'

'The stick?'

'Yes.'

'It's part of the hanger in my wardrobe, where I do hang my clothes. It got broken.'

'So, you are saying it's part of the clothes hanger?'

'Yes.'

'When we searched your room, we found a signed letter written by Jude to his mum and it said:

Dear Mum,

I am fed up of the way Chima's mum has been beating me. She gives me scars on my hand and leg. Please, Mum, I want to come over to Cape Town as soon as possible. I hope everyone is doing well. Send my greetings to them, and I am sorry I did not send anything to you. I've got no money. I know you will be sad for me. Please try and be happy but I will not forgive Chima's mum because she is a monster.

And that is signed by Jude and was found in your bedroom.'

'Have you seen that letter before?'

'Yes.'

'So, why would Jude write such a letter?'

'Because of the bad things he does.'

'Really?'

'Yes. Besides, it's not Jude who wrote the letter, that's not Jude's writing. I can show you something written by Jude.'

'So, do you know who wrote the letter?'

237

'I repeat that's not Jude's writing.'

'That's Jude at the start of his signature because I've got his signature. He writes *Jud* and crossed it out.'

'I don't know.'

'More to the point, then, this letter is signed from somebody I believe at this time is Jude. It is addressed to his mum; it has your home address on it, and he is describing how unhappy he is because of what you are doing to him and that he can't forgive you. He thinks you are a monster. Why would he write that?'

'Because of the evil he does as well.'

'So, he just does it because he's a bad boy and was that what you kept referring as being naughty?'

'No comment.'

'I have nothing further to add. Is there anything at this time that you would like to tell me in relation to these allegations against you?'

'Nothing.'

'Well, based on that fact then, I'll stop the tape.'

The young constable had twisted every question he asked to sound the opposite until Nkem admitted without realising she was agreeing with the facts the interrogator was raising. Some of the statements she made were inconsistent, which broke down the entire fabrication.

From all indications, it seemed the police had enough grounds to press charges.

Chapter Sixteen

While Nkem was facing a court case and on the brink of receiving a possible sentence for child violence in South Africa, there was a dangerous probability that some unexpected changes would yet happen in my life. The Chief Executive Officer of the company where I worked released an announcement to all employees on the very first Monday following our end of the year party.

That announcement was what first greeted us as soon as we switched on our computers to begin the day's work. Some of the most senior employees swapped places, which affected Mr Ben Johnson, my immediate boss at that time. Under the new arrangement, Mr Johnson would become the new head of the procurement department while Mr Gerald Bako became my new boss.

Mr Bako was from the middle belt, with deep, thick tribal marks that could make any individual easily believe he must be inconsiderate in relating with other employees. He was tall and chubby and, later, I got to know he was a no-nonsense fellow who had no known intimate friend.

The top managers' movement was to happen quickly. Those affected were all to pack their belongings in their present units and go to their new offices without dilly-dallying about it. Only the chief executive of the company could explain what necessitated the changes and why it was necessary for the people affected to act without dragging their heels.

As workers and executives in all the departments were absorbing the news of the unexpected reshuffling that would bring in a female for the first time as the head of the human resources department, many were wondering whether that would mean good times for the employees in general. People throughout the company were forecasting the likely fallout from the reshuffling and guessing what changes, if any, might be in store. Most workers seemed to think that the changes would be few and small.

Before Mr Johnson left, he pushed out a series of files and documents to my desk. The impromptu directive must be the reason those documents were left untreated because Mr Johnson was somebody known to always take his time. Some of the documents he pushed out were those requiring further action by the man who would replace him while he wanted me to file away the others.

It was not long before Mr Bako who had shortly arrived at his new office, where I was, stood in front of my desk, asking to see a one-page document Mr Johnson told him he had made some notes on for immediate attention. I quickly called Mr Johnson, now my former boss, to provide further clarification on the said document.

'It is a one-page letter from Henharry Consult,' he explained. 'It's about an international exhibition coming up in two weeks' time.'

I searched everywhere on and around my desk but could

not find the document. I never remembered seeing it anyway. *Where could it be?* I wondered. 'Please give me time, I'll find it,' I told Mr Bako. He seemed reluctant to leave but instead showed his willingness to assist in the search. He lifted the files one after the other and flipped through every sheet of paper he could find. When he got tired, he walked back to his new office with a look which I felt was resentment. I presumed he had built a negative first impression about me.

I would not have been much worried if not that the document must get to the Finance section to enable them to raise some money for the international exhibition scheduled to take place in Ghana.

Half an hour after, Mr Bako spoke in the loudest tone of voice from his office, 'Any luck?'

'No,' I replied. 'Please, sir, give me some more time. I'm still searching for it.' Fortunately, by the time I was to give up, the document just dropped off from one of the files ransacked earlier. Out of joy, I shouted, 'Praise God!'

'What?' Mr Bako enquired.

'I found it.'

'Good. Let me have it then.'

Immediately, I went and handed it over to him. He collected it and bent again, glancing through the big file jacket containing hundreds of other documents. Inside that jacket was also the handover notes, which marshalled out all the tasks the department should accomplish before the end of the second quarter of the year.

As I stood in front of him, waiting to hear if there was something else, I tried to read his mind, whether he was pleased with me or not. I was yet to study him and it would take me time. He looked up after a while and said nothing so I walked away.

No one could have been like Mr Johnson in the whole of that office. Mr. Johnson was easy-going, kind and patient. He often believed that no one was above error and that no matter how careful one might be, one could still fall into the trap of some grievous mistakes. His leniency was a big advantage for me in accomplishing my tasks without any hassle.

But for Mr Bako, after I had worked with him for a few months, I could say that he was a man of stringent rules who had zero tolerance for faults. I understood he bagged his Ph.D. in Sociology when he was only 24 years old. Despite his academic excellence, he was a dodgy individual, with an itching palm and had little or no regard for integrity. What happened the following week proved that. As soon as I reported to work, he pushed out a purchase requisition form that he had carefully completed. He had also signed the section meant to be signed by the head of department, which he was anyways, but usually, the initiator was supposed to sign first. Later, he came out of his office. 'Chidi, could you please put your name on the form I dropped on your desk and act as the initiator of that process,' he said.

'But, sir, I know nothing about the items on the form,' I quickly replied. 'Not that alone, I'm not familiar with the vendor.'

'Yes, I know but all I need you to do is to append your signature.'

'I'm very sorry, sir. I will find it difficult to do because it will be against my Christian belief,' I sounded blunt.

'Okay, I'm sorry too. I regret involving you in this in the first instance. I didn't know that your Christian belief wouldn't allow you to sign a requisition form that you did not initiate.'

His face dimmed and he became completely gloomy. It was as if he swelled instantly like someone with festering internal wounds. I could see something unspoken in him, as if he was questioning my bravery by not doing what he wanted me to do. Although, we did not talk about the matter again but from that time, his behaviour changed towards me. Whenever I put a personal request to him, it would stay on his desk for days and he would not attend to it. Occasionally, he would give a flimsy excuse why it would not be possible to have it approved. I knew he was paying me back in my own coin. The longer I worked with him, the more I thought I would soon get used to him. However, I never did.

One day, I went to his former department to ask people who had worked with him previously on the best way to manage him. 'Mr Bako has a rigid behaviour and doesn't give room for argument or new ideas,' one colleague told me. 'His major weakness is his strong dislike for male subordinates and people who carry themselves about, openly declaring their stand as Christians,' he continued. 'Sometimes, when he came out from a management meeting his eyes would be red and his aura tough as though he had received some rebuke from higher authority. We were usually not bothered if we were sure we had not done anything that would have contributed to his receiving a bashing from the chief executive. At that time, he would avoid everybody and would not converse with anyone or delegate responsibilities. He would usually be on his own.'

Soon, I discovered that not only me but also almost everybody found Mr Bako very hard company, as a boss or colleague. Sometimes, he would come to the office and initiate discussions first thing in the morning, spending up to half an hour in front of my desk before entering his office to begin the day's work. He would talk about personal issues of life, ranging from the previous night's menu to football league results.

I was not surprised when I learnt he had not been married before even though he was forty-eight years old at that time. Yet, he seemed so calm and appeared not to be anxious, thinking or talking about marriage. He had a female cook and another mistress who acted, more or less, like his wife, except that they were not living together. The woman's name was Grace who had a gangling look that sometimes I felt she had better not be walking alone because I was afraid any light wind could throw her down. She visited Mr Bako very frequently while at work. Someone told me she was working in a government office very close to our company. She looked nourished and was not in any way deprived fiscally. And nobody could take her for granted.

One day, Grace came to visit Mr Bako and refused to leave. Her voice went up and she insisted that Mr Bako must pay her back the money he borrowed from her. She seemed to have had her revenge well prepared. As hard looking as Mr Bako was, he was begging Grace not to disgrace him. We all felt glad that there was somebody who could subdue Mr Bako.

'Mr Bako is my friend but doesn't deserve mercy,' she insisted when I approached her. 'He wants mercy but he is not merciful,' she said. 'And what does the Holy Book say? Blessed are the merciful for they shall obtain mercy. He's bent on firing his cook despite my pleading,' Grace pointed out. After much persuasion, Grace later cooled down and left.

Not long after, the cook entered pleading that Mr Bako should not sack her as he had decided to do as soon as that month ended. Mr Bako was still contending despite the fact that he had hit her several times on the head with a frying pan because she mistakenly put too much oil in the fried egg that she had served him over the weekend.

Some of us in that office joined in to beg Mr Bako not to fire the woman, but he refused, saying that she must leave at the end of that month. In my heart, I was wishing that God had paired Mr Bako and Nkem, my wife, as a couple.

In those periods, when I got home from work, I would retreat into my bedroom, leaving Mary to be wondering if it was all because of Nkem and Chima's disappearance. Many a time, she would enter the room and say, 'Uncle, please don't skip your dinner, come and eat before you sleep. Things will be all right someday. You will smile over a very happy home one of these days.'

I was almost ashamed that such a girl, still in her teens was admonishing me on that kind of subject matter. Whenever I heard her words, water would dim my eyes and she would see it but would quickly take her eyes away.

'Oh! How I miss Chima. I miss aunty too,' she would sometimes utter.

Her longing to see Nkem again drove me crazy, making me to wonder if her mental stability was still intact, judging from all she went through at Nkem's hands.

That time, whenever I was late to reach home from work, Mary would be on the street, looking out for me and she would race towards me to pick up my office bag as soon as she sighted me. She became very free with me. She would then ask me, how my day was. She would also ask what I had for my lunch and what time I left the office.

One day, I returned from work and refused to take my dinner despite Mary's persuasion and she too rejected hers.

But for me, there was a very good reason why I suddenly lost desire for food. I had my half-yearly performance review with Mr Bako and he had rated me so poorly. That year, for the first time, I did not receive any financial reward and some other associated benefits. It had never happened to me since I started work in that company. It pained me so much.

Six months later, we came to work as usual and the news spread that the company was planning a serious restructuring that was going to result in releasing about seventy employees. It was a cold wave across the company. Work virtually halted as employees were discussing the matter at every corner. The company did not make the details of the plans known to employees but they, perhaps, related to certain demands to comply with the recommendation of the Technical Committee on Privatisation and Commercialisation of government firms.

Efforts by the workers union to intervene in order to ensure that there was no unfair play in the selection process of employees to be shown the way out after it was suggested that workers should be made to work on a rotational basis or a cut in salary were in vain. Later, when the chief executive officer explained the move further, he said, 'The exercise is to inject new life into the organisational system owing to a continued growth of expenditure.' The criteria he spelt out included frequency of sick leave, warnings and queries, lateness, absenteeism, old age and any record of adverse report.

There were the untouchable people who the exercise would never affect. Those who were one hundred percent sure, even when it was going to be based on prejudice. I, for one, was having worried feelings. It was going to be a big disaster to be out of work and at the same time not to have a woman in my home to console me.

We were all going to work on a daily basis not knowing whether we would return the following day with our names still on the payroll. The air was charged. The management members, who participated in the dialogue of identifying the employees who would eventually leave, already knew those pencilled down. When those managers passed, all eyes would be on them in order to read their body language. But they kept their gesture the same, making it extremely difficult for anyone to read their minds.

When the time drew near, the chief executive officer gathered us together again at the staff canteen to prepare our minds and reiterate the inevitability of the exercise. 'When the work ends for you, I encourage you to be strong and look elsewhere, as it is not the end of the world,' he said. 'In order to make the exit less painful for those of you who would be affected, we have worked out what we thought to be reasonable gratuity and ex-gratia as the case may be. Out of two hundred and seventeen staff, about seventy would go, leaving one hundred and forty-seven behind. By this time next week, we shall be distributing the white envelopes containing the letters of those touched by this exercise. When you get it, if you are affected, please remember that it is the beginning of another journey for you.'

Nearly everybody had become tired of waiting and wanted the human resources group to share the envelopes as quickly as possible in order to end the hapless anxiety. But the company would only act according to its agenda and not any person's wishes.

Many were already gathering their belongings and some were copying important information from their computer systems. Some other employees' desks had by now, become

247

clear and tidy as if they were new staff. Those who had recently obtained company's loan were frightened the most, doubting if they would be able to withstand the heavy financial burden that would probably soon follow.

The few officers involved in typing out the release letters were having sealed lips. People were now skipping their lunches, tight-fisted, acting as if they had learnt to maintain low quality lives. Many suddenly became judicious spenders.

Eventually, came that day everybody was talking about. No one was sure whether the global formula of *last in, first out* was the order. No doubt, people were sure some would unnecessarily be favoured because of the godfather syndrome. It was the bane of our society at that time, even until now. It often played a part in situations like that, even in multinational companies, how much more a government firm like ours.

Soon, top managers went over to the human resources department to collect the letters of those affected in their units but those letters would not be handed-over to the people according to the directive until the very last minute to the close of work. It meant the folks who were to stay behind would not know those leaving. There would not be time for those individuals who would be staying behind to say goodbye to their colleagues taking their leave and would no longer show up for work the next day.

When it was exactly ten minutes before five p.m., Mr Bako called me into his office. My heartbeat rose. I summoned up the courage and went in. He had left his desk to the specially designed office double sofa close to the window. 'Come right in,' he uttered as I got in, waving his arms for me to come over to where he was seated on the twin sofa. 'Sit down, Chidi,' he said. The sofa was so low that I was worried if I was not going to have trouble getting up. He paused a little, looking at me and I could tell the expression of sympathy written all over his face. For the first time, I saw feelings of compassion coming from him. How genuine it was, I could not tell. 'Well, I can see suspicious expression on your face, and I regret to tell you that your inkling is right as you are one of those affected by the ongoing downsizing exercise. That is not the end of the world. You have to dust your certificate again and believe you can still find another job elsewhere.' Now he put forth his hand with the letter. 'I wish you the very best,' he added. 'Feel free to use me as your reference and I'm sure Mr Johnson would oblige you the same too.'

My composure deserted me for the first few minutes as I could not wrap my head around the fact that I had lost my job. My throat felt as if it were full of broken bones. I hesitated for a while before stretching my hand to collect the envelope after sighing heavily. Straight away, I went to my desk, gathered my few belongings, and bade a few of my colleagues who I could see, goodbye. I went to Mr Johnson's office to say goodbye to him too. He was stunned and could not believe that such a thing would ever happen to me, yet it was too late for anyone to intervene.

When I got home, Mary knew that something devastating had happened but she was not bold to confront me this time around.

Chapter Seventeen

The case of the allegations of child abuse against Nkem opened at the beginning of the following year. The state assigned the trial to a young black woman of Zambian origin who appointed two assessors to help her evaluate the case and reach a verdict. Section thirty-five of the South African Bill of Rights provided, that "Every accused person has a right to a fair trial, which includes the right, *inter alia*, to be tried in a language that the accused person understands, or, if that is not practicable, to have the proceedings interpreted in that language".

The courtroom was packed with people, with other onlookers gathered outside for other cases. One of the officers led my wife to the stand and shortly after, the judge stepped into the courtroom from the door facing the public gallery.

'All stand!' hollered the clerk, with an unexpected amplified voice.

Everyone obeyed and there was silence as the judge came in with great dignity and power. There was a roll of red carpet leading up the steps of the throne where she later sat, very tall in her robe of justice.

'The case file, please,' the judge ordered, with every

weight of authority.

The clerk walked to her with the file and she stretched her left hand and collected it with not an iota of humility. She stared and then flipped through. 'The court session shall be held in English and I hope you are comfortable with that or do you require an interpreter?'

'She can cope with it, my Lord,' the defence lawyer responded.

In the opening statement, the prosecutor, Moyanga Smith poured out the charges, noting that the abused cases against my wife was on circumstantial evidence, highlighting that there were no eyewitnesses to the incidents.

In the opening statement read out by my wife's lawyer, Barrister Thompson Kobi, my wife admitted to all the marks found on Jude's body but concocted a snowball of lies by saying they were domestic accidents. He also admitted that she had the responsibility of correcting both Chima and Jude whenever they misbehaved and never, at any time, deliberately inflicted injuries on them. If she could raise a reasonable doubt in her favour that she did not cause the marks found in Jude's body, she was entitled, under South African Law, to an acquittal on the charge of child abuse. If otherwise, the court with all other requirements assumed, will convict her of child abuse.

On the second day of the trial, a young man named Moputu, testified to hearing cries on a regular basis coming out from my wife's apartment, especially in the mornings and late evenings. Another witness testified to what she described as a child's screams on the evening preceding the day the police took Jude and Chima into social workers' custody. 'I heard a young boy crying loudly in a high-pitched voice and shouting, "Please, I'm sorry, Mummy.". It was a cry of anguish,' she added.

After assessing the gravity of the matter, the prosecutor later brought an application for an independent specialist to assess my wife's mental condition under article seventy-eight of the South African Criminal Procedure Act.

The next day, the judge ordered an evaluation of her state to take place as an outpatient at one of the city's hospitals in Soweto. It was to be week days, between nine a.m. and four p.m., starting from that weekend and lasting for two weeks.

In the end, the evaluation found that my wife was not in any way mentally incapacitated to the extent that she would like to dehumanise children. Similarly, the judge directed that a medical practitioner should carry out a DNA investigation and soon after that, it revealed that she was the real mother of Chima, with a 99.99 per cent chance.

On the day of the judgement, the judge stared very angrily at my wife and said, 'The persecutor proved beyond reasonable doubt that you are a first-degree abuser capable of causing great harm to children and possibly death. I saw in your lips the signs of your own guilt. Indeed, you are a woman with a peculiar temper, who uses excessive force to deal with children. I hereby find you guilty as charged.'

Before the sentence, my wife admitted, 'This has been a huge life lesson for me and I regret it every day,' she apologised in the court. 'My mother brought me up very well and I have grown to be a good mother myself to the two boys…'

'I totally disagree with you,' said the judge. 'You did not treat the two boys the same way. Although you might be a good mother to your son, Chima, which I even doubt very much, you are not to Jude.'

'Your Lord, I plead that you tamper justice with mercy,' the defence lawyer said. 'I therefore, would like to recommend a two-year community sentence with twenty hours of community service per month, My Lord.'

The judge rejected the lawyer's submission and delivered a seven-year jail term to my wife, without parole, with two years community service of two hours daily, Monday to Friday, to be served when she is out of jail. And the judge added, 'After your release from prison and the completion of your two years post-release control that will run concurrently with your community service period, you shall be removed to Nigeria where you came from on the basis that you are an over-stayer who has no right to work or recourse to public fund.'

After listening to the sentence, one eyewitness speaking about my wife said, 'She was broken, she was screaming, she was crying, she was also praying.'

One other man who saw her said he saw her true person that day whilst another woman said she was merely acting and that her emotional responses were insincere.

Soon after the sentence, one of the police officers who stood behind the counter where my wife positioned, which the officer of the court had bolted with an iron hook, handcuffed her, and led her out through the back of the courtroom without any opportunity to talk to anyone, straight to the waiting prison van. As she and the police officer stood waiting for the driver to open the door of the van, her lawyer approached her. 'Nkem, I did my best but the evidence against you were glaring,' he told her.

'I know,' my wife responded in a very calm voice yet looking so distressed.

'My efforts resulted in your not bagging the maximum jail term for the offence, which is twelve years.'

'Yes, I know.'

'I encourage you to be strong and serve your term. Very soon, you will be out but you must learn your lessons. Or will you like to appeal?'

'No,' she said, nodding at the same time.

'Is there any other thing you will like me to do for you?'

'Please help me move all my belongings to storage until I'm out. My two bank cards are inside a wallet on top of my wardrobe in my room. I have sufficient funds in my account that would be able to cover the store rent for the period. Thereafter, hand over the key of my apartment to John, my neighbour, who should take it to the property owner when my rent is due in seven months' time. Will you do that for me?'

'Take it as done.'

At about the time the driver of the van appeared and was opening the door, Juliana, Jude's mother, came running towards the courtroom and as she noticed that the court had ended the session, she started finding her way towards the back of the court. She probably had an idea what usually happens after every court's sentence. But she would not be allowed to get near the van or talk to my wife who was about getting in the van. She stood gazing, as my wife was locked-up in the van and driven away.

Hesitantly, Jude's mother turned back and was not too sure which way to go and how to locate her son. Nevertheless, she made the right decision when she decided to show up at the police station to make enquiries about Jude. When the police researched their records, they were able to let her know where Jude and Chima were, and how she could meet with them.

Jude's mother appeared to be the opposite of Nkem. She understood what motherhood was all about. She knew that her son needed her as the counsellor that would always be there for him and comfort him. She was never crossed-out or became easily whacked like most other women. She would apologise to Jude whenever she felt she was at fault. She would not say that just because Jude was small and her child that she was not going to own up to her faults. She was never a bully, domineering or sarcastic. She had respect for Jude. She would never push anything down his throat. She knew that genuine love was essential to a child's upbringing. She thought all women were like her and had little or no knowledge of what Nkem was capable of doing. If she knew Nkem was the person she now proved to be, she would never have left her only son with her.

The next morning, she was able to secure a meeting between her and Jude who was currently in the same foster home with Chima. Both Jude and Chima screamed as soon as they caught sight of her. It was quite a cordial meeting as both boys expressed their wish to be with her. It was obvious they were thirsty for warmth and care by someone they were already acquainted with. Children generally like to feel loved, accepted and nurtured. 'Why did you go away for so long?' Jude asked his mother.

'I'm so sorry, Jude, and that won't happen again, I assure you.'

'Is it because Chima's mother is a monster and I don't like her. I don't want to see her again in my life.'

'Stop saying that,' Juliana cautioned.

'It's true, my mother is a wicked woman,' Chima

255

concurred.

'No, no, don't ever speak ill of your mother again,' Juliana stated. No doubt, she very much understood the children, and knew what they meant. She realised they were right but she was not going to let them know it.

A couple of days later, the Social Services department released the two boys to Juliana to look after and she treated both of them alike. Chima enjoyed being with Jude's mother more than his and he expressed his feelings that he would not like to see his mother again.

Chapter Eighteen

While Nkem was in jail in the South African prison, I was on the street drifting from one company's doorstep to the other searching for a new job. It was contrary to my initial belief that I would immediately get another job, but six months later I was still job hunting and my savings had dwindled.

To make ends meet, I moved from one menial job to the next, sometimes teaching in a private school for a very steady meagre remuneration.

I knew nothing about Nkem's life in prison and I never heard from her throughout her stay there neither did I know the whereabouts of Chima. Like a child's play, seven years past and she eventually got out. The authority subjected her to the supervision of the Correctional Services agents for another two years. So, she stayed nine years without making any contact with me. In the end, immigration removed her from South Africa to Nigeria. When she landed at the airport, she called me after the Nigerian immigration had again detained and queried her.

It was on a rainy Saturday morning and I must say that I had almost forgotten everything about her, taking life as it came. My handset rang and I picked it. 'Chidi, how are you?

It is me, Nkem, and I'm at the airport. Please could you come and pick me up?'

I could not remember exactly what I said, but I recalled saying to her, 'But I didn't take you to the airport in the first instance.'

Quickly, I called our new pastor, Brother Cletus Wike—the former one having retired a year before—to let him know about the surprise package, but amazingly, he was more anxious and excited than I had anticipated. 'Chidi, that is good news. We must immediately go and pick her up. Are you at home this very moment?'

'Yes, I am.'

'Call her back and ask her to wait. I will drive down to your house in a couple of minutes.'

'Well, she seemed to have called from a public telephone,' I said. 'Maybe she would call again.'

Now, I was beginning to trust that God must have used those periods she spent in jail to remould her. I hoped I would be right. I hoped I would still recognise her. I had heard of the perpetuation of evil that went on in the South African jails especially if the inmates were from the West African coast. I heard that sometimes, the prisoners went without food, resulting in rioting that could lead to the death of some of the inmates and warders. Therefore, for her to survive and be out must be the miracle of God.

One Nigerian, Silas Abbass, who told about his prison experience in South Africa after the judge sentenced him for fraud, said that sometimes, the prison officials treated the inmates inhumanly, torturing and frustrating them with the government refusing to deal with their grievances, making them feel totally disregarded and disparaged.

Besides, there were the issues of overcrowding, lack of bedding, clothing, dietary needs, and no medical attention. There was always tension in those prisons and chaos and rioting were commonplace. In extreme cases, prisoners resorted to cutting themselves with sharp objects so that the authority could investigate their case.

People claimed that the architects designed some of their cells to house about forty inmates. They ended up accommodating up to a hundred, making some sleep in the toilets or shower floors.

Rapes and sodomy were common, according to Silas, in a few of the most notorious South African prisons. Some of the cells were literarily the last stops to hell and not many came out with their sanity and humanity intact. Again, there were lots of strain on sanitation, ventilation, and health care. Widespread rumours had it that many of the prisoners were usually kept locked for up to twenty hours out of the twenty-four hours a day, with no adequate cross-ventilation, leaving thick cigarette smoke and the possibility of contracting any dangerous diseases like tuberculosis and rashes. With all of that, I had great fear for Nkem.

Not long later, the pastor was in front of my door. I was downcast and confused, not too sure, if I was acting correctly by accepting to go and pick Nkem up as she waited at the airport.

The pastor saw the negative expression on my face and he quickly said, 'Chidi, you don't have to delay. God must have worked in her. Let's go.'

My mind went back to six, seven and eight years before. I could still remember the heat Nkem used to produce in my home. Could it mean consenting to yet another era of unrest in my now quiet domain?

Mary, who had now finished her primary school and was in year four in the secondary school, would be so sad and dismayed to hear that her atrocious aunty was due to return to the house. Was it going to be the end of the peace and tranquillity that Mary and I were now enjoying? Yet, again, the pastor tapped me on the shoulder. 'Let's go, Brother Chidi.'

Very reluctantly, I walked into the room and came out in fresh clothes and entered the car. The pastor drove so fast on the way that I became petrified and thought the car was going to crash into a trench. We got there safe anyways.

By the time we got out of the car, we could notice Nkem from afar, still holding the silver-coated trolley bearing her luggage. I was looking out for Chima, which was my primary concern but could not identify him from among some teenagers who stood with their backs turned on us. Maybe he had changed so much that I could no longer picture him from a distance. When we got closer, I could then easily see that Chima was not with Nkem. My heart jumped as if it was going to come out of my chest. Unknown to us, Nkem had seen us as soon as we alighted from the vehicle. She did not act like someone who was yearning to see the people she left some years back.

She was now darker than I knew her to be and very skinny too. Though her hair still fell on both shoulders with some hanging on the upper side of her back, all twisted and rolled clusters like pork sausages. The prison experience must have taken its toll on her, I imagined. Her face was sad with no ecstasy of delight, even though Pastor Wike kept smiling at her. She was looking slightly blue because she was cold and was not breathing easily. Gradually, she began to push the trolley towards us.

'Where is Chima?' was my first utterance, with a twisted face. She ignored the question and proceeded with her hands opened to receive a hug from me.

I quickly stepped out of her grip. 'Greet me, Chidi,' she said. 'We've not seen each other for years and you are not even prepared to give me a hug?'

To cover up, Pastor Wike went in between us and embraced her but it was as briefly as the lightning and she did not seem to like that.

'Where is Chima?' I asked again.

'Is he more important than me? Chima is fine. I'll explain to you when we get home. Nevertheless, he's very fine and he's in school.'

Pastor Wike began to haul her luggage: three giant suitcases two medium sized ones; one large heavy carton covered with cellophane; her hand luggage; and her handbag. She must have packed all that were hers without leaving anything behind. As soon as we got to where we parked the car, I intercepted the pastor and lifted all her belongings, one after the other into the tiny boot of the pastor's car. The boot was so small that it would not take all the boxes so the rest were on the back seat with Nkem folded at one side.

When we got to the house, the car was off-loaded and on stepping into the sitting room, Nkem went down on her knees on a whim, weeping profusely and holding one of my legs. 'Get your hands off me,' I said on top of my voice.

I knew she was asking for forgiveness. However, time changes things but no one could say, for sure, if all of that was from the depth of her heart. Was twelve years enough to curb her early-life violent behaviour that had earned her the

Margaret Thatcher of United Kingdom or the Angela Merkel of Germany or the Ellen Johnson Sirleaf of Liberia, without leaving any remnant of such brutality hiding in her?

The pastor stood away from us, silently watching, perhaps not knowing what to say or calculatingly withholding his opinion. He knew I had not enjoyed the marriage. He knew that anyone with the right judgement would vindicate me if I treated Nkem with howls of derision assuming it was morally permitted. He knew all of that and more.

'Chidi, please listen to her,' the pastor pleaded. 'May be this is a new era in your marriage.' He stretched his hands towards Nkem and lifted her up. 'Sit down both of you,' he instructed. Nkem's head still bowed, finding it extremely reprehensible to rise. The whole of her face had now been wet by the pool of water dripping down her eyes, unhindered. With her face still bent towards the rug on the floor, she moved backward as if she was counting her steps, throwing her hand behind to feel the seat at her back. Then she took her seat without bothering to smooth her dress under her as she sat.

We all heard Mary's steps quietly moving towards the sitting room from the kitchen where she was making the breakfast. She opened her mouth as she pulled the kitchen flexible wooden curtain and screamed, 'Aunty!'

I quickly made a shooing motion with my hand, urging her to go away. She was too excited to listen.

'Mary, could you please give us some seconds?' the pastor whispered.

'Ah!' she again screeched and ran back. She could still not believe her eyes. Now we all could hear the sound of running water coming from the kitchen. The impulse to check when she heard several voices approaching the living room must have made her forget to lock the kitchen tap. The water was splashing noisily on the unwashed dishes that lay disorganised in the sink.

'Sit down, Chidi,' the pastor commanded, persuading at the same time. 'Today is like a fresh wedding day for both of you. You must henceforth stop looking back and focus on the future,' he said. 'We can't change the past but we can change the future if the change begins now. Chidi, please don't think otherwise. I know how you feel and I feel for you. Nkem is still your wife. Take her back from the depth of your heart and let's see what God will do. Now, the two of you get up.' He turned to Nkem and said, 'Bring your hand and hold him.'

Nkem nervously drew my right hand towards hers and held me quite loosely. The pastor noticed it and whispered, 'Hold him firmly.' Nkem tightened her hand on mine. 'Now, repeat after me. I, Nkem, take you Chidi to be my husband, my partner in life and my one true love. I will cherish our friendship and love you again henceforth, today, tomorrow, and forever. I will trust you, respect you and honour you. I will laugh with you when you laugh and cry with you when you cry. I'll love you faithfully through the best and the worst times, through the difficult and easy moments. Come what may, I'll always be there for you. As I've given you my hand to hold, so I give you my life to keep.' He now turned to me and asked me to make the same vow. But those were the same vows I made about fifteen years earlier, yet things turned sour. He could sense I was exceedingly finding it dispiriting to go over the same convention. Hesitantly, I consented, and he requested that we close our eyes in prayer. 'Oh God of Heaven and Earth,' he prayed. 'Thou hast said that what you have joined together, no man or woman should put it asunder. You have also said that no man or woman has the right to put his or her partner away. You told us that the institution of marriage is for life. Above all, you admonished that we should always forgive one another no matter the gravity of the offence as thou hast forgiven us. You said that even when there is enough ground to separate that we should come together again so that the enemy will not triumph over us. Please, Oh Lord, give this couple the heart to forgive and to love each other again as in the beginning. Amen! Chidi, please embrace your wife.' Slowly and casually, we embraced each other. Not too long after, the pastor left.

Minutes later, I called Mary who quickly appeared. 'Aunty, welcome,' she said. 'How about Chima?' she asked.

'Chima is fine,' she responded. 'Hope you are doing very well?'

'Yes, Aunty.'

'You now look quite big.'

'Thank you, Aunty.'

'And have you heard from your parents lately?'

'Yes, Aunty.'

She moved closer to her and rubbed her back telling her, 'I'm very sorry if I'd wronged you in the past.'

'No, Aunty, you have never wronged me,' Mary responded very naively. She could not believe that a woman, who had so dehumanised her at one time, could now stand side by side with her rubbing her back and engaging her in a conversation. 'Why did Chima not come with you?'

'He will come when schools are on holiday,' she responded.

'Now move all the bags to the room,' I instructed.

'Everywhere has changed. This place is better than the

former house. This apartment is lovely. What happened to the old house? Why did you pack out of that house? You changed the cushion. Did you sell the old refrigerator? I guess this is a new one. The fans too are new...'

She spoke on and on without any reply coming. This time her pitch was low, soft and natural even though the voice had cracked, and she now spoke as if she was a woman with an inborn baritone voice. The tone was no more with the usual hostile expression. She noticed I was acting like one covered with frost. 'Chidi, please don't be cold towards me. I know it'll take you time to trust me again, but I have learnt my lessons in a very big and ugly way.' She now pulled the sleeve of her blue and white button-down top to reveal a frightening deep scar on her left arm which she said she got because she said, 'I fought the warder while in jail, a week after I was sentenced, when he ordered that all inmates should move into their rooms when it was still four p.m.; five p.m. was usually when a senior warder gives such orders. I questioned him, and he tried to push me and I fought him to a standstill until the other warders came and rescued him. Despite my wounds, the authority immediately placed me on super maximum segregation custody. I ended up staying there for six months, under a lockdown condition. Nevertheless, they treated me for my wounds. After those months, they then transferred me to a new maximum security at the borders of Cape Town. Prison life is not a good place for anybody. It's not a thing that anyone should wish to live and it's not a place to go for a second time. I will tell you the rest of the story later,' she promised.

'Nkem! Nkem! Nkem! You know very well that you should never have passed through such horrifying moments.'

'Please, Chidi, let's not talk about it again.'

***

The next Sunday, Nkem was the first to get up and went straight into the kitchen to prepare our breakfast. Without any coercion, she had agreed to go with us to the church. She was at the driving end, reminding me we must be ready on time in order not to be late. She personally polished my shoes and ironed my tie. When the breakfast was ready, she served it, and took it to the dining table and insisted that Mary must have her breakfast on the same table with us. Mary blatantly rejected that offer. Yet, the sudden roundabout turn in my wife's behaviour was not enough to deaden my pains as I continued to panic and anticipate that sooner or later, she could show her genuine identity. However, the previous day, she revealed that apart from her ugly experience in jail, the period she spent with the Corrective Services Department transformed her life a great deal. But seeing was believing, as far as I was concerned.

I watched Mary's retreating figure and could not pass any blame on her. She kept treading softly. She had not forgotten all that she suffered at the hands of Nkem when she first came to the house.

I was tempted to trust that God had done a positive work in Nkem's life after she repeatedly told me that her life had changed and pledged to do everything to make the marriage work again. She later narrated that before they moved her to another prison, she witnessed how some inmates were tortured, maltreated and dehumanised. She said she escaped rape once and watched how some warders raped another inmate. She said she observed how a gang of three officers approached that woman to sleep with her but she refused. 'All

266

of a sudden, they hit her with a paddle-lock, which knocked her down and soon she found herself lying naked in the porter's closet and they threatened that if she dared to report the incident, they would slaughter her,' she narrated. 'That made me join a group of worshippers and I began to trust God to keep me safe throughout my stay in that prison. I made a vow to God that if He brought me out without making me a rape victim, that I would do whatever he would want me do.'

As soon as we got to the church, everybody was happy to see her, many not knowing all that had transpired. From that time on, she never missed Sunday School Service.

Two weeks later, one night, Nkem said there was something troubling her heart that she would like to divulge to me. Communication between us got better. After our dinner, I was ready to hear her. 'I don't know how to begin my story,' she started. 'I hope that after telling you what I have got to say that you will find it in your heart to forgive me.'

'I thought we had talked over all of that before and we are now looking forward.'

'Yes, I know but this is something I have not said before.'

'Okay, go ahead, I'm listening.' Somehow, Nkem had proven to me that she was now amiable, candid and thoughtful in the way any man would have expected his wife to be. I made up my mind, though I did not disclose it, that whatever it was, I was going to forgive her straight off. 'Nkem, please talk, don't worry,' I reassured her. She dilly-dallied and just in one fell swoop, kowtowed and held my feet in the same manner she had done the day she first arrived. She now wept profusely. I watched and waited patiently for her to empty her feelings. When I could no longer hang on, I said, 'Nkem, stand up and stop crying. Tell me what the matter is and I promise it would be over.'

'Chima would not be allowed to return to Nigeria until he is eighteen years old. He would be held in a foster home until he gets to that age.'

'Have you not said that before?'

'No.'

'I too read it somewhere that once a child is taken into custody, that child would be there until they become an adult, when they would be capable of living alone. As I learnt, the condition can only be different if there is somebody in the family who is willing to accept the custody of that child. Anyway, is it possible to pay him a visit in future, if it's worked out? I can also indicate my willingness to take custody of him.'

'Yes. Nevertheless, all of that is not the point.'

'What's the point then?'

'Emm… Chima is not your son,' she uttered suddenly and became restless. She began to weep once more.

'You said what?' I spoke as loud as I could.

'You are not the rightful father to Chima,' she reiterated.

I opened my mouth and could not close it back that very minute. She now began to wail boisterously, like she had never done before. I was dazed to the marrow. In another moment, it felt as if my head went blank.

'I had already been put in the family way before I came to your house that first day we stayed together,' she explained. Chima's father is currently in South Africa. He travelled to South Africa soon after I became pregnant because he'd said he was not interested in getting married to me. I agreed to marry you with the intention and sole objective of covering the shame and evading the wrath of my parents.'

'Stop!' I shouted. 'I can't bear to hear this irking

deposition,' I squealed. I stopped looking at her face. I was irritated and felt like disowning her and letting her off to be in someone else's arms if she cared.

My breathing discontinued for a few seconds as my head seemed completely empty and light and I realised that if not for God's mercy and grace, I would have passed out. I felt as if someone had hit me hard below the belt, like a punch to the gut. Quickly, there came strange pains like a hailstorm in some part of my head. I felt as if I had completely lost everything in my life. In some ways, it was a trauma for me.

My mind went back to that night she fell into labour, how I kept vigil until the daybreak. I recalled the several trips I made to the hospital to give Chima a better life; the huge amount I paid before the doctors agreed to operate on him.

The next few minutes, I felt insane and the ensuing moment it was panic and shivering. No doubt, I had been humiliated, cheated and betrayed. There was no need to begin to rewind the reels of my life to discover where the fault came from. It was from me.

In another moment, I stood up and went to the living room. It was too much for me to swallow, but I recollected promising to forgive her a moment before, no matter the severity of the matter. At that point, I struggled to gather the zeal to keep to my promise. It was hard, I must acknowledge.

As I reassessed the whole account of my life, the story of an ex-convict popped up in my head. Not many, perhaps, had been recorded able to forgive the degree of injury that man did. One day, he had left his home and stumbled into a place minutes after a murder had been committed. The police arrested him, and they tried and sentenced him to twenty-five years in prison, with hard labour. For eighteen years of that time, he endured severe punishment that was always meted out to hardened criminals, sometimes, kept in an underground cell, twenty feet below the ground, with no light. He would be there with chains on his legs and wrists. He served his term and later came out homeless, looking for a job with nothing to eat. Not long later, he had the opportunity to come across a man who committed that murder that sent him to jail for twenty-five years. The man was begging for forgiveness. He thought of the lashes he received, the gunshot he got and the underground prison experience. It was too much for him to think of. But within a jiffy he forgave.

Despite all of that, the beans Nkem had just spilled were in my judgement a huge hurt that would take a decade to heal. Can I ever shrug off the weight of my grim past and start all over again with all the experiences of unrelenting mental discomfort?

Nkem later summoned up the courage and came to where I sat. 'Now listen to me, Chidi,' she said. 'I offer to be your maid and no longer the wife I used to be, if that would give you the potency to pardon me.'

With those words, I could not hold back my own tears. My heart melted and I stood up. She rose too. My legs wobbling, yet sluggishly I could utter with a very inaudible voice, 'I let it go; I forgive you, my dear wife. I won't let you be my maid but my wife who you have always been.'

She hugged and kissed me, promising to make me happy again. She pledged to do whatever I asked her to do, go wherever I wanted her and never again to speak whenever I was speaking. From then on and for a while, we lived together happily as husband and wife. It never lasted.

***

About a month after, Nkem woke up one morning to discover a small lump in her left breast. We took a trip to the hospital and after a preliminary test, what looked like bad news came. It was cancer. The cold, hard reality of the strange tumour abruptly eclipsed her dreams. It was a bad report for both of us.

The next day, I had a thirty-minute telephone conversation with a doctor who explained the ailment very well to us and answered many of our questions. He also provided additional information about cancer to us and advised that we visit a cancer specialist at the general hospital. We adhered to his advice and Nkem quickly registered as an outpatient. A further examination revealed another lump in her right breast. Later the doctor said the cancer had metastasised to her brain, lungs, kidney, liver, back, neck and chest wall. We were advised that the only option left was immediate multiple surgeries involving bi-lateral mastectomy, hysterectomy, and brain tumour removal. The hospital conducted an X-ray and the result looked grim.

Fate was now testing the warrior in my wife. I would constantly kneel beside her and prayed that God should spare her life. It was a terrifying moment for both of us. Sometimes, drops of tears would come out from her eyes and whenever she was not crying, she kept asking, 'Why me? No one in my lineage ever had cancer.'

Nkem started the treatment by receiving radiation for five days a week for two months. In all, she had about forty radiation treatments. She also had hormone therapy for one month. Towards the end of the radiation treatment, she had some side effects, which was her inability to breathe very well. The doctor fought hard to alleviate the side effect. That doctor was doing everything that he was required to do. All the people attending to us in that hospital were very good people. They helped us in reducing the stress we would have experienced in coming for the treatment. No hospital in that municipality seemed as good as that one. It did not even smell like a hospital. The toilets were free of any bad odours. There were tiles everywhere and the paintings on the walls were immaculately white. A painter whose job was to retouch the walls with fresh paint, on a daily basis, was regularly available. There was a standby gigantic generator in case of any power surge.

The hospital also served very healthy meals, three times a day with fresh entertainments of pineapple juice and biscuits for people visiting any of the inpatients. However, the trauma, the care and the cost of attending to such a high-class ailment overstretched us.

Within a short time, Nkem changed physically by the treatment she was taking. She experienced loss of hair, nails and weight at the same time. I looked at her eyes and I could see that she was struggling to live; she did not want to die at that time.

After staying in that hospital for more than five months, it seemed she was gradually giving up on herself and was saying goodbye to everyone. Her fighting spirit had diminished. At a point, her father, her mother, her friends, Mary and I were all beside her. Her mother, who was by now confused, was endlessly sobbing.

As her naked condensed body lay beneath the hospital thick blanket, I knew her time was nearing its end. I could then feel the chill of her anaemic hands and the once beautiful complexion and rosy skin were now leaner and pale. She was no longer looking like herself.

Finally, the worst news came. The doctor told us that her body could no longer handle the treatments needed because her immune system was no longer working well. In less than thirty minutes, death struck and did its worst. Her mother threw herself to the floor and started rolling, unconscious of the fact she was at the hospital. The friends screeched while her father bent towards the glittering floor, biting his lips and pulling his moustache. Mary could not be consoled.

By this time, my memory fizzled out and I became cold as I contemplated. In the days running up to that moment, I guess she had seen me as a loving and light-hearted husband. Suddenly, I could not find her to cross-examine her whether my assumption was right. I looked at her face, which I once loved; it was no longer as comely. To brood over the fact that when she promised hope and honour, the brutality of death unexpectedly cornered her away, to a cool rest, did not afford me any room to give a chuckle of delight.

As for those who believe in resurrection, death was supposed to be a moment of rejoicing as the soul of the saint of God goes to the maker. I now had one fear. Where would she go? Would she go to Heaven or Hades? I did not know what she would face. Only God could answer that.

The nurses came and pulled the bed where she lay to where they intended to wash her body with diluted cold water. She would then be dressed in a grave cloth, to await her interment. They plugged some pieces of cotton wool in her ears and nostril and balanced her aptly, waiting for the casket to arrive.

I owed her my last respect, which was to give her a befitting burial, not to allow her now dehydrated body to decompose in the morgue, or float along the street or be cast into the garbage-swollen canal because I had not come forward to claim her body.

Exactly a week after, everything had been set for the impromptu burial. The body was cast into the neatly constructed mahogany wooden coffin, reinforced with a Formica timber surface and off-white silky material lining that protected the flaps of the interior. It was cheap but so beautiful and only good for the dead.

We moved straight to the church where a short service was held before her committal to mother earth. We laid her body in state for a few minutes.

The lid of the coffin was open for all who wished to glance at her face for the last moment. As my eyes caught her well-dressed corpse, my heart was drenched by dread and my eyes blinded by water. That stiff, lethargic, warm body under that dress once belonged to me. My whole body being burned with ache to tears as my chest rocked on and on, on the harsh wave of doubt. There lay my dear and lovely wife, Nkem, with her face up, body frozen and figure utterly still, stretched across the casket, making it obvious that she was truly dead.

She wore a priceless unpierced purple lace material, the colour she cherished most. All her beauty and elegance were no more, only the tiny traces of her dimples remained, poking out like her old self. Her mouth, that previously was so quick and sharp to speak vulgarity, was shut. And when I remembered that her flesh would soon be cast to the dust to rot and the once perfect bones concealed in the soil among the dirt and rubbles in the church graveyard, popularly known as "The

Trumpet Shall Sound Yard" my sobs became louder and louder. I could not bear to look for more than a few seconds before I walked off.

Though, she was favoured by fortune in both birth and marriage but she now lay without any known accomplishments. There was nothing on earth, which she idolised more than money and possessions, yet there she was inside the casket, now carefully sealed with concrete nails and I could unmistakeably assert she acquired nothing, my evidence being that when I looked into her bank account, there was not a single legal tender in it.

I was in a black suit and a dark sunshade that bore a resemblance of swimming pool spectacles, in a slowly moving procession into the church. Mary was behind me. She was dressed in a well-fitted black gown that almost rode the ground, with one elderly woman by her side, holding her as she wept profusely as if the lost was to her alone. The casket bearers pushing the flatbed trolley with ornate brass handles bore solemn faces as though they knew the deceased more than anyone else but were steady in their march.

Those blowing the wind instruments, nearly all of them consisting of a row of hollow pipes, made of wood or bronze and the choir blew across their tops to produce the solemn funeral music that touched every heart, simultaneously alternating their pitches.

The casket gleamed in the late morning light that streamed through the church windows. The preacher began to sermonise and I was hearing what I had heard repeatedly before but the centre of my heart could not hold. I needed something more than comfort at this time. My world was on its hardest slope, it appeared.

Moments later, while at the graveside, I found it so hard to come to terms with the dictions when the choir rendered the last song:

> *When peace like a river, attendeth my way,*
> *When sorrows like sea, billows roll;*
> *Whatever my lot, Thou has taught me to say,*
> *It is well; it is well with my soul.*
> *It is well... with my soul,*
> *It is well; it is well with my soul.*

As soon as the song ended, the two flat logs holding the casket across the grave, the logs which had been well positioned in conjunction with the twines to bear the casket tentatively, were taken away. The casket, which was now left on the doubled stretched thick twines held by four of the corpse bearers, two at each side, now went down to the grave as the corpse bearers gradually released the twines.

As the gravediggers began to put together the sand that was spread around the grave, to cover my wife, my feet stuck to the ground. It was all like a nightmare. Slowly, I walked back and ready to make my way back home.

I could now sight a number of other fresh tombs dug and left uncovered, awaiting the sparkling new caskets that would be accompanied by heartbroken relatives. I could also see some undersized already covered graves that I was sure were for an unknown number of children. It was a place where the bodies of the old and the young, the weak and the strong, the poor and the rich were all taken by the worms when the time was up. A cloud of darkness enveloped my mind. For how long would I remain in that state, I did not know?

Chapter Nineteen

As I turned to leave the graveyard, Pastor Wike was waiting in his car to drive me home, along with Mary and Nkem's parents. The car was a wagon. One sympathiser was in the front with the pastor and another by Mary's side, in the back seat. Nkem's parents were in the middle where I sat. As I sat, I hugged the grief to my bosom. I was now inexplicably, a widower, having been ambushed and attacked unexpectedly by sudden loss.

As soon as we got home, I went and sat on the single sofa near the window and started staring into my lap, this time I was very exhausted. It now dawned on me that a clearly gaping hole had erupted in my life, more than ever before. I never dreamed my world would turn to what it was now. In my mind, I moved from wing to wing, in the clinic of my anguish.

Anxiety, confusion and depression all hijacked me. My status had suddenly changed and I had to remake my future. Would I ever recover and be normal again?

Nkem was in some way woven lately into every nook and cranny of my life after she begged for forgiveness. Yet, when I thought of her, I thought of her in tears, for her thoughts were giving me sorrow and not comfort because three-quarters of her existence was out of my grip and filled with greed and desperation.

A good number of sympathisers sat around me, including Matthias and Martin, both of whom were my old friends and church members, they all stayed in absolute silence.

Then the pastor broke the silence and said, 'We do not know what to say but we feel your pain. We may not exactly suffer the pain the way you do but God in heaven does know precisely how you feel and will comfort and raise you up again. We just pray that our prayers help a bit.'

I understood the words he said but they were not having meaning and effect on me at that moment. 'It's just enough to know you are standing by me,' I managed to utter. 'I feel better that I can lean on you and you are like a pillar on my porch. Thank you very much,' I said with a sincere sense of gratitude.

Soon after the pastor's words of encouragement, the people began to leave one after the other and, at last, it was so painful to see myself all alone.

By the following day, it got worse when Nkem's parent took their leave and decided to take Mary along with them. Mary would have loved to stay but her staying would have no meaning without Nkem, especially now that she was a fully grown-up woman, ready for any man of her choice.

As Mary gathered her belongings, tears glittered down her cheeks. She wished she could make a decision for herself. She intermittently glanced at my face thinking I would do something to stop her from leaving. I looked into her eyes; they were red, sad and covered with water. As she packed her things one by one into her lofty portmanteau, her hands shook and because of that, she was merely dropping the stuff in the box without caring to organise them. 'Don't worry, Mary,' I said. 'I do realise I mean the whole world to you but there is so much for you to be happy about that you are going away. Thank God, you have finished your secondary education and there is the possibility you can study further if you choose to. I shall always be there for you. I will never forget the gap you have come to fill in my life. I will cherish your memories forever. I will always remember you.' Despite my soothing words, I could still see the agony of parting written all over her.

'It is not the parting that hurts but the flashbacks,' Mary responded in a shaky, sad voice.

'Please don't grieve over the past. It is gone. Look forward to the future.'

As Mary stepped away with Nkem's parents, I could not utter a word or stand from where I sat glancing at the empty space. I was yet to know what a world of total vacuum was about to emerge in my home.

Within a few days, I started dividing Nkem's stuff for charity so that I could easily forget her and move on with my life. Nkem had kept a lot of stuff since she came into my home so it was like going through her life memories again.

After some days, I decided to intensify my effort to get a better job so that I could get myself well occupied but nothing worked. That was putting me down a great deal. I had no close friends around my age. The only person I was used to visiting was Matthias who lived across the road. He had already said to me, 'You need to start your life anew.' But from where exactly would I start?

To worsen the case, I began to dream about Nkem's final moments on a frequent basis and would wake up most times, sad and afraid.

Exactly seven weeks after Nkem's funeral, I woke up one morning with an acute illness that was marked with severe flu and body rash. I was also fatigued with joint pains. After taking some self-medication, I discovered that those symptoms subsided, but soon cropped up and what later followed were vomiting, cold, dry cough with choking and shortness of breath.

At that time, my temperature rose to all time high of about thirty-nine degrees. I had also completely lost my appetite. I became frightened and decided to see the doctor.

The doctor directed the laboratory technologist to run a number of tests on me. Later, when the result came, he told me that I had pneumonia and the early symptoms of toxoplasmosis, meningitis and Kaposi's sarcoma. I received what he said were the appropriate treatment for those symptoms. He assured me that after a few weeks, I would begin to recover and feel better especially when those diagnoses came early.

At the end of the sixth week, I went back to the hospital, as there was no significant improvement. The person in the lab ran another series of tests, following the doctor's advice. The next day when I went for the result, the doctor told me that I had Human Immunodeficiency Virus. I was practically dumbfounded and nervous. H.I.V? How did that happen? How did I contract the disease knowing that Nkem was the only woman I had ever known all through my life? I felt as if my death was around the corner. My whole world fell apart. Although, the doctor who broke the news to me was so amazing, telling me that he had known people living with the disease for over twenty-five years. I made great effort to latch on those bolstering words, but it was almost impossible.

How was I going to survive? It was certain I was going to face discrimination while looking for a job that I needed so badly at that time, since medical tests would often be required. It was going to be a big issue for any organisation who may be interested in my service. Anyone employing me would know that he or she would be employing a drug user. Was it not even better that I die rather than face a situation of no wife, no child and no job, after more than twenty years since I started? I thought.

Not long after, my health started to deteriorate physically, mentally and emotionally as well. How pale I began to look. After a whirlwind romance of about eight months, following Nkem's return from what seemed to me a jamboree in South Africa; a deadly disease welcomed me. It was like a special gift she brought back to me.

I began to take the most highly active drugs for the illness—antiretroviral therapy alongside drugs like zidovudine and stavudine. Despite those drugs, at the early stage, I was constantly throwing up after food, running repeatedly to the toilet because of diarrhoea and at a point, my life became hectic, as I could no longer walk very well. I looked into my life now and must admit it was one of great disappointment and distress. I was gradually shutting down in all aspects. I remember standing in front of the mirror with tears streaming down my face.

I began to long to see my parents who both had only sent words of consolation for the loss of my wife. I owe them lots of restitution. I needed to tell them how sorry I was by not sticking to their advice and caveat before I put a diamond ring on Nkem's finger. I knew my life was like an indignity to them as I came through the torment of a failed matrimony, loss of everything marriage could promise and had become shattered. I prayed I would have their clemency.

I made up my mind, it was only better I go and be with them for a while. Age must have told so much on them. It had been like twenty years since I left the village, though I was in constant touch, visiting only once in the last seven years. My mother was still attaching herself to her now ancient sewing machine under the cashew tree. That cashew tree could not have been the one standing there twenty years before. My uncle must have cut the old one away and replanted another since that time. My father was still tilling his farmland but not with the strength and vigour he used to do years back. After about twenty years, I could neither fully support them, as was their dream years back nor give them a grandchild that could make them happy. Both my father's arm and eyes were now gradually failing him. And if there was any time he needed assistance most, it was now.

My uncle had become much weaker than my father had, though he was older. He was no longer the acclaimed farmer that he used to be as he could no longer make his regular trips to his farm. Out of his five children who used to be very small that first time I bade them goodbye, when I was leaving the village finally to go to the city, two were working and then constantly supporting him especially after he lost his wife four years back.

As I made that journey back home to meet my parents, my heart pounded because I knew it would not be to their delight. When they see me, no one would explain to them that my life had taken a dramatic turn-around.

On that fateful day, as I came out of the vehicle that carried me that mid-afternoon, I met my parents at the dinner table. Their skins were now slightly wrinkled but my mother, in particular, was still carrying a faded beauty. They both spontaneously lost their appetite for their meals as soon as they sighted me with my frail looks when I stepped into that portable mud-house built many years back.

My mother immediately got up and embraced me, holding me with tight fists until she inhaled the unpleasant and intolerable smell of my flesh. She knew before this time that I lost my wife but not my physical looks. We stood in silence for ages before she could call out my name. 'Chidi! Is this really you? Is it because of the death of your wife that you have so much lost your flesh and balance?' she spoke in a worrying tone.

'How I wish it is only that, Mama,' I replied.

'Is it your job?'

'That too is minor, even though it was giving me concern.'

Meanwhile, my father was speechless. It was not as if it was his choice to remain mute. He was taken aback, seeing my physical condition the way it was. As I stepped forward to find a seat, I saw myself instantaneously getting weaker and weaker. My father was quick to notice my wobbling balance so he got up to render a helping hand. Then he realised that my white eyes unexpectedly dilated with force, taking away the splendid dark pupil. That was all I remembered. When I opened my eyes minutes later, I saw myself drenched in water. They had splashed me with cold cups of water when I suddenly slipped into coma. As I wangled my eyes, I could notice that a number of other villagers, in addition to my parents, were surrounding me and had kept vigil by my side, watching for signs that I might open my eyes. It was only then that my father spoke. 'Chidi, what is the matter with you?'

'I was diagnosed with Human Immunodeficiency Virus—HIV.'

They all shouted at the same rhythm, like the sound of monkeys chased by the hunter's gun. I was still unstable and now the bones in my neck, chest and arms projecting in a very ugly form, in their eyes.

When I got myself back fully, the people later dispersed, leaving me with my parents. I could not look into their eyes. My mother's eyes were wet with tears while my father continued to stare at me in tearless grief. His next utterance tore my heart apart. 'Chidi! No matter how careful we may be or how well we might have planned our future, things could still go wrong due to a combination of circumstances. When things go wrong and they are traced specifically to our wrong decisions or actions which we had the opportunity to have altered, then we merit no empathy or encouragement while going through the pains of the aftermath of the hasty choice we made.'

'I apologise, Papa, for not listening to you both. You have no idea of the intensity of my emotional pains and pang of guilt in my heart. I deserve what I got. As you forgive me, I pray that God in heaven would too.'

I remained with them for months until I began to recover in a very wondrous manner. In those days, I had both good and bad times. The days I woke up with no memory of the source of my ailment was my good times. The day I woke up and the thoughts of my late wife enveloped me was my bad time.

I continued to struggle day and night until one fateful day, I saw myself walking down the aisle of our church colourful edifice in a golden suite almost similar to the one I used for the wedding to my late wife. And by my side was the real woman of my dreams whom I had every evidence she was God's chosen for me. Her name was Magdalene. My face beamed with the smiles of a gallant celebrated figure. Our strides were admirable by all who surrounded us and had come to grease the occasion.

Now and finally, I had to share my life with the woman I won after nights of prayer. A treasure more valuable than anything the world could offer. Something I cherished and wished for more than silver or gold. Like the moon at night, she suddenly lit up my broken heart and plunked me into shreds of comfort from plain disaster. At last, I was going to rebuild after the storm. With her, my life shall never be the same again.

As we marched side by side after the officiating minister had joined us together to the podium for a group photograph, my arm around hers, glued together, and our eyes stared gracefully at the unfamiliar crowd. And as I turned to her, I uttered, 'As long as I live, I shall continue to love you. What about you?'

She smiled brilliantly and her lips parted and as her response was about to come, I opened my eyes; it was a dream. It unrolled the scroll of my agony. My tongue hung out and I wept.

But as the weeks and months passed by, my parents never gave in. Great parents are so valuable and I had so much to thank mine for. Their love for me was limitless and unconditional. They were ever ready to walk over burning coals for my sake, despite my pig-headedness. They kept up with me, giving me all the necessary care and comfort, I was unworthy of. They were fetching all the local herbs they could lay their hands on, which I was consuming along with the drugs prescribed by my doctor. They never gave up on me and I hated to see them struggle to make me survive. Indeed, they were both embodiments of love, true legends, hero and heroine of huge proportions, even though unsung. Their love for me and mine for them became the last strength I had.

I could not but see my self-confidence substituted with an infant sense of guilt, especially when I realised it was I who let myself down and disappointed my parents too. If I ever recuperated, I had learnt my lessons in a very gruelling way and I had paid the towering price. If I ever pulled through, I would have to start life anew after more than twenty years of taking a stride wide off the mark, and I would follow their commands, letter by letter without skipping any.

If I ever have the occasion to go over my life again, and were to look for a companion, I would keep a round-the-clock vigil, days upon days, nights upon nights, seeking God's favour, so that my dream would come through. Even when I find the favour I hunt, I would yet ask for a sign.